FORSAKEN

THE FORGOTTEN: BOOK TWO

M.R. FORBES

Published by Quirky Algorithms
Seattle, Washington

This novel is a work of fiction and a product of the author's imagination. Any resemblance to actual persons or events is purely coincidental.

Cover illustration by Tom Edwards
tomedwardsdesign.com

ACKNOWLEDGMENTS

THANK YOU to my readers, for staying with Hayden and Natalia as their story continues. I hope you enjoy the ride!

THANK YOU to my beta readers. This book would be a much harder read if you didn't exist.

THANK YOU to my wife. This book wouldn't exist if you didn't.

1

"HAYDEN, WE'RE GOING TO BE LATE," NATALIA SAID, RAISING her voice slightly from the bathroom of their cube.

"We won't be late," Hayden countered. "We're only going two blocks, and we have ten minutes before the Governor will start to wonder what happened to us."

"You're forgetting that the lift is offline again. I've got Mae coming to look at it while we're meeting with Malcolm, but we still have to slog down the stairs."

"Plenty of time," Hayden insisted. "Do you think they'll have steak?"

Natalia emerged from the bathroom. She was wearing a blue dress that sat tight across her shoulders, the distressing of the worn cloth causing it to fade into more of a light blue and then a white as it crossed over her breasts and bulged out at her stomach. It made a rounded shape there before tucking back in at her legs and ending with a looser flare just below the knees.

Hayden stood near the door to their cube, staring silently at his wife.

"What?" she asked, smiling at him.

"I don't know," he replied. "I just don't know. I can't believe how lucky I am to have a wife as beautiful and intelligent as you. I can't believe how honored I feel that we're going to be parents. I'm grateful for everything we have, but especially for you."

Her smile got a little bigger. "I feel the same way."

"I know things in Metro aren't always easy, but I feel like together we can make a difference."

"We already are making a difference. That's why Malcolm is treating us to this dinner." She took on a deep voice to mimic the Governor. "A small token of my appreciation. I'm bringing a surprise from my special stash."

"What do you think it will be?" Hayden asked, laughing.

"I'm hoping for chocolate," she replied. "He brought a few pieces to Engineering a couple of years back. I haven't forgotten the taste. I want you to try it."

"And I want to try it."

Hayden walked over to Natalia, putting one hand on her face and the other on her stomach. "I love you."

"I love you, too."

Their lips met. Small kisses at first, but growing as they maintained the connection.

"We're going to be late," Natalia said beneath his mouth.

"We can skip the dinner," Hayden suggested.

She laughed. "Not this time. But I'm sure you can make it up to me later."

He kissed her one last time before pulling away. "I would be honored."

"Good. Come on."

They left the cube, moving out into the hallway, hands clasped together. Hayden had never felt happier in his entire life. He had everything he ever wanted. A great job. An incredible wife. A growing family. Not everyone on the

Pilgrim got to have children. It was special to win the lottery.

They made it to the stairwell and started to descend. The lift had died only an hour before and would be repaired by the time their dinner with the Governor was over. Hayden didn't mind the steps. He could use the exercise.

They were on the twelfth floor when Natalia came to a sudden stop. She was silent as she gripped her stomach, but Hayden noticed immediately.

"Nat, are you okay?" he asked.

"Just a second," she said. "A little cramping. That's all."

He put his arm around her shoulders. "We can go back up?"

She shook her head. "No. I'll be fine. I just need. Ahh-" She clenched her teeth, a pained expression on her face. "Oh, Hayden. Get Doctor Hun."

Hayden's heart began to race. "Here, just sit. I'll see if she's in her cube." He helped Natalia down, a sense of panic rising in his chest. He wouldn't let her see him worried.

She sat, still clutching at her stomach. He sprinted back up the stairs, out onto their floor and down the hallway to Doctor Hun's cube. He knocked on the door.

Doctor Lin Hun opened it, her expression immediately concerned.

"Sheriff? What's wrong?"

"Natalia," he said. "She's in the stairwell. She's having pain."

"I'll be right there. Call Medical and have them bring a transport."

"What?"

"Do it."

She closed the door. Hayden returned to his cube, grabbing his badge from the table and tapping it to activate the transceiver.

"Medical," he said. "Emergency."

"This is Medical," a voice said immediately. "Sheriff Duke, what do you need?"

"It's Natalia," he said. "Doctor Hun said to have you send a transport to my Block."

"Of course, Sheriff," the woman replied. "We're on our way. Hold tight."

Doctor Hun was already at the door to the stairwell when Hayden left the cube and ran down the corridor. They descended together, back to where Natalia was sitting. She had tears in her eyes, a sight that broke Hayden's heart.

"Hayden," she said, her lip quivering. "I can't feel her."

"Stay calm, Natalia," Doctor Hun said. "The transport is on the way. We're going to get you to the Hospital."

"It's too late," Natalia replied tearfully. "It's too late. I can't feel her. I don't understand. I don't know what happened."

"It's going to be okay," Hayden said.

"No. It isn't. She's gone, Hayden. I know she is. Our baby is gone."

Hayden felt the words like a knife to the chest. He couldn't breathe, but he had to breathe. He had to keep telling her it was going to be okay, to keep her calm until Medical arrived. Even if it wasn't going to be okay. Even if it was already too late.

He put on a show for his wife, calm and confident and strong. Let the doctors do their job. We don't know anything yet. There could be a thousand reasons you don't feel her.

Inside, he knew she was right. He knew it by her face. By her tone. By her words. She was too damn smart, too damn in tune to be wrong.

Inside, his entire body was burning with the agony of the loss.

Outside, he was burning, too. So hot he could barely stand it. So much pain he could barely keep from crying out.

"Shhh," the man said, leaning over him. "You need to stay quiet."

Hayden's eyes fluttered open. He looked up at the man. A bushy, ragged white beard. A wrinkled face. Sad eyes. It hurt so damn much. He could feel the moisture in his eyes. What the hell was happening?

"Dad, you have to keep him still," someone else said.

A light was flickering around them, making it hard to see. His entire body felt like it wanted to explode. There was so much stinging, so much throbbing, so much pressure.

"I'm trying, Jake. I'm not as young as I used to be."

Hayden noticed more of the intense pain coming from his left. He turned his head slightly, noticing the corrugated metal above the bearded man's head. Where the hell was he? Where was Natalia?

"You need to stay still, mister," the younger voice, Jake, said. "Real still. You don't want me to grep this up."

"I don't understand," Hayden said weakly. "Where am I?"

He tried to sit up. His left arm was being held down, but his right was free. He swung it out, trying to push the old man away. He knocked something off a table beside him and heard it shatter on the ground.

"Damn it, Dad," Jake cursed. "Look, mister. If you want to die, you keep flailing like that. If you want to live, if you want me to do something about that missing hand of yours, stay the grep still."

Hayden flipped his head to look at the man. He was older than his voice sounded, with a thin beard and a handlebar mustache that made Hayden want to laugh. He was leaning over him, over his arm. He had some kind of tool in his hand. It was nothing Hayden had ever seen before, primitive and greasy.

It wasn't grease. It was blood. His blood. Hayden squeezed his eyes closed, trying to remember. There had been so much blood it had run down Natalia's leg. The baby. His little girl. They had lost her. By pure chance, bad luck, they had lost her.

"Natalia," he said, choking out her name.

"I don't know who Natalia is, son," the old man said. "But if you want to see her again, you have to calm down and let Jake work. He knows what he's doing."

Hayden clenched his teeth. He kept his eyes closed. The pain was intense. Almost unbearable.

Natalia.

An image of a man in a white suit, wearing a white-brimmed hat. He was holding onto Natalia. Taking her away.

The monsters. They were right behind him. Towering over him. Foul and ugly and horrible.

His wife. Where was his wife?

Where the hell was he?

"Who are you?" he managed to whisper.

"Nobody special," Jake replied. "Just a man trying to save another man's life. There isn't enough of that in this world. Not nearly enough."

"Why?"

The old man laughed. "Because you brought my horse back, son," he said. "Those asshole Scrappers took him from me two months ago, but you brought him back. And judging by your wounds and some of the words you've been babbling, it sounds like you did that group of hyenas well and good. It's about time somebody stood up to them."

"I would have saved you from the infection anyway," Jake said. "The replacement is payment for killing Pig."

"Pig?"

Hayden tried to remember the word. The name?

What did he mean replacement, anyway?

The sound of the drill drowned out his thoughts. The whirring reminded him of the machine in Medical.

The one that took their baby away.
The pain drowned out his consciousness.

2

"STAY STILL," THE OLD MAN SAID, THE NEXT TIME HAYDEN opened his eyes.

It was still dark around him, the single small light the only source of illumination. He was in the same place. In the same position. It was as though he had never slept at all.

He was calm enough now, sane enough now, to heed the old man's words. He remained still, moving only his eyes. He was in a room of some kind. Wood, real wood, surrounded him. It was weathered and worn, and it smelled wet. It was a new smell for him. He tried to make sense of it.

He tried to make sense of all of it.

He remembered now. Everything that happened before, though he was sure he was missing a few days. Metro, the xenotrife, the Scrappers. He remembered Pig. And the giants. How would he ever forget the giants?

"Where am I?" he asked, voice hoarse.

The old man leaned over, picked up a metal flask and held it over his face. "Water."

Hayden let his mouth fall open. The old man dumped the liquid in. It was cool and crisp. Hayden had never tasted anything like it. He was so used to the recycled water of the Pilgrim. This was the real thing. Fresh. Not processed out of urine.

The old man put the flask on the table beside him. "You have a name, son?"

"Duke," he replied. "Sheriff Hayden Duke."

The old man laughed at that. "Sheriff? As in, a man of the law?"

"Yes."

"There hasn't been any law but the law of survival around here for, I don't know, a hundred years. Probably more. Where did you come from?"

Hayden noticed his left arm was burning, close to the elbow, not down near the wrist where he had lost the hand. Pig had cut it off, trying to get to his identification chip, not realizing it didn't have access to Metro. He started to turn his head, but the old man reached out, putting a hand on the side of his cheek and holding it straight. The hand was weathered and dry.

"It's best not to look at it just yet," the old man said. "It takes a little getting used to."

"What does?"

"The replacement."

"I don't know what that means."

"My son, Jake, he's a Borger. Do you know what that means?"

"No."

"Then I'll repeat my question. Where are you from? Your clothes are strange, but not that strange. We figured maybe you made the trip across Central, which already makes you pretty damn impressive. But you should know what a Borger is."

"What's your name?" Hayden asked, instead of answering the question.

He knew the Pilgrim was valuable to the Scrappers. So was Metro. How did he know it wasn't valuable to this man and his son, or people they knew?

He remembered what the old man had said about the horse. They were no friends of the Scrappers, that was for sure.

"Hank," the man replied. "Hank Jackson. It's a pleasure to meet you, Sheriff Duke."

He smiled, a hint of mirth lining it.

"You don't need to patronize me," Hayden said. "I might be a stranger to this place, but I'm not an idiot."

Hank laughed. "I love your spirit, Hayden."

"What happened to me?" Hayden asked.

"You'll have to tell me that, once you trust me a little more. And you will. Me and Jake, we're what someone calling themselves a Sheriff would call the good guys. The Scrappers, the militia you got mixed up with, they're the bad guys."

"I figured that much," Hayden said. "I killed their leader. Pig."

"No. You killed one of their Sergeants. A pretty notorious one at that, but Pig was nowhere near the top of the Scrapper food chain."

"I was afraid you were going to say that."

Hank laughed again. Hayden's eyes shifted when part of the wall opened. No, it was a door. A hidden door. He could see past Jake, out into another dark room.

"You're awake," Jake said. "Good."

He was holding something in his hand. A bowl. The smell rising from it made Hayden's mouth water instantly.

"I brought you some broth. No solid food for you yet, I don't think you'll be able to keep it down." He handed the bowl to Hank, who set it down on the table.

That was when Hayden noticed the man only had one arm.

"What happened?" he asked, looking at the stump that ended just below the elbow. It was bleeding slightly, the wound relatively fresh.

"Scrappers," he said, using his hand to pick up a spoon from the edge of the soup bowl. "I'll have to do the feeding for now. You shouldn't move yet."

"When can I move?" Hayden asked.

Jake sat on a small stool next to Hayden. "You had an infection in that wrist of yours. I see someone tried to cauterize it, but whatever they used it was a lousy tool for the job. You also had a fragment of metal in your back, and a number of lacerations and bruises. You showed up looking like you'd been through hell."

"It felt like it at times," Hayden admitted. "How did I get here?"

"You were lucky," Hank said. "Cass knew the way home. She showed up here early morning, a couple of days ago, with you slumped over the saddle."

"Cass?"

"Cassiopeia. My best breeding mare. Or she would be if the Scrappers hadn't taken all of my other horses."

"That was Pig's doing," Jake said. "Most of the Scrapper Sergeants leave us alone. They barter for the horses instead of outright taking them because they know we provide an important service. He said he had extra burden he needed beasts to carry." Jake smiled. "Before you killed him."

"I was sick, then?"

"Very. We weren't sure you would survive. I cleaned out your wounds, cut out the infected part of your arm and hit you with some penicillin. You're lucky some people still know how to make that."

Hayden was aware of his arm again. It felt different. "You did more than that."

"Have some broth," Hank said, dipping a spoon of it toward Hayden's mouth.

He opened it and let the man pour the broth in. The taste was bland, but it was real. He savored it for a moment.

"I need to get out of here," Hayden said. "As soon as possible. The Scrappers have my wife, Natalia. She's the reason I'm here."

He started trying to sit up, but Hank put the spoon back in the bowl and used his hand to press his chest back down.

"Hold up. You won't make it two days out there in your condition. You need to stay alive if you plan on finding your wife."

"I hate to be the bearer of bad news," Jake said. "But you'll need to do a hell of a lot more than that if you intend to get her back from the Scrappers."

"I'll do whatever I have to."

Jake didn't argue. "I don't doubt that, mister-"

"Where are my manners?" Hank said. "Jake, meet Sheriff Hayden Duke."

"Sheriff?" Jake said. "Like in the old videos? Wyatt Earp?"

"Yup," Hank said. "A lawman."

"There are still places out there with lawmen?"

"At least one," Hayden said.

"Nice to meet you, Sheriff Duke," Jake said, with the same expression as his father. "The world could use more men who believe in laws, instead of assholes like King."

"King?"

"Pig was a Sergeant. King is the Five-star General," Hank said. "He's in control of the Scrappers. He's in control of everything around here."

"Does he wear a white suit and a big, white hat?" Hayden asked.

Hank's expression changed. "You saw Ghost?"

"If that's his name. He had my wife. He pulled her into a vehicle of some kind, and they went away. Right before these giants attacked the building we were in. They attacked the Scrappers. What the hell are those things?"

"You definitely aren't from around here if you don't know the goliaths," Jake said.

"I thought they were everywhere," Hank said. "From the States all the way to Australia."

"Not where I'm from," Hayden said. "What are they? Where did they come from? They picked up the Scrappers and ate them."

Hank smiled. "Yeah, that's what the goliaths do. They wander around the countryside, eating pretty much anything that has two legs. They aren't very smart, though. As long as you keep quiet, they'll pass you by."

"And they're easy to hear coming, on account of their size," Jake said. "As for where they came from? Nobody knows. Or nobody remembers. They came after the invasion, after the fall of our last true civilization. Most folks think they're from another planet, like the trife."

"The trife are still out here?"

"Of course," Hank said, feeding him another spoonful of soup. "You can't get rid of the trife. It's impossible. The world learned that the hard way."

"Which may be what brought the goliaths here," Jake said. "Though some think the goliaths are the ones who seeded the planet with the trife, to create an ecosystem they could survive in."

"They don't sound smart enough for that," Hayden said.

"No, they don't. But we don't know that much about them. We don't know if they have an intellect that's just different. They seem dumb when they come to scoop up poor souls who can't keep their mouths shut, or to root out a nest of trife and devour them. But that's the only way we know them. They could have a city somewhere. They could have starships. Who knows?"

Hayden considered that while he swallowed more of the broth. According to Jennifer, someone had dumped the trife on Earth. Was it the goliaths?

"As for Ghost," Hank said. "He's King's top Courier."

"Courier?"

"Moving stuff around here is always dangerous, even for the Scrappers," Jake said. "Everybody has to deal with the trife and the goliaths and assorted problems, other humans included. Couriers are the answer."

"They aren't just messengers," Hank said. "They're assassins. They're diplomats. They're whatever the person paying them needs them to be. The bottom line is that in the tree of survivors, they're at the very top."

"And Ghost is on top of that," Jake said. "If he took your wife, you can bet he's bringing her to King."

"So I need to find this King," Hayden said. "It sounds like it won't be that hard."

"To find him? No. To find your wife alive? That depends. If King wants her, she must be special. But he doesn't think anything is more special than him, and he's got a reputation for destroying things that other people would covet."

They weren't the words Hayden wanted to hear, but at least they were honest.

"All the more reason for me to be on my way," Hayden said. "I've been enough of a burden to you already, and I have no way to repay you."

"Are you kidding? You had a pocket full of Notes when I found you. Enough to pay for your treatment and your replacement. If I would accept payment from you, which I won't."

Notes? Hayden realized he must be referring to the scraps of paper with the USSF eagle logo on them.

"You're not ready to leave yet, son," Hank said, taking on a more fatherly tone. "You'll die out there."

"Natalia is everything to me, Hank," Hayden said. "I'd rather risk dying out there than keep sitting in here."

"Just hold on a minute, Hayden," Jake said. "I promise, we'll get you on your way as fast as possible. I can see how much you love your wife. I can't imagine what you've already been through to find her. I want you to have a chance out there. We both do. What I'm trying to say is, please, trust us. If you don't know the goliaths, then you have no idea what's waiting outside these walls. Wherever you're from, you're not prepared, and you'll need to be."

Hayden shifted his eyes to stare at Jake. A big part of him wanted to get up and go. But the man was right. He hadn't been expecting any of what he had discovered since leaving Metro, and especially since finding his way off the Pilgrim. Right now it was an effort to move at all. He needed time to heal. Ghost hadn't come for Natalia to kill her. Engineers were valuable. King wanted to use her mind, not destroy her body.

Patient. He needed to be patient.

But not too patient.

"Okay," Hayden said. "You're right. But I don't want to sit here anymore. I want to get up."

Jake nodded. "I understand, Sheriff. Before you do, we need to run a calibration sequence on the replacement."

"Calibration sequence?" Hayden asked.

"He doesn't know what a Borger is, Jake," Hank said.

"Oh," Jake replied. "It's a bit of a shock when you're expecting it. Depending on your mindset, this could make the calibration easier or harder."

"Can you both stop tiptoeing around whatever it is you don't want to say and don't want me to see?"

"Sorry," Jake said. "It's part of the process. You need to see it first."

"See what?"

"Are you sure he's ready, son?" Hank asked, glancing at Jake.

"If our Sheriff here were most men, I would say no. But he isn't like most men. I can see that in his eyes." Jake paused, staring at Hayden. Hayden stared back, keeping eye contact. "What you want to do is turn your head slowly, start at your left shoulder and let your eyes work their way down. Don't rush it."

Hayden nodded. Jake had done something to his arm, beyond healing the infection. But what? He turned his head toward his shoulder. He winced when he saw the cuts and bruises. He had really taken a beating. The kid had told him to go slowly, but he didn't think that was going to help. Whatever had happened, he wanted to face it on his own terms.

He turned his head quickly, snapping it to his wrist.

It was dull and dented, scratched and decayed. It looked older than he was by a long way.

It was still a hand, but it wasn't his hand. It wasn't anybody's hand. It had been made, of metal and wires and who knew what else.

Replacement. Now he understood.

Pig had taken his hand.

Jake had given him a new one.

3

HAYDEN STARED AT THE APPENDAGE FOR A LONG TIME. HE didn't speak. He didn't react. He examined it, shifting his eyes up along its beaten surface to a fresh ring of metal near his elbow. He stared at that for a moment and then tried to wiggle the fingers.

One of them shifted slightly. The others were still.

"Wow," Jake said. "You've got sync already. I haven't even run the calibration yet."

Hayden didn't respond. He kept trying to move the hand while Jake reached down into something at the side of the bed and lifted out a rectangular block of plastic. He opened it, revealing a display and keyboard. The USSF logo appeared on the screen. He lifted out another item, a cable, and plugged one end into the computer and the other into the band of metal on Hayden's arm.

"What did you think I would do when I saw it?" Hayden asked. "Be horrified?"

"Most people are. Most people would rather live without than use a replacement, mechanical or otherwise."

"I had nothing, and now I have something."

"That's the spirit," Hank said.

Hayden turned to look at Hank's stump, and then back at the hand. "This was yours," he said, making the connection.

"Now it's yours," Hank replied.

Hayden shook his head. "I can't accept this."

"Too late," Hank said, smiling. "It's already been connected, and in few seconds it'll be synced. It always treated me well; I'm sure it'll do the same for you."

"I've never seen anything like this before," Hayden said. "I think you should take it back."

"Nope," Hank insisted. "I'm old, and I wouldn't need her for that much longer. She's better on someone who's going to get some use out of her. If you want to repay me for my generosity, you can tell us where you're from. If only so we don't die from curiosity."

Hayden cracked a small smile. "Have you ever heard of the Pilgrim?" he asked.

They both shook their heads.

"It's a starship. A generation ship. It was supposed to leave Earth almost four hundred years ago, with fifty-thousand colonists living in a city inside. It was scheduled to reach a planet in the Trappist system they named New Gaia about ninety-six years ago. Natalia and me, we're the only ones on board who know the Pilgrim never left Earth. The rest of the people are still there, still locked inside. They think they're in space, headed to New Gaia."

Jake and Hank were silent for a moment. Then Jake whistled.

"Shit, Sheriff," he said. "If you weren't so green I wouldn't be able to put my mind far enough around that idea to believe you. You're saying there's a starship laying around not that far from here?"

"I don't know how far it is. You'd have to ask your horse." He smiled a little wider to show them it was a joke. "But yes. It's underground. The Scrappers know it's there. They're trying to reach the city. They were after me because they think I can get them in."

"Can you?" Hank asked.

"No."

"But you got out," Jake said.

"That's why they think I can get in. It was a one-way trip to find my wife. I didn't know when I did it if we would ever be able to go back. I didn't know this was out here, either."

"This is going to hurt a little bit," Jake warned.

He was typing something on the computer, and as he hit one last key, a round of stinging shockwaves passed through Hayden's arm. He grunted in response to the pain, watching the fingers on the alien hand open and close. After a few seconds, he realized he was able to feel the movement in his mind, as though the mechanical fingers were his fingers. When the pain stopped, he was able to control the digits, as well as the hand and wrist they were attached to.

"Perfect," Jake said.

"You're more than lucky, Sheriff," Hank said. "Only a few Borgers this side of the States could have replaced you with my hand."

"The muscles and nerves are similar, but not even close to being the same," Jake said. "The ring," he tapped on the metal band as he unplugged the computer from it, "is an interface between your brain's version of things and the replacement's version of things."

"It's impressive," Hayden said, manipulating the hand.

"It's old tech, left over from the war. There was a time when hands like these were common. That's where the Borger title came from. Cyborgs. Part human, part machine.

A long time ago, our military started repairing soldiers this way so they could keep fighting the trife. The cyborgs were more effective at first, but the trife evolve in a hurry. Try squeezing your fist."

Hayden clenched his left hand into a fist. He heard the soft snap of a spring, and three twenty centimeter claws extended from the top of his forearm, jutting out past his hand

"You'll find those claws can cut through more than just flesh," Hank said. "They're stronger than steel, and in my opinion better than a human hand any day."

"If your goal is to kill Scrappers, anyway," Jake said.

"Where did you learn how to do this?" Hayden asked.

"There's a Borger named Castillo in the town closest to here. Haven. I did an apprenticeship with him until he was killed a couple of years back. Some people thought I should take over his shop for him, but I don't want to live in Haven. I like it out here. It's quieter, and most of the time that makes it safer. I go into town when somebody sends for me. I charge an arm and a leg."

He laughed at his joke. Hayden couldn't help but laugh, too.

"So, Sheriff," Hank said. "You were saying you came from a starship?"

"Yes." He paused, suddenly remembering the trife's contagion, and that contact with infected blood could cause problems. "I may be infected with their disease."

"I hadn't thought of that," Jake said. "But don't worry that you passed it on to us, Sheriff. We've been immune for a long time. I assume no one in the colony was infected?"

"No. The protocol." He paused, remembering how Malcolm had gunned down the people who had gotten too close to the trife. "They killed anyone who might have been exposed."

"I've heard when the war started, they did the same thing here, too, for a while," Hank said. "A grepping mess."

"Is there a cure?" Hayden asked.

"No," Jake replied. "We never needed one. Genetics took care of who lived and who died before we had a chance to come up with an immunization. You and your wife will either survive or perish. That's up to your DNA."

He knew the odds. They weren't good. There was a ninety percent chance he would die.

"Sorry, Sheriff," Hank said. "I didn't think anybody needed to worry about that form of death anymore."

"It's okay. I understand. That's why the people of Metro are better off staying in Metro. One of the reasons, at least. "

"You said you couldn't get them out, anyway," Hank said.

"No. I can't," Hayden agreed.

He could have before. He had thrown Malcolm's chip away. It was better for everyone to stay locked inside Metro, at least for now. Maybe one day it would be safe to come out, but he doubted it.

He noticed now that Jake had stopped moving. He was looking at Hayden, a suddenly fearful expression on his face.

"Sheriff, you said the Scrappers think you can get them in?"

"That's right."

"How badly do they want to get in?"

"Pretty damn bad."

"Did any of them see you escape?"

Hayden caught on to what Jake was thinking.

It didn't matter if they thought he should stay and rest.

He wasn't safe here.

Maybe none of them were.

"I left a whole group behind, outside the Pilgrim. They had your other horses. I doubt they would have come up while the goliath was tearing the place apart. Unless they got trapped, they know I got away." He paused. "Ghost saw me, too."

Jake threw the computer into the bag at his feet and stood up, lifting it with him.

"We have to go."

4

"What do you mean, we?" Hayden asked.

"Help me help him up, will you, Dad?" Jake said, ignoring him.

He took Hayden beneath the shoulder and at the elbow of his left arm, while Hank moved to the right.

It should have been awkward to have a mechanical arm attached to his own, grafted on with the metal band that made the limb controllable. By the magic of that same band, it wasn't. The hand felt natural to his mind, providing the sensation and motion that he expected and satisfying his mind's desire for a symmetrical form. It looked awful and out of place, but he could live with that.

"I said, 'what do you mean, we?'" he repeated.

His feet landed on the floor. He tried to stand, finding the limbs still weak. For all of his talk about getting up and getting out, he could barely stand.

"You're in no condition to travel alone," Jake said. "And besides, you have no idea where you're going."

"This is my fight," Hayden said. "My hunt. I've already put you in danger."

"A risk we accepted when we took you in," Hank said.

They started helping him walk toward the hidden door.

"I can't ask you to get involved in this," Hayden insisted.

"Too late," Hank said. "We made a decision to get involved. Somebody had to, or you would have died."

"Then you should have let me die, damn it," Hayden said. "Everyone who's tried to help me so far has been killed. Sarah, Jonas, Jennifer. They all died."

"Welcome to Earth, Sheriff," Jake said. "That's the way the world is now. A lot of people die for a lot of stupid, senseless reasons. But you didn't. Not yet. Maybe you can make a difference."

"We need good men," Hank said.

"I'm not a good man," Hayden replied.

"You took on the Scrappers. You killed Pig. That makes you good in my book."

"Bullshit. I didn't do it because I was trying to help you. It was self-preservation, plain and simple."

They reached the door. Jake pushed it open. At the same time he did, a door slammed open above their heads.

"Shit," Jake whispered. "Stay quiet."

"Hank, you mangy old cuss," a rough voice shouted above them. "Where the hell did you get off to? I need to talk to you."

"Gregor, is that you?" Hank shouted.

"Dad," Jake said.

"Take him out the back way," Hank said. "I'll keep Gregor busy."

"It's me. Where are you, Hank?"

"In the basement. I'm coming."

"Don't let him see your hand," Jake said.

Hank nodded, slipping out from beneath Hayden, leaving him dangling from Jake's arm. Hayden planted his feet, testing his legs again. The strength and feeling were slowly returning.

"I've got it," he said. "Let me go."

"Let's not take any chances, Sheriff," Jake said.

They moved out into a small, narrow hallway with a stairwell at each end. Hank turned to the right and kept walking. Jake pulled Hayden to the left.

"This way," Jake said.

Hayden let the kid guide him. They could both hear Hank's footfalls on the stairs and then the floor above them as they moved.

"Gregor," Hank said. "To what do I owe this pleasure?"

"Grep your pleasure, old man. I want pleasure, I go to Haven and pay for it. I'm looking for someone. He stole one of the horses we took from you."

"What does that have to do with me?" Hank asked.

"We thought maybe your mare brought our person of interest back here to you. He was pretty badly injured."

"More likely he fell off the horse," Hank said. "Cass came back all right, but there was nobody on her. I figured she broke loose of you lot."

"You're sure she was alone?" Gregor asked. "It would be a shame if any more trouble came down on you, wouldn't it, Hank? It already cost you your hand and your wife."

Jake and Hayden were moving toward the stairs at the opposite end when Hayden heard that. He froze in place, looking back at the distant steps, and then at his new appendage.

"Sheriff," Jake said. "Don't. We have to keep moving. You start trouble here, you'll get us all killed."

"There's only one of them," Hayden said.

"There's never only one of them unless it's Ghost," Jake replied. "How are your legs?"

"Weak," Hayden admitted. "You were right about me not being ready to move."

"I wish we had another choice. Here's what we're going to do. These stairs lead to the back of the house. You wait there while I sneak around and grab Cass. We get to her, and we get out of here."

"What about your father?"

"He can handle himself. It's not strange for me to be gone. I go to Haven a lot."

"How far is it?"

"Thirty miles. I'm not saying they're easy miles, but I've done it plenty of times before."

"Pozz," Hayden said.

"Pozz?" Jake asked.

"It means yes, or affirmative."

They reached the stairs.

"Got it. Wait at the top. Stay silent."

Jake helped Hayden to the top of the steps, blocked off by a closed door resting horizontally at the top. He unlatched it and slowly pushed it open, scanning the area. When he decided it was clear, he climbed out. Hayden saw Jake's feet quickly crossing a small clearing before the door settled closed.

"Gregor, I promise," Hank said. "Why would I lie to you? Do you think I'd protect some half-dead stranger if he did show up at my door? What good would that do me?"

"You've denied us before, Hank. Don't forget about that. You could have given Pig your wife, but you had to make him take her, right along with your arm. She might still be alive if you hadn't been so damn stubborn."

Hayden felt his face flush. So that was why the old man and his son were helping him.

"No man has a right to whatever he wants just because he wants it," Hank said. "Not even Pig."

He could hear the Scrapper laughing. "You see, Hank, that's exactly what I'm talking about. It's a good thing for you Pig is dead."

A few seconds of silence passed before Hank spoke.

"Good riddance."

More silence. Where the hell was Jake?

"You don't sound very surprised," Gregor said.

"I. I." Hank froze again. "I just don't know what to say. Who? How?"

"The grepper we're looking for, that's who. Burned his brain right out with this."

"What is it?" Hank asked.

"A laser pistol," Gregor said. "Our target dropped it outside the building we were holing up in after a pair of goliaths showed up and killed most of our crew. Lucky for me, I was underground when it happened. Do you want to see how it works?"

"Uh. Gregor, I. Ahhh."

Hayden didn't hear anything, but he knew the laser pistol didn't make any noise when it was fired. Where had Gregor shot Hank? The arm? The leg?

"Where is he?" Gregor shouted.

"I. I swear I don't know," Hank said between moans of pain. "Shit, Gregor, I grepping swear."

"What happened to your arm, Hank?" Gregor said. "Where's your replacement? Where's your fool son, for that matter?"

Hayden wanted to go up there, to help the old man who had helped to save his life. He had unwittingly brought the Scrappers to them. It didn't matter if they had decided to help him.

Where the hell was Jake?

The door upstairs opened. Something thumped onto the floor.

"I found the Borger outside. He was leading the horse somewhere."

"I see," Gregor said. "Where were you going, Jake?"

"Grep you," Jake said.

"Jake!" Hank shouted. "Don't."

"Dad?" Jake said, apparently seeing his father had been shot. "You didn't have to hurt him. He doesn't know anything."

"Well, then what do you know, Jake?" Gregor said.

"Please," Hank said. "Leave my son alone. You've already taken my wife. Isn't that enough?"

Hayden bit his lip as he forced himself to his feet. He couldn't sit there and let them both die for him. He couldn't let the Scrappers get away with this.

He pushed on the cellar door, shoving it open and stepping out. There was a brick wall directly behind him, the foundation of the home. A pair of steep hills were on both sides of the home, a natural barrier against the goliath. A small field with a run-down stable sat further back.

He made his way along the house until he reached the corner. He looked around the side. Four more horses were waiting there. He recognized them from the airlock inside the Pilgrim. His eyes shifted to the house, to the two guards waiting at the door in front of it. They were still wearing the roughspun robes, but they had removed their masks. What was the apparatus for if not to prevent them from getting the xenotrife disease?

He could see the revolver resting on one of the guards' hips. Could he reach them before the guard could draw, aim, and fire the weapon?

He had to.

He took in a few quick breaths, flexing his legs a few times to make sure he wouldn't collapse on the way.

Then he charged.

"Raaaaaa," he shouted, drawing their attention as he ran at them.

Both guards were taken by surprise, and they fumbled for their guns, giving him the time he needed. He reached the first as the heavy sidearm came to the guard's hand, slashing hard with his new claws. They passed easily through the man's throat, nearly severing his head and killing him instantly.

He caught the body with his other hand, holding it up as the second guard planted a slug in it. Hayden used his momentum to throw the corpse into the guard, following behind it as the man stepped aside, only to be greeted with a set of sharp claws slicing through the side of his face. Flesh and muscle, bone and brain were all torn aside by the surgically sharp blades.

Hayden's legs were burning, but he changed direction, heading for the door. The third Scrapper was in the middle of trying to pull it open to get at him, and he saved him the trouble, stabbing forward with the claws, smiling savagely when they went through the wood and into the Scrapper's chest.

He kept pushing, moving the dying man out of the way. He bent at the entrance, retrieving the Scrapper's gun. Then he entered the house. He was in a small foyer. A handmade vase of wildflowers rested on an old wood table. A faded color photograph of a woman hung above it. To his right, he could see the Scrapper, Gregor, had the laser pistol up against Jake's head.

"Stop," Gregor commanded. "Or he dies."

Hayden took a few steps forward, leaning on the frame of the doorway to keep himself from falling.

"I said stop," Gregor said, pushing the muzzle against Jake's head.

"Kill him," Jake said. "Or he'll kill us all."

"I killed Pig," Hayden said, acting tougher than he felt. "You look like a little piece of shit compared to him. Drop the gun, and you'll get out of here alive."

"I'll kill him," Gregor said. "Don't grep with me, Insider."

"Did you come for access to Metro? Is that why you're here?"

"King will reward me for bringing you in."

"I can't open it. I can't open the hatch. Nobody can except the Governor, and he's Inside."

"I don't believe you. Pig said you could get us in. He said there's treasure in there. He heard the stories."

"I don't care if you believe me. It's true. If you kill these people, then I kill you. Or you can drop the gun and walk away. Nobody has to know you were ever here."

"You can't reach me before I burn a hole in his head."

"Are you sure you want to take that chance?"

"I-"

Hank shifted, lunging toward the Scrapper.

"Hank, no," Hayden said.

Gregor turned the pistol on the old man, squeezing the trigger at the same time Hayden fired the revolver, whose muzzle had been placed against the flimsy looking wall of the farmhouse.

Hank's body hit the floor with a thud; a fresh hole burned right through his brain. Gregor was knocked sideways by the impact of the heavy slug, a spray of blood launching from him as the round hit him in the shoulder.

Then Hayden was on him, claws slashing hard across the Scrapper's chest, cutting him open from collar to pelvis. Gregor crumpled back and didn't move.

"Dad," Jake said, crawling to his father on his knees.

Hayden fell to his knees, too, failing to keep himself steady.

Jake reached down, putting his fingers on his father's

neck and searching for a pulse. Hayden knew he wouldn't find one.

"No. Damn it. No." Jake looked at Hayden. "He's dead."

"I'm sorry," Hayden said. "I tried."

Jake's face tightened against the pain. He nodded. "I know. And I know Gregor. He would have killed us both and then found you anyway. You saved my life."

"I led them right to you."

"You didn't," Jake insisted. "Cass did. You weren't even conscious when she turned up. It isn't your fault."

"I wish I could have saved you both."

"That's because you're one of the good guys, Sheriff." He looked back at his father, but he didn't let himself sob. "He's with my mother now. Where he belongs."

He put his hand on Hank's shoulder and whispered something under his breath. Then he pushed himself back to his feet.

"We have to go," he said. "When Gregor doesn't report in, they'll be coming to find him."

Hayden grimaced as he fought to get to his feet. "Take the pistol," he said. "It's a good gun."

"We'll take more than that," Jake replied.

5

Hayden finished wrapping himself in the Scrapper's robes, appreciative of the way they covered his new hand as long as he kept it at his side. Jake was close by, digging through one of the horses' saddlebags and tossing the stuff he didn't want to the ground.

"Are you looking for something specific?" Hayden asked.

"Yes," Jake replied. "The Scrappers usually carry fire-bombs. I want to burn the farmhouse down."

"Burn it down? This is your home."

Jake stopped and looked at him. He had taken one of the other Scrapper's robes. It had a bloodstain on the shoulder. "This was my home, Sheriff. I stayed with my Dad, to help him as he got older. There's nothing for me here now."

"I'm sorry," Hayden said again.

"I know. And I know that no matter how many times I tell you not to be, you still will be. I like that about you."

He resumed his search, finding what he wanted a few seconds later. He lifted it out. A glass cylinder with liquid at the bottom and a rag stuffed into the top. It was a primitive thing.

"The Scrappers were wearing those masks inside the Pilgrim," Hayden said, pointing at one of the discarded devices. "Do you know why? I thought it was to keep from getting infected, but you said they're all immune."

Jake looked down at the mask, which was connected to a small, square tank by a short tube.

"A lot of them wear these," he said. "They're filled with nitrous oxide. They use it to get high, and stay that way."

"A narcotic?"

"In a sense."

"Are drugs illegal here?"

Jake laughed. "Sheriff, nothing is illegal here. As long as you don't cross King, you're pretty much free to do whatever the hell you please."

"I don't understand."

"What's to understand? The world went to hell. It's as simple as that."

"But we were fighting the trife."

"We lost. Years ago. It's been a long time, Sheriff. A really long time. The farmhouse here, it was built two hundred years ago. By who? I have no idea. My parents happened across it while they were trying to migrate from Haven. They decided to stay. Then, my Dad, he came across some wild horses and managed to tame them. And you're saying you were on your starship almost twice as long as that."

"But humankind is still here. We didn't go extinct."

"We're in a constant state of flux. The whole planet is. We change, the trife change, the goliath change, and so on and so on. The bottom line is that we haven't been able to mount any kind of lasting defense. We haven't been able to restore stable lines of communication, maintain industry or large-scale agriculture, or any of the other things a society needs to grow and organize. We're spread out and cut off. It's been that way for a long time, and now most folks just accept it. A hard life, local justice, or tyrants as the case may be. It's like those old movies. The wild west. Four centuries ago, the trife came, and civilization ended. Full stop."

Hayden was silent for a moment.

"So men like King come into power?" he asked. "They make all the rules?"

"Pretty much. Like I said, local justice. You wrong me or mine, and I have every right to wrong you back. Unless you're a Scrapper." He spit on the mask at his feet. "Grep that. They took your wife. They killed both my folks. As far as I'm concerned, you and me, we're at war."

"I don't want to be at war."

Jake laughed. "You shouldn't have sliced those men's heads off then, eh, Sheriff? You shouldn't have gutted Gregor or killed Pig. The Scrappers might take you alive, but only until they get what they want from you or you finally convince them they can't."

"There has to be more, though."

"What do you mean, more?"

"A way to start rebuilding? A way to destroy the trife? Something? The Pilgrim had a research module in it. They were working on the way to make the trife sick, the way they made us sick. They weren't the only ones."

"There may be people out there doing what you say, Sheriff. I only know what's happening between here and Haven. But I wouldn't count on it. Four hundred years is a long time to be trying to work something like that out. If it could be done, you'd think it would have been done already."

"Is all of that history really lost?"

"A lot of it is. Lost and forgotten."

Jake turned away from him, digging into his pocket. He pulled out a small device, pressed a switch, and put it to the rag. A second later, the cloth was on fire.

"Here's to the future, Sheriff," Jake said, heaving the cylinder toward the house.

It hit a window, going through it with a crash. A thump followed a few seconds later, and the inside of the farmhouse lit up as the flames started to spread.

Two hundred years, and it was going to vanish just like that.

Just like human civilization.

"We better get moving," Jake said, turning away from the place as smoke started pouring out the broken window. "You can take Cass; she seems to like you. I'll take Virgo. The rest of them will go back to being free, I suppose."

Hayden was standing next to the mare, who seemed unaffected by everything going on around her.

"Jake," Hayden said. "One small problem."

"What's that?"

"I don't know how to ride."

"You found your way here, Sheriff. You know how to ride." He smiled. "Maybe just not how to steer. I'll show you the ropes once we're away from here. The smoke's going to attract the trife, and the trife might attract a goliath. If we're lucky, a few Scrappers will wind up in the middle of that mess."

Hayden put his boot in the stirrup, pulling himself awkwardly into the saddle. Jake hopped onto Virgo, a larger brown stallion who didn't seem nearly as calm as his ride. The horse snorted as Jake took the reins, bringing him to Hayden and picking up Cass' lead.

"All you have to do right now is hang on," Jake said.

"I can do that," Hayden replied, keeping a grip on the saddle.

His body was still sore, and when they started walking every jostle hurt. He would deal with that pain for as long as he needed. It was a small price to pay to be moving forward again.

The next ten minutes passed in silence, both Hayden and Jake lost in their own thoughts.

Then the ground shivered softly, and Jake's horse tossed its head and whined.

"I was right," Jake said, turning his head back toward the house.

Hayden looked back, too. The vague outline of a goliath was coming into focus on a hazy horizon.

"What kept the trife away from the house before?" Hayden asked.

"Who said they stay away?" Jake replied. "They don't have any interest in horses, but the horses get real worked up when they're close. We always heard them making a fuss in plenty of time to hide. I knew the smoke would bring them back."

Cass' head shifted, and she whined loudly, joining Virgo. It was a powerful outburst compared to the animal's usual calm.

"I take it this is worked up?" Hayden asked.

Jake nodded, reaching over to the side of his mount and grabbing an old rifle. Hayden followed his lead, reaching for the laser pistol he had placed in one of the saddlebags.

A series of hisses rose from within the brush, seemingly from all around them.

The trife were coming.

6

"DAMN SCRAPPERS MUST HAVE DRAWN THEM OVER ON THEIR way in," Jake said, head swiveling back and forth as he watched for the creatures. "The trife don't usually gather on this side of the creek. They don't like water all that much."

The landscape here was hilly and green, with sparse trees on either side of them and plenty of thick vegetation lining both sides of the trail. A part of Hayden was in awe at the sight of so many plants, but there was no time to relax and admire the beauty of the scenery.

The bushes on the left ahead of Jake moved. He rotated in the saddle, bringing the rifle to his shoulder and tilting his head to sight down it. The trife appeared a moment later, bounding out of the greenery and charging.

The shot echoed through the air, the round hitting the trife square in the chest. It hissed softly as it was thrown back and to the ground. It didn't get back up.

The bushes on both sides of them started to move, disturbed by the creatures passing through them. Hayden gripped the pistol, waiting for the demons to emerge.

The ground was shaking more heavily.

Hayden risked a glance back. He could see the goliath more clearly now. It was at least fifty meters tall, a mass of mottled flesh clinging to dense bone. It moved slowly, its head slightly lowered, eyes searching the area. It lifted a massive leg, taking another step that would bring it ever closer to them.

"Sheriff!" Jake shouted, breaking Hayden from his stupor.

He whipped his head back as a pair of trife broke from cover, leaping toward Cass. He fired as she spun, hitting one of the trife in the arm before the change in momentum pulled him from the saddle. He rolled off the side of her, landing hard on his back. Waves of fire lanced up through the area Jake had stitched, and he fought to keep his eyes open against the pain.

"Damn it," he heard Jake say.

Then one of the trife was on top of him, claws angling down toward his neck. It was definitely different than the ones he had encountered on the Pilgrim. Every part of it was smaller, and it was much heavier than the hollow-boned creatures he had fought before.

He reacted without thinking, bringing his replacement hand up to block the attack, catching the trife's claws with his own. Seeing the hand, the creature hissed more sharply.

Hayden managed to hold onto the pistol when he fell, and blocking the trife's attack gave him the seconds he needed to put it to the creature's chest and pull the trigger. It screeched as the weapon burned a hole in it and then fell on top of him.

The ground shuddered, the goliath drawing closer.

Hayden cursed as he shoved the trife, pushing it off him. He forced himself to get up, finding Jake standing next to Virgo, holding both Cass and the stallion's leads. There were four dead trife on the road, including the one he had shot.

"What are you doing?" Hayden asked.

"Shhh," Jake replied, putting a finger to his lips. Then he motioned Hayden to join them.

Hayden limped to where Jake was standing, the fall from the horse causing one of his legs to lock up in spasm. His heart thumped heavily, his breathing froze as the light filtering onto the trail vanished, blocked out by the goliath.

He turned around and looked up as the ground shook again, almost hard enough to knock him over. An awful smell wafted across the area, the goliath's scent preceding its arrival.

"Stay silent," Jake said. "Try not to move."

Hayden stared up at the giant. They were standing in the center of the trail, completely exposed. How were they supposed to not be seen?

Then the goliath was right on top of them, one of its huge legs crashing through the brush a few meters away. The smell of it was nearly unbearable, like the waste recycling system in Metro when it backed up and broke down. Hayden remained completely still, frozen in fear at the sight of the thing towering over them.

It huffed as it leaned forward, long limbs sweeping across the ground behind them. Something screeched, and then he saw a huge hand move to the goliath's heavily-toothed mouth, depositing a trife into it.

It turned on its hips, reaching down with its other arm, scooping up another of the creatures and devouring it. Then it paused, still standing over them, eyes sweeping the area. Hayden's breath caught in his throat as the large, blue orbs angled directly toward them, definitely looking their way.

They didn't stop on the spot, passing over the pair without concern. The brush was shifting nearby, and Hayden watched as it reached toward the area for the trife that were active there.

The trife that were coming their way.

"Jake," Hayden said, realizing their paths were going to cross at a bad time.

"Shit," Jake said at the same time, noticing the same thing. "Stay close to the horses. It won't pay attention to anything that doesn't look human."

Hayden was having a hard time believing something so large was so selective about what it ate, but he did as the other man said, pressing against Cass' side as they moved further down the trail.

One of the trife burst out of the brush behind them, hissing in fear. Hayden glanced back as it saw them, rushing in their direction. He could see the goliath's arm behind it, trying to grab it as it moved.

He raised the pistol toward it.

"Don't," Jake said. "Too much noise."

Hayden fired. The laser burned silently through the creature, causing it to drop. The goliath scooped it up a moment later.

They remained in place, waiting while the behemoth continued its hunt. Large hands crashed through the area around them, grabbing a few more of the trife. Then it straightened up, eyes scanning the landscape.

They waited a minute. And then another. Hayden's heart was beating so fast it hurt, his level of fear causing him to shiver where he stood. He stayed quiet. They both did. The horses shifted and nickered beside them, but as promised the goliath paid them no mind.

Instead, it slowly shifted, turning itself around to face the burning farmhouse once more. Something must have caught its attention there because it started walking heavily away.

They didn't move for another five minutes. It was long enough that the goliath had made it all the way back to the farmhouse. Hayden could still see part of it through the trees, leaning over and reaching out to grab the trife there.

"Too close," Jake whispered. "I forgot that thing doesn't make a sound. You saved our asses."

"You did just fine on your own," Hayden said. "I only killed two of them."

Jake smiled. "You don't survive out here alone without learning how to shoot," he said. "That pistol of yours is priceless."

"It's also one of the reasons the Scrappers want me so badly," Hayden said. "There are probably more of them inside the Pilgrim. There's a whole cache of weapons, armor, and vehicles beneath the colony, sealed in where they can't reach."

Jake whistled at the description. "Wheee-ewww. But how do those assholes know about that?"

"That's the winning question, isn't it? I'd love to know the answer to that myself."

"Maybe we can ask King once we get to him?" Jake suggested.

"Once Natalia is safe," Hayden replied. "Nothing else matters before that."

"We better get moving," Jake said. "The trife come out in greater numbers at night, and we've got a ways to travel. There's a safe house at the halfway point. We can rest there, but we have to reach it first."

Hayden grabbed Cass' saddle and pulled himself up. Jake climbed back onto Virgo.

"What are we waiting for?" Hayden said, looking back at the farmhouse and the fading silhouette of the goliath one last time.

For all of their fearsomeness, it was obvious the giants were also helping keep the planet's trife population under control. He couldn't help but think back to the Research module and the corpses he had discovered there, bent and twisted into monstrous things.

Were the goliaths really another invading species, or had they been made? If someone had made them, where were those someones now, and what else did they know? If they could create monsters, could they cure him and Natalia of the xenotrife's disease?

Maybe some things were better off forgotten, but some things definitely weren't.

7

HAYDEN MANAGED TO FIND A LITTLE BIT OF ENERGY TO MARVEL at the landscape as they made the ride from the farmhouse toward the rest stop Jake referred to as Crossroads. He gaped at the sheer volume of greenery around them. The trees. The plants. The flowers. The bushes. He also stared wide-eyed at the numbers of different animals they passed along the way. Birds, mostly, of various shapes and sizes, but also a number of insects and smaller creatures.

Some of the plants and animals he recognized from the PASS. The others, Jake named for him, offering him a brief description. When a squirrel scurried past in front of Cass, he told Hayden a story about how one of the creatures had gotten into his house once, and how difficult it had been to get it back out. When a deer happened by, he mentioned he was surprised to see one. The animals were good for food and getting harder and harder to find.

The kid was a good talker, and well-educated. Considering the condition Hayden had been in when he escaped from the Pilgrim, he had been incredibly lucky to wind up in his and Hank's care. It was the only reason he was still alive.

It was the only reason he might see Natalia again.

He could still sense the biting emptiness his fevered dreams had caused. It was a small pit in his soul, a blank hole that had never really been filled, only covered over. They had planned to name their daughter Hallia, an aggregation of both their names. They had been excited as any expecting parents could be. And then came the night on the stairwell, when something had gone horribly wrong. It had been made even worse when Medical couldn't give them a solid reason for the loss.

"Sometimes, these things just happen," they had said.

He hated the words. Things didn't just happen. There was always a reason. They didn't know what the reason was. The same way he didn't know the reason for the xenotrife or the goliaths for that matter.

Neither had just happened.

The green started to fade over time, replaced with browns and grays of dirt and stone, a wide swath of it that cut across the landscape. There were signs of a long lost civilization littering the chasm, where heavily rusted hunks of metal sat in random patterns on both sides and plants pushed their way through every crack and crevice.

"This is the common road to Haven," Jake said. "The Crossroads is about a three miles west of here. We'll stick to the side of the pavement. If we hear anything, we find cover immediately. Okay, Sheriff?"

"Pozz," Hayden said. He paused a moment. "Where did this come from?"

"The world before the trife," Jake replied. "It used to stretch for thousands of miles, across the entire continent from one ocean to another. Some parts of it were destroyed in the war, other parts have decayed over time. King maintains the segment from here to Haven and then north all the way to the Fortress, so his Scrappers have an easier time getting from place to place."

"Ghost came this way, then?"

"You can bet on it."

"How far does King's control reach?" Hayden asked. "You said the road stretched thousands of miles. He can't go that far?"

"No. Not yet, anyway. The Scrappers have been clearing further east, pushing their empire outward, not only with violence but with the machines King and his crews have been able to restore. Right now, they control an approximately three hundred mile radius around the Fortress, give or take, minus the part of that territory that's all ocean. There have been rumors of a floating city out there somewhere, self-sufficient and safe from the trife. There's always some fool passing through Haven with the idea of building a boat to take them there."

"You don't think it's real?"

"No. Nobody's ever met anybody who came from there, and people who head out to find it never return."

"Maybe it's just a great place to live," Hayden said.

Jake laughed. "You're welcome to build a boat of your own, Sheriff."

"No thanks."

They were both silent for a few minutes, letting the soft clopping of the horses' hooves be the only nearby sound. Then Jake broke the silence.

"A little rundown on Crossroads," he said. "It's a safe house, designed to provide rest and relief to travelers at nightfall. What that means is there are serious consequences for anyone who makes trouble while inside, including the Scrappers. It's supposed to be neutral ground, and the proprietor is the last person on the planet you would ever want to screw with. Got it?"

"Pozz," Hayden said.

"Once you leave the grounds is another story. It isn't uncommon for people to be jumped and killed on their way out, and if we run into any of the wrong people, the same thing can happen to us."

"Are you sure you want to go there?"

"It's going to be dark in an hour. The trife are bad enough during the day, but they're nearly invisible once the sun goes down. You don't wander around at night unless you're stupid, desperate, or part of a large group of well-equipped individuals."

"Like the Scrappers?"

"Not even the Scrappers want to be out at night. Crossroads is pretty safe, the trife have learned to stay away from there."

"They're intelligent," Hayden said. "In a different way than you and me, but they're smart."

"You won't get an argument from me on that. I've read old studies that were done on them. They adapt better than we do. They evolve more rapidly, and they pass some level of instinct or understanding down to their offspring through the serumen; the gloppy, sticky shit they secrete when they're reproducing."

"The trife we encountered before looked a lot different from the trife on the Pilgrim. Smaller and denser."

"I've heard if you head further south there are trife with wings if you can believe that."

"I'm ready to believe pretty much anything," Hayden admitted.

Jake smiled, opening his mouth to say something else. He didn't, his face freezing instead. He stopped Virgo, shifting around to face the other way.

Hayden heard it, too. A low hum in the distance, getting louder by the second. He swiveled his head to look along the road to the east. A small cloud of dust was visible on the horizon.

"Find cover," Jake said.

Hayden took Cass' reins, the way Jake had shown him during the ride. He kicked the horse lightly, asking her to follow Virgo as the stallion carried Jake off the road, toward a larger, rusted hulk of metal.

Jake dismounted when he got there, tying Virgo off on a rusted metal crossbar that was visible through the foliage before taking his rifle from the horse's back. Hayden tied off Cass, grabbed his pistol, and joined the man at the back corner of the junker.

The humming was much louder now, a rhythmic rumble that Hayden found oddly soothing. It echoed across the wide road, causing the horses to whinny as they tried to decide if they were afraid of it or not.

He could see the source of the noise now. A car. He had seen them before in the videos stored on the PASS and the movies brought by the colonists. He couldn't believe they were still out here, still operable nearly four hundred years later.

This one was long and low, a black brick on wheels. Armor plating had been mounted to portions of it, the metal sculpted into ridges that would probably impale anything that tried to jump on it. The tires were barely visible beyond even more plating, rusted and riveted steel protecting them from bullets and claws. A short pole jutted out of the back, a scrap of purple cloth waving from it.

Jake had been watching it approach with his rifle raised, sighting down it. He lowered the weapon now, straightening up.

"Stay hidden," he said, ducking further behind their cover. Hayden did the same.

The car went by, rocketing past at high speed. They watched the back of it vanish down the road.

"Who was it?" Hayden asked.

"Just a second," Jake said, holding up his hand. He was still listening.

Hayden stayed quiet. A few seconds later, he heard a fresh round of noise. They both returned to the corner of the scrapped vehicle, watching as three more cars approached. They all looked different, though they had a few things in common. Large, thick wheels, violent armor plating, cockpits open to the air but protected by heavy steel cages. Each had four people riding inside. One was a driver; another stood behind a mounted rifle. The other two were both armed, balancing from the sides of the machines. A USSF flag whipped in the air behind the lead car, a blue eagle and star logo plainly visible on a red and white background.

"Damn," Jake said.

"What is it?" Hayden asked.

"Scrapper Road Enforcers. They're monitoring the stretch between Haven and Lavega. If they're chasing someone, it means they either killed a Scrapper or refused to pay the road tax." He paused. "Or the assholes just want their car."

"It looks like they're making a run for Crossroads," Hayden said as the cars zoomed past.

"Any enemy of the Scrappers is a friend of ours," Jake replied. "I hope they make it."

8

DAYLIGHT WAS FADING BY THE TIME CROSSROADS CAME INTO view, the darkness slowly overtaking them and casting the wide road they were riding on into long shadows where Hayden could easily imagine a trife's dark flesh disappearing. They had followed in the wake of the Road Enforcers and their quarry on the way to neutral ground, keeping a steady, urgent pace that wouldn't tire their mounts or themselves and would still get them to safety on time.

The perimeter of the Crossroads slowly materialized out of the horizon. A mixture of settling mist and dust was hanging in the air, keeping visibility low as they approached. Even so, Jake let out an audible sigh of relief to have made it to their destination before the sun had completely given up on them, and Hayden's tired and sore body relaxed in response.

They had made it.

It seemed like an accomplishment, even if they hadn't run into any other trouble after leaving the farmhouse and escaping the goliath. The overlying potential for confrontation hung ominously around them with every step they took, a dark cloud Hayden knew might never lift.

For them or for what was left of humankind.

Crossroads sat a half a kilometer off the main stretch of road, along a secondary track that passed beneath the one they had traveled on, still suspended by its original moorings despite the passage of centuries. One of the supports was cracked and broken, no longer holding up the heavy stone bridge, but it seemed the remaining two were enough to keep it upright. For now, anyway.

They hadn't been able to see the safe house from up there, thanks to the dust and fog. They had followed a winding path around to the bottom, to the place where the Crossroads derived its name. The intersection of another road, one that Jake said didn't go very far before falling into ruin. The name had stuck though.

The first thing Hayden noticed, the first thing anyone noticed, were the guns. They sat on large, cement blocks along the Crossroads perimeter, spaced evenly apart, a dozen in all. They were large, violent things, with massive barrels jutting out of steel casings, most of which had been dented and scuffed by bullets coming back toward them. At the moment, the turrets were at rest, facing downward. Hayden didn't see any people nearby to man them.

"Wow," he said, almost without thinking. He had never seen weapons like them. Even the limited military gear he had discovered on the Pilgrim looked ineffective in comparison. "We had guns like this, and we still lost to the trife?"

"The guns weren't the problem," Jake said. "The bullets were." He shrugged. "We just couldn't make them fast enough. Have you ever seen ants, Sheriff?"

"We had a few nature videos on the Pilgrim," Hayden replied. "I've seen fire ants. They swarm together during a flood and make a raft until they find some other floating debris, and then they catch onto that. There were thousands and thousands of them."

"Imagine those ants are trife and imagine the debris is a building like Crossroads."

Hayden couldn't see the building yet, not in detail, but he could make out the structure in the fog. It was at least ten meters tall, a solid block of concrete. There were spaces for windows, but it looked like they had all been filled in. He pictured the trife swarming it, covering it up.

And getting inside.

"A million bullets," Jake continued. "Could kill a million trife, and there would still be a million more."

"But not now."

"Not after the goliaths came. We don't even know how many of them there are, or how many trife they eat every day. It has to be a lot considering how big they are."

"A lot, but not enough."

"Things were worse before. We've been able to get some kind of civilization going, but it isn't easy, I'll give you that. We've got the basics. Clothing. Food. Shelter. Well, some of us, anyway. There are still plenty of poor to go around. King's an asshole, but he's been getting some things done. He's making concrete. He's producing new bullets and guns. He's putting together cars. I've heard he has an aircraft, but nobody knows how to fly it."

"I can only guess how he's planning to use all of that. I have a feeling it isn't to continue the war against the trife."

"Not so far," Jake agreed. "He's been focused on expanding his empire and lording over folks like my dad and me with threats and fear, using his Scrappers like hungry dogs. If he has any intention of doing anything about the trife, he's got a funny way of showing it."

Crossroads came into full view as they passed between two of the turrets. The guns were even larger up close, coming up to the top of his head despite his height on the horse. Ahead of them, a single dark hole was the only break in the concrete of the massive building, an entrance to the safe house. To its left, he could see there had been a different type of doorway once, hundreds of years before. A round sign of filthy red and white rings was still hanging over the blocks of concrete that had covered over the entrance, and even that concrete was aged and cracked and covered in moss, showing it had been there for quite some time.

"What was this place?" Hayden asked.

"A store, a long time ago, before Wiz took over."

"Wiz?"

"She's the proprietor of Crossroads. Smartest woman I've ever met. And most dangerous."

"How so?"

Jake looked over at him. "You did see the guns, right?"

Hayden smiled. "Right."

They led the horses into the hole, which was hiding a ramp leading downward. A guard was stationed there, the first person Hayden had seen who wasn't Jake, Hank, or a Scrapper. A man in patterned cloth that reminded him of military fatigues. He was carrying a rifle just like the one Hayden had found on the Pilgrim.

Where had he gotten it?

The guard waved at Jake as they rode past, apparently recognizing him. Jake waved back but didn't speak. Then the man looked at Hayden, eyes landing on the small portion of the mechanical hand jutting out from his robes and lingering there for a few seconds, as though he understood what it meant. He didn't react at all to the fact they were dressed as Scrappers.

Neutral ground.

"Ten more minutes, you would have been locked out," the guard said, deciding to say something after all.

"I know," Jake replied. "It doesn't matter now."

The guard chuckled. "True, true."

That was the extent of the conversation. They continued down the ramp. It curved around as it descended, bringing them further beneath the building. The horses' hooves echoed off the concrete as they reached the first level. Hayden could see the ramp continued deeper, but Jake led him off there.

The subterranean space was lit by dozens of bulbs strung to the supports that lined the ceiling, each of them giving off slight but valuable light. The first thing Hayden noticed were the cars. There were nine or ten in total, and he immediately recognized the three Scrapper vehicles with the big tires and the long, black car they had been chasing. The others were all modified similarly, with extra metal plating to protect the occupants and the vehicle itself from attack.

The next thing he noticed were the people. They were interspersed around the floor in individual small camps. Most had little more than small bedrolls and backpacks stuffed with possessions. A few were more organized, with cooktops like the one Pig had used, pop-up shelters for privacy, and game that had been hunted on the way there. They were all dirty, all tired looking. Hayden didn't see the Scrappers among them.

"They paid for an upgrade," Jake said. "To the upper floors. These people are travelers, mostly. On their way to Haven or the Fortress to join up with King."

"Join up with him?"

"For most, what he offers is better than what they have."

"It doesn't matter how he gets it or how he uses them?"

"Not to most. Everybody needs to eat."

"Needs to eat what? The Scrappers I ran into were cannibals."

Jake's face paled. "Yeah. Some of them are."

"I want to go up to where they are."

"Why?"

"I want to get to know them better. This seems like the best place to do it."

"You're still thinking like a Sheriff?"

"It's all I know how to be."

"It'll cost."

"You said I could pay."

Jake smiled. "You can."

Jake brought them over to one of the camps, dismounting as an older woman stood up.

"Jake," she said. "Good to see you."

"Good to see you too, Vera," he replied.

"On your way to Haven for some work?"

"You know me. Still making herb runs?"

"We all do what we know how to do. Doc Klegg pays me well enough to keep it worthwhile." She glanced at Hayden. "Who's your friend?"

"Hayden," Jake said. "He's a stranger, turned up at my door half-dead. I put him back together as best I could."

"Why?"

Hayden was surprised by the way she said it. Like Jake was an idiot for helping someone out for no other reason than because they were injured.

Jake lowered his voice. "He killed Pig."

Vera looked at him with fresh eyes, her entire expression becoming warmer with the words. She smiled at him, showing him a mouth missing most of its teeth. "In that case, you're my new best friend, Hayden. That grepping asshole took my daughter, and when he gave her back." She shook her head, and then spit on the ground. "Good riddance."

"Vera, can you keep an eye on Virgo and Cass for us? We're heading up."

"Come into some money, have you?"

"Not me," Jake said.

Vera kept smiling at Hayden. "I see. Well, you keep this up, you'll be a legend around here in no time."

"I'm not looking to be a legend," Hayden said. "I'm just looking for my wife."

Her smile vanished as suddenly as it had appeared. "Don't tell me-"

"Ghost took her," Jake said.

Now she was afraid. "Ghost? Hayden, if you know what's good for you, just let her go now. Save yourself the trouble."

Hayden wanted to yell at her like he had yelled at Jennifer. But she didn't know him; she only knew the people he was against.

"Can you watch Virgo and Cass?" Jake repeated.

"One note each," she said.

"One note for both," Jake replied. "I can find someone else down here to watch them."

"Fine," Vera said.

Jake dug into a pocket, pulling out a single torn piece of paper with the USSF logo on it. He handed it to Vera, who glanced around to make sure nobody was watching before putting it away.

Hayden climbed off Cass, patting the side of the horse's head before turning over the reins. The horse leaned in, nuzzling him for a moment.

"I don't know why she likes you so much," Jake said.

"Me neither," Hayden replied. He reached into his saddlebag to retrieve the laser pistol, tucking it under his robes.

"You won't need that in here," Jake said.

"I'm done taking chances," Hayden replied.

"Suit yourself. This way."

They walked through a ragged aisle that split the camps, across the floor to a doorway. A guard was stationed there, a woman with another one of the Space Force rifles.

"Two notes each to go up," she said.

Jake already had the scraps ready, and he handed them to her.

"Good to see you again, Jake," she said.

"You too, Sally."

"You know everybody around here?" Hayden asked as they entered the stairwell.

They could go up or down, but they hadn't paid to go down. They started to climb.

"Everybody who works here. I've been coming here at least twice a week for or so for the last ten years. Vera, she's a good woman. She knows plants, and she collects herbs and stuff for Haven's Doctor, Klegg."

"Sounds dangerous. I didn't see a gun."

"She doesn't have one. Most people don't realize the trife don't attack everyone. If you aren't a threat, they leave you alone."

"How do they determine if someone's a threat?"

"Men are always a threat. Women? Usually by age."

It was another interesting fact about the trife he would never have guessed. Where had the strange aliens come from, and why?

They reached the next floor, and Jake pushed open the door.

He nearly hit one of the Scrappers in the back with it as he did.

They were standing in a semi-circle in front of a wall, blocking whatever they were surrounding from view. The man they had almost hit turned around and glared at them.

"If you know what's good for you, you'll walk your asses right by."

Hayden kept staring, managing to get a peek through the human barrier. One of the Scrappers had a woman pressed against the wall, a knife to her throat.

What the hell happened to neutral ground?

9

"I'M NOT GOING ANYWHERE," HAYDEN SAID.

"What did you say?" the Scrapper asked.

Jake looked back at him, fear in his eyes. "Remember what I said about once we leave Crossroads?" he whispered.

Hayden remembered what he said. He didn't care. "I said, I'm not going anywhere. Whatever the hell you think you're doing, it stops right now."

The man turned around. He was bigger than Hayden by a head. He looked him over, recognizing the Scrapper robes.

"Do I know you, mate?" he asked. "You don't look familiar to me."

"I'm a Courier," Hayden said. "Name's Pozz."

He almost winced when he said it. It was the first thing that came to mind.

"You new or something, Pozz?" the Scrapper said. "You don't get how the family works?"

Hayden realized the other Scrappers had turned to look at him. He glanced over at the one in the center. The man was still holding the knife to the woman's throat, but he was looking back, too.

"I get it," Hayden said. "Thing is, I've been chasing that bitch for two days. My effort. My reward."

The man in the center laughed. "Is that right, mate?"

Hayden nodded. "That's right."

"What'd she do to you?"

"I was sent to deliver a package to King. She stole it from me. She's got it in that big ugly block of metal downstairs."

The woman was looking at him now, confused.

"No wonder she jumped our checkpoint," the Scrapper said. "I'll tell you what, Pozz. You knock me down; she's all yours. I knock you down; she stays with me."

"Pozz," Jake said, trying to warn him against it.

"Deal," Hayden said.

The man laughed. "Move aside, boys."

The half-circle opened to let Hayden in. The lead Scrapper let go of the woman, shoving her over to one of his lackeys, who grabbed her before she could get away. She struggled against him for a moment before settling, staring at Hayden, still trying to figure out what his game was.

"My name's Orion," the Scrapper said. "Here's the rules." He paused and then laughed. "There ain't no rules."

Then he lunged toward Hayden, leading with his knife. It was a large, thick hunting knife, sharp and ugly.

Hayden's first surprise was that he was ready for the attack. He had already learned from Pig not to trust these assholes with anything.

His second surprise came when he reached out with his borg hand, wrapping the metal fingers around the blade of the knife and squeezing so hard it snapped off the handle.

The motion left Orion off-balance, and Hayden followed up his first movement by throwing his balled right hand into the Scrapper's face.

The other Scrappers mumbled to one another behind him

as Orion straightened up, his face angry. "You got a borg? That's grepping cheating."

"You just said there ain't no rules," Hayden replied, grabbing his pistol and pointing it at the Scrapper. He had been right to bring it after all. "Why don't you fall? Now."

Orion stared at the weapon for a second. Then he threw himself to the ground.

Hayden put the gun back under his robes. He turned to the Scrapper holding the woman. "I'll take her," he said.

"Uh, Pozz?" Jake said.

Hayden looked over at him. A trio of guards had materialized in the hallway, and they had their rifles trained on the entire group.

"You all know the rules," Sally said. She had emerged from the stairwell. "No conflict. No violence. You're all spending the night outside. Anything you brought in becomes property of Wiz."

Orion bounced back to his feet. "What?" he screamed. "Are you grepping kidding me, you little bitch? Do you know who we are? Do you know who we work for?"

"Save it, Scrapper," Sally replied. "This is sovereign ground. Even King recognizes that."

"Grep your sovereign bullshit," Orion complained. "I ain't sleeping outside, and I ain't leaving my ride with you."

"Officer," Hayden said, getting her attention. "I'd like to point out that there was no violence taking place. No blood. No bruises. We're all just having a little fun. No harm done."

"Yeah," Orion said. "What Pozz said. We're all just having fun." He laughed uncomfortably. The other Scrappers laughed with him.

Sally looked at the woman. The Scrapper had let her go, leaving her standing on her own with the group. "Is that true?"

The woman eyed Hayden again, hesitating. She was

trying to decide if she could trust him or not, at least enough that being inside with him was better than being outside with her enemies.

"Yeah," she said. "These boys were just having a friendly little game to see who would be the lucky one to take me to bed tonight."

Sally looked them over, unconvinced. Then she put her hand up to her ear, distracted for a moment.

"Here's the deal," she said. "You, you, you, and you are coming with me." She pointed at Hayden, Jake, Orion, and the woman. "The rest of you can go grep yourselves."

"I ain't coming with you," Orion said. "You're going to throw me outside."

"The remains to be seen," Sally said. "But I can guarantee with absolute certainty you'll be put outside if you don't come."

Orion groaned but capitulated. "Meet me by the rigs in the morning, boys."

The other Scrappers headed back into the stairwell, leaving the four of them alone with the guards.

Sally glanced at Jake. "What's really going on here, Jake? You're no Scrapper."

"What?" Orion said.

"Can we talk about it in private?" Jake asked.

"Pozz, you a Courier for King or ain't you?" Orion asked.

"No," Hayden replied. He looked at Sally. "I'm not."

"Who the grep are you then?" Orion asked.

"I don't care if you are or aren't," Sally said. "My job is to get the truth about what was happening right here." She looked at Orion. "Your boys did a pretty good job blocking you from the camera. You didn't think she'd send us up?"

"Not that fast," Orion admitted. "But nothing was happening. Like Pozz said."

"Bullshit," the woman said, getting Sally's attention. "The

truth is, this asshole was going to bring me to his room and do who knows what to me if this guy, Pozz, or whatever the grep his name is, hadn't shown up. I blew the Road Enforcers' checkpoint about twenty klicks out, and they chased me all the way here."

"That's our job," Orion said.

"I made it here ahead of you," the woman replied.

Sally put her hand up to hear ear again. She had to be wearing some kind of transceiver. Then she returned her attention to Hayden.

"Were you screwing around or not?" she asked.

He could tell she, or Wiz had already decided what the truth was. But they were giving him a chance to choose how to handle it.

Orion was staring at him, doing his best to use his eyes as a threat. They were safe in Crossroads, but they still had to leave sometime. If he helped get the Scrapper off the hook, maybe they would let him pass. Maybe.

The other option was to deal with the fallout in the morning. At least they would have time to prepare for the inevitability.

"Well?" Sally asked, getting impatient.

"It wasn't a game," Hayden said. "As far as I'm concerned, this asshole can rot in Hell."

"Seconded," the woman said.

"You little piece of shit," Orion said. "Just wait until you leave, I'm going to-"

A single, sharp crack echoed in the hallway. A splatter of blood appeared on the wall behind Orion's head. His body slumped to the floor against it.

Sally holstered her sidearm. She was calm and steady.

"Wiz wants to speak to you," she said, looking at him. "All of you."

10

"My name is Hayden Duke," Hayden said to the woman, holding out his hand.

They were walking beside one another with Jake slightly ahead, sandwiched between Sally and the other two guards. He still hadn't gotten to see the first floor of Crossroads, because the guards had immediately started leading them up to the top floor.

She stared at it for a few seconds, trying to decide if she wanted to make his acquaintance or not. Finally, she took it. Her hand was tiny compared to his.

"Chains," she said.

"That's not a name," Hayden replied. Her grip was firm.

"It's the best you're going to get. That's what everyone calls me, anyway."

"I can see why," he said.

Chains was tiny, her head barely making his chest, her frame slight enough that he could probably pick her up with his single human hand. She had a shaved head, and a pair of thick silver rings in each of her ears, with rows of thin silver chains hugging her scalp and creating a fake hairline before connecting back to the rings. She was wearing a thicker pant than he had seen before, black and low slung. It showed off the bottom of her stomach before sliding over her hips and down. She was also wearing a dirty leather vest that left her arms exposed. More chains wrapped around them as well, starting at metal rings positioned just below her elbows and terminating at her fingers. He imagined she probably had more of them on her toes, too, though he couldn't see them beneath her boots.

The look was definitely unique.

"Why'd you jump the Enforcer's checkpoint?" he asked.

"Why'd you get involved?" she retorted.

"I don't like the Scrappers much."

"Does anybody who isn't a Scrapper? Most people don't intentionally start with them. Especially to help a stranger."

"I'm different."

"I can tell. You have a funny accent, too. Where are you from?"

"You wouldn't believe me if I told you."

"I don't know about that. I get around."

"You haven't been where I'm from."

"You sound pretty sure of yourself."

Hayden smiled. "I am."

They reached the end of the stairwell. Sally pulled open the door and ushered them through.

The space was large and open, one huge room that took over the entire top level of the building. Dirty, cracked tile gave way to carpets and rugs of a number of sizes and shapes, arranged in a jigsaw pattern to direct traffic from the entrance to different areas on the floor.

The one that immediately caught Hayden's attention was a line of displays against the north wall, and a second line of computers below them. A simple wooden table sat in front of it all, and he could see the red glow of a projected keyboard and a braid of long blonde hair spilling over a low-backed chair. The displays were feeds from a number of cameras arranged in and around Crossroads, giving the viewer an accurate picture of everything that was happening nearby. Hayden noticed one of them was showing them, standing at the entrance to the floor.

The braid moved, its owner getting to her feet, reaching up to the side of her head and tugging something from her ear. Then she started over toward them.

Where Chains' look was unique and exotic, Wiz's look was ordinary. She wore a plain blue dress that fell to her knees, cinched by a black belt that also supported a sleeve of pockets, which were filled with tools of different kinds. A small face with a large nose holding up a pair of horn-rimmed glasses, leading to hair pulled back tight. The only thing that stood out on Wiz was a nasty scar that ran from her lower left lip all the way down her neck.

"Sergeant," she said to Sally. "Thank you for escorting our guests here."

"Of course, Madam," Sally replied.

She took a moment to look over each of them. Her eyes lingered a little longer on Chains, but that didn't surprise Hayden. The woman had a unique look worth spending more time on.

Then she fixed her gaze on Jake. "Jake. I don't appreciate trouble at Crossroads."

"I know," he replied. He looked uncomfortable.

"How is your father?" she asked.

"Dead."

Wiz didn't apologize or offer condolences. She turned away from him, her expression flat. Her eyes fell on Hayden.

"You were in my home for all of five minutes, and you started a fight. Why?"

Hayden met her glare with his own. He could tell she wanted to intimidate him. That wasn't going to happen.

"He didn't start the fight," Chains said. "Orion did. The Scrapper your girl capped downstairs. Didn't she tell you that?"

"I'll ask the questions if you don't mind," Wiz said. "Be a good girl and shut up."

Chains' face wrinkled in anger, but she stayed silent.

"He was carrying this," Sally said, handing out the laser pistol.

Wiz took it, giving it a closer look. "Interesting." She flipped it over in her hand, finding the switch. She was surprised when it turned on. "And it has a charge?" She looked at Hayden again. "Where did you get this?"

"Do you know what it is?" he asked.

She motioned for him to follow. They moved as a group, with the guards behind them, over the rugs and across the floor to a walled-in section of the space. It had a few tables on it, and some shelves that reminded Hayden of the USMC module on the Pilgrim. The shelves were lined with weapons of all kinds, most of which he didn't recognize.

Wiz walked over to one of the shelves and lifted a familiar weapon from it. A laser pistol, just like his.

"I have four of them," she said, showing it to him. "But I've never found one with a live battery pack. Until now." She smiled. "Thank you for this."

"That's mine," Hayden said.

"It was yours," Wiz said. "Now it's mine. Unless you'd prefer to spend the night outside?"

"Wiz," Jake said. "Hold on."

"Don't tell me what to do, Jake," Wiz said. "Your new friend broke the only rule I have here. No grepping fighting. Orion paid for it with his life. You can pay for it with your gun." She laughed. "Hell, I don't even care about the gun. Just the battery."

"He was trying to help me," Chains said. "One nice guy in a sea of thousands of assholes."

"Didn't I tell you to be quiet?" Wiz said. She paused for a few seconds. "How about this? You tell me where you got it, and you can have it back. Fair?"

Hayden shrugged. "You won't believe me."

"You might be surprised. I haven't always lived in Crossroads. I traveled extensively in my teens. I was one of the top Collectors in the area. I might look like a beautiful waif now, but I'm not one to be crossed. I earned what I have." She motioned to her scar.

"Collectors?" Hayden asked.

"Artifacts of the old world," Wiz said. "The world before the trife, and immediately after, when the United States Armed Forces were still producing high-end tech. I specialize in arms, in case you hadn't guessed, but I also collect technology of other kinds. I've learned to restore it. I used it to make this place what it is. The guns outside are automated, activated when we lock up for the night. Anything gets too close; it gets obliterated. I wrote the software myself."

"What about the goliaths?" Hayden asked.

"I don't waste bullets on them, and as long as nobody makes too much noise in here, we don't have a problem. It's one of the reasons for my rule. The other is because nobody would pay to stay in a safe house that wasn't safe."

"How did you learn to write software for old tech?" Hayden said, curious.

"Let me show you."

She led them out of the area and to another space, where a shelf of books were resting. Hayden's eyes widened at the sight of them. It was an entire collection of manuals like the ones he had seen on the Pilgrim.

"Where did you get those?" he said, realizing his mistake as soon as he finished asking.

"You recognize them?" she said. "Interesting."

"I've been around, too," he said.

"And yet you don't know what a Collector is?"

Hayden glanced over at Jake. He looked frightened.

"Let me ask you again, Mister?"

"Duke," Hayden said. "Hayden Duke."

"Let me ask you again, Mister Duke. Where are you from?"

Hayden hesitated.

"It isn't a hard question," Wiz said. "Where are you from?"

She was getting impatient.

"Where did you get these?" Hayden asked instead.

"I bought them from a man who said they were in his family for generations," she replied. "He said they came from a starship that never made it to the stars, and the computer I took from him after I killed him backed that up. The ship was named the Wanderer. It was overrun with trife before it had the chance to launch. They killed everyone on board. I can show you the recordings if it would help you answer my question. But I already know the answer to my question, don't I, Hayden Duke? You carry an old weapon that shouldn't still function, but does, and you recognize manuals recovered from a generation ship." She paused, staring at him. He still didn't speak. "One of four constructed on the west coast. I had heard there was a launch site not far from here, but so far the Collectors I've hired to find it have either come back empty handed or they haven't come back at all."

She stepped up to him, her face nearly level with his.

"Who are you, really? A Courier? A Collector? A stranger, for sure."

Hayden stared back at her. Did she know he was a colonist?

"Let me tell you something about myself," Wiz said, taking a step away from him when he didn't answer. "I'm not afraid to go to extraordinary lengths to get what I want. Sally."

Sally grabbed Jake, throwing him to the floor. Wiz held out the laser pistol, putting it against his head.

"Wiz?" Jake said. "You know me."

"Do you know him?" Wiz asked. "One of you tell me the damned truth, or I swear there's going to be a corpse in this room in the next ten seconds. Nine. Eight. Seven."

She ticked off the time, giving them both a chance. They shouldn't have come here. He should have stayed down and out of sight and not attract attention. There was nothing he could do about it now.

"Three. Two."

"The ship is called the Pilgrim," Hayden said, not waiting for her to get to one.

Wiz smiled, immediately pulling the gun away from Jake's head. "That wasn't so hard, was it? I already know the name of the ship, and now I know you're telling me the truth. I've never been sure if the Pilgrim had launched or not. Some of the ships made it, some of them didn't. The ones that didn't, they hold treasure beyond imagining. Relics of the world before the trife brought us to this. Ever since I learned about them from that old man, I've been hoping I might unlock their secrets one day. And now here you are."

She reached out, grabbed at the robe covering his mechanical hand and pulling it back.

"Where's your hand?" she asked. "Your real hand."

"I lost it," he replied.

"Jake?" She whirled back toward the Borger. "This is Hank's. You replaced his hand. Where is it?"

"Wiz, I-"

She put the gun back to his head. "Where is it?" she shouted.

"It was already missing," Jake said. "Damn it, Wiz. This man didn't find the Pilgrim, he's from the Pilgrim. The colonists are still inside. They don't know the ship never left Earth."

Wiz glanced back at Hayden. Then she started to laugh.

"You can't be serious," she said. "They don't know they never left? That's the most adorable thing I think I've ever heard."

"The Scrappers found the Pilgrim first," Hayden said. "They beat you to it."

She stopped laughing. "What? Did they get inside?"

"They can't get inside. Nobody can."

"You can," she said.

"I can't," Hayden replied. "If you wanted to see my hand, you know the colonists have an identification chip. Only the Governor's chip can open the outside doors to the colony. I wasn't the Governor, and I don't have any chip at all. The Scrapper, Pig, cut off my hand trying to get in before I killed him."

"I see," Wiz said, surprising him by not insisting that he could do what she claimed.

"You killed Pig?" Chains said.

He wasn't going to tell her a trife had helped him do it.

"Yes."

"Good."

"There has to be another way in," Wiz said. "Is the bridge still intact?"

Hayden nodded.

"Then I can figure out how to bypass the door controls." She walked over to the bookshelf, lifting a thick manual from it. "I'll need some time to study this." She carried it back to Hayden. "Who were you on the inside, Mister Duke?"

"I was the Sheriff," Hayden said.

"Sheriff? I'm impressed. But then, I should have guessed, shouldn't I, the way you tried to rescue the damsel in distress like any good lawman would do?" She laughed again. "Damn King for being who he is. I liked him better before he started claiming control of this area, but what can you do? I want what's on your ship, Sheriff. Anyone who knows anything about the Generation ships does. How did you wind up out here, anyway?"

"One of the hatches glitched and opened. Pig grabbed my wife before it closed again. She's on her way to King."

"And you came looking for her?"

"Yes."

"How sweet." She put her hand on his face, touching him gently. "I hate to be the bearer of bad news, Sheriff, but she's going to have to wait. I need you to bring me back to the Pilgrim."

"I can't," Hayden said. "She needs me."

Wiz laughed. "Oh, I'm sorry. Did that sound like I was giving you a choice? You will bring me back to the Pilgrim. Once I'm inside, maybe I'll let you go try to pry your wife away from King. Though it would be better for your health if I didn't."

"I can't stay here," Hayden said. "Bringing you back there won't change anything. You need the master code, and there's no way to get it from the bridge. Only the PASS can print it, and the PASS is on the inside."

"I'll be the judge of that," Wiz said. "Jake, you're free to carry on with whatever it was you were doing before you crossed paths with this one." She turned to Chains. "As for you, I think it's best if you stay here for a few days. The Enforcers are going to blame you for getting Orion killed, and it would be a shame for someone as beautiful as you are to be killed as soon as they left in the morning."

"I'll take my chances," Chains said.

"No, you won't," Wiz replied. "Sally, take these two to a room for holding." She held up the manual again. "I need to spend some time with this before we go. We'll leave in two days."

"I can't wait two days," Hayden said.

"I don't care," Wiz replied. "You haven't learned enough about our world yet, Sheriff. But you'll come to realize there are two kinds of people in it. Those who take, and those who give. You gave of yourself, and look where it got you. I take what I want, and look where it's gotten me. The sooner you change your worldview, the better off you'll be."

Hayden glared at her, holding in his anger. He was stuck. Trapped.

"Thanks for the advice," he said.

Sally pointed her rifle at him. "Let's go."

11

"THAT BITCH!" CHAINS SHOUTED, THE MOMENT THE DOOR OF their room was closed behind them. "All I wanted to do was get my shit to Haven and get the hell back to Lavega. Those grepping Scrappers. Grep them all!"

She stormed around the room, cursing and shouting while Hayden took in their surroundings. The room was on the second floor of Crossroads, one of a number of living spaces that branched off from two main corridors. It had a bed against one wall, a separate toilet and shower in a room to the left, and a small table opposite them. A pair of bulbs hung from wires over their heads, providing all of the light.

Hayden returned to the door and tried to turn the knob. As expected, it was locked. He was sure one or more of the guards had been left outside as well.

"'Pick up the parts,' he said," Chains said, still yelling. "'It'll be a piece of grepping cake,' he said. 'Easy grepping money,' he said. 'Just don't let the Enforcers see what you're carrying.'"

"Can you possibly calm down?" Hayden said.

She whirled around to face him. “Calm down? Your shit got me stuck in this prison with you.”

“It was your trouble that got us both stuck in here. If I hadn’t tried to help you, we-”

“And who the grep asked you to try to help me?” she said. “I don’t remember requesting a guardian angel.”

“You seemed grateful twenty minutes ago.”

“That’s before I got locked up by the owner of Crossroads. She may want you to help her plunder some old wreck. She wants me for something else entirely.” She shook her head. “Ewww.”

“She said she would let you go in a couple of days.”

“Said the spider to the fly. Yeah, right. I believe that. You might have just crawled out from under a rock yesterday, but I didn’t. She’ll let me go right to her boudoir, and that’s about it. No thank you.”

“In that case, we both want the same thing, which is to get out of here as soon as possible. So why don’t you take a few breaths and then we can start working on this problem together?”

Chains glared at him for a moment, and then nodded and sat on the edge of the bed, closing her eyes and taking the requested breaths.

Hayden used the time to enter the bathroom. A dirty mirror was propped against the wall behind the sink, and he was able to see his face for the first time in days. He hadn’t realized Jake had shaved him. He put his fingers on the smaller bruises there, and a sewn up cut below his eye. When had that happened? He looked awful.

“I’ve seen asses that look more like a face than your face,” Chains said, entering the bathroom. She unbuttoned her pants, pulling them down and sitting on the toilet, starting to pee before he could move.

“Don’t mind me,” he said.

"Clearly, I don't," she replied.

She grabbed a small bit of tissue from beside the toilet, wiping herself and then standing.

"I figure a man who left the warmth and safety of a protected colony and mixed it up with Pig to find their wife has no interest in anyone else, so why be shy? Am I right?" She pulled her pants back up, buttoning them closed.

"That's not the point," Hayden said.

"Isn't it, though?" She laughed. "So you really came from inside a starship?"

"Yes," Hayden said.

"And the other people there really don't know they're on Earth?"

"No."

She kept laughing. "That's rich. So, you're like a planetary virgin. You're more of an alien than the grepping aliens are."

"I guess you could put it that way. Can we focus on finding a way out of this?"

"How do you like our little ball of dirt so far?"

"I'm not convinced it's our ball of dirt."

"True enough. We've had to learn to share. It can be a hard life, I'm a prime example of that, but us humans are an adaptable lot. We keep fighting, and one day we'll get rid of the trife and the goliaths."

"Do you really believe that?" Hayden asked.

"Sure, why not? Either that or maybe we can take a starship like yours and get the hell out of here? Is that what you were planning to do once you found your woman?"

"I don't know. I haven't gotten that far yet."

"You need a plan, Sheriff," Chains said. "What is a Sheriff, anyway? Wiz said you're a man of the law?"

"I was. I made sure people followed the rules that were put in place for the health and safety of everyone in the colony."

"Rules. A quaint notion." She smiled. "The only rules here are King's, and his only rule is what he wants, he gets. Takers or givers, like Wiz said." She rolled her eyes. "Except I don't want her to take me."

"Then we need to get out."

"There's no getting out. Not right now. We're stuck here together until daybreak at the least. I'd say we could play cards or something, but we haven't got any cards." She paused, eyeing him mischievously. "There is a bed. Are the people in your colony monotonous?"

"You mean monogamous, and yes, we are."

"Okay, so that's out, too. Damn, I wish I had something to do. I go crazy when I'm awake and not moving around."

"So do I," Hayden said, regretting helping her more with every word out of her mouth. "I want to get out now."

"Funny," Chains said, still smiling. "At least we still have our sense of humor, right, Hayden?"

"I'm not joking."

The smile vanished. "No. Uh-uh. No way. I know you're new around here, but going out there at night? That's suicide. Even if the trife aren't massing, the turrets will tear you to shreds. And that's assuming we can get past the guards, you know, like the one standing right outside the door?"

"I'm willing to take my chances. I killed plenty of trife getting out here."

"With varying levels of success," Chains said. "You lost your hand, and you're covered in cuts and bruises."

"Pig cut off my hand. If we can get to Wiz's armory, she has enough firepower to keep the trife at a distance, at least long enough for us to escape in your car."

"Us? My car? I don't think so. We can break out together, but then I'm going it alone."

"You said you were going to Haven."

"I am."

"So are we."

"That's not the point."

"Isn't it, though?"

She stared at him, biting her lip.

"Trust me, it isn't because of your winning personality," Hayden said. "But we have two common enemies and a common goal. It makes sense for us to stick together, at least until we get to Haven."

"What's wrong with my personality?"

Hayden didn't answer.

"Go ahead; you can be honest."

"You're a little abrasive," he said.

"Abrasive? What you call abrasive, I call interesting. You're duller than a 50cc scooter."

"I don't know what that is."

"It doesn't matter. The point is, if we try to escape now, we die. Period. End of story."

"We need to catch them off guard. They won't be expecting us to try to run right now."

"For good reason."

"When it comes down to it, do you want to take your chances in here or out there?"

"Honestly? I like being alive."

"More than you like being free?"

She sighed. "Damn. You got me there, Sheriff. This is crazy, you know?"

"I'm desperate."

"What's the plan?"

"Can you fight?"

She smiled, reaching up to the chains connected at her elbows. She disconnected a few of them on each side, quickly wrapping them around her knuckles.

"They don't call me Chains for nothing."

12

NATALIA DUKE LEANED HER HEAD TO THE SIDE TO LOOK OUT of the front windshield of the car as it began to slow. A pile of old cars had been assembled ahead of them, a stack ten husks tall that stretched from a chokepoint in the center of the wide road to both the left and the right, extending twenty meters in each direction. A separate vehicle sat in the middle of the barrier, an armored behemoth of a truck, heavily armored and featuring a long barrel that extended from the center. A dozen men and women in sand-colored robes, half of them wearing breathing masks and tinted glasses, stood on the armored car and on the junk pile, rifles in hand, waiting for her vehicle to near.

"Where are we?" she asked, looking over at the other passenger in the car, a lanky man in a white suit. His large brimmed hat was resting in his lap, his hands hidden beneath it.

He barely turned his head to look at her, but his eyes shifted far to the left. He paused deliberately before he spoke.

"We call it Sanisco," he replied. "It is King's home city.

You'll be able to see the Fortress once we're beyond the checkpoint."

Natalia didn't respond. She continued watching the people on the wall. She didn't want to see the Fortress. She didn't want to meet King. She didn't want to be here at all.

Her hands rubbed the hem of the dress they had given her. It was a white, frilly thing with a high collar and an elaborate checkered pattern, in better condition than anything she had ever worn in her life. A gift from King, to hear her captor tell it. A peace offering. A welcome.

She hated it.

She looked down at her active hands. There were marks on the backs of her fingers where she had dug in her nails, creating a small sense of pain there to help manage the pain of her present experience. There were bruises, too, sustained when she had resisted, first when the large, tattooed man had grabbed her from the other side of the secured hatch in Section C, and then maintained by every other effort she had made to escape from these people.

She didn't belong here. None of the people of Metro belonged here.

She closed her eyes. They were supposed to be in space, on the way to their new home. They were supposed to have escaped from Earth, a planet she had learned was overrun with alien creatures bent on destroying them. She should have been with Hayden, back in their cube, in the bedroom making good on the Governor's gift.

Not here. She would rather be anywhere than here.

The truth hadn't completely settled. Not yet. There was a part of her that still felt like she would wake up, turn her head to the right, and see Hayden there, sound asleep. She would listen to him snore for a few minutes. Then she would close her eyes and pass the entire thing off as a bad dream.

Only it wasn't a dream.

It wasn't a nightmare, either.

It was worse.

It was reality.

She could feel the tears welling in her eyes. Hayden had been real, too. She could still see him there, sitting on the back of a horse of all things, a gun in one hand and... he only had the one hand. The other was a stump, bloody and burned. How could he even survive something like that?

He had come for her. He had found a way out of Metro and had given chase to the people who had taken her. She was as amazed by that truth as she was afraid of it. She would have given anything for Hayden to be back in the city, to be safe and sound behind the heavy doors that divided them from this harsh truth. She would have given anything for him to remain ignorant and in the dark, unaware that there was no new home, only the old one.

He had come for her, bruised and bloody and desperate, only to lose her at the last moment because he had a horse, and his captors had a car.

She opened her eyes, glancing over at the man on the seat beside her. Ghost. That was what they all called him. The tattooed man, Pig, had treated him with all the deference in the world. He had been afraid of Ghost.

Terrified of him.

Natalia hadn't known why when he came to meet the Scrappers inside the Pilgrim. There was nothing about him that looked particularly frightening. He was skinny instead of muscular, soft-spoken instead of loud. His movements looked clumsy, not easy and smooth. He reminded her of Hoskins, one of her Engineers. He was smart, but he was no fighter.

Then the monsters had come.

They had attacked Ghost, Pig, and the others, surrounding them with a force nearly two dozen strong. The

Scrappers weren't afraid of them, not the way they were afraid of Ghost. She had seen the result when of the demons killed one of their number. It had charged past her and into Metro in the dozen or so seconds the hatch was open. Just long enough for it to enter. Just long enough for Pig to pull her out. She hadn't intended to tell him she was an Engineer, but he had threatened to kill and eat her, and in her surprise and fear she had believed him. She didn't know then the Pilgrim had never left Earth, and Engineers were important on a starship.

She had learned they were equally important planetside, in the wake of humankind's loss to the creatures, a story Ghost told her in that whispering, gentle voice of his. She had seen how important firsthand when Ghost had jumped in front of the creatures, two small knives transferring from somewhere on his body to his hands. He had cut them down with a measure of dexterity and power she had never witnessed before.

By the time the last of them was dead, she was afraid of him, too.

She had begged him not to kill Hayden when her husband appeared on the horse, static in front of them in a state of surprised shock. She had whispered to him, "Please. Please don't."

She was still surprised he hadn't, but she had come to understand why later.

He didn't expect Hayden to survive.

Not in the middle of a Scrapper camp.

Not injured the way he was.

Not with an even bigger, more frightening monster bearing down on him.

Ghost had spared her from having to watch her husband die. That was all.

She reached up to wipe the tears from her eyes. In twelve

seconds, her entire life had changed. In twelve seconds, she had lost her innocence. She had lost her husband. She had lost her freedom.

She didn't know what came next, but she had already decided on one thing:

One way or another, she was going to kill the man who had killed Hayden.

She was going to kill the one they called King.

13

THE ARMORED VEHICLE WAS DRIVEN OUT OF THE WAY, GIVING the car the space it needed to pass through the barrier and into the outer reaches of Sanisco. There was an eight-meter high, solid wall here, made of concrete and steel, wrapping around this portion of the city all the way back to the water. A gaping wound was visible directly ahead, a jagged cliff of bent metal and sharp stone. The junked cars had been piled one on top of the other to help seal it.

"They built the wall too late," Ghost said quietly. He always seemed to know when she had a question on her mind before she could begin to ask it. "And they didn't build it high enough. The trife, they stormed up to it, hundreds of thousands strong, if you can imagine. An entire sea of black-skinned bugs, scaling one another to reach the top. They fired a uranium tipped missile into this section. It killed thousands of them, and plenty of people, too. It didn't stop them. Not in the end."

"You mean the creatures got in here?" she asked.

"It was a long time ago. The smart ones hid like they always did. The smart ones didn't trust the wall."

"Why patch it, if it doesn't keep them out?"

"Trife aren't the only things we have to worry about."

"You mean the goliaths?"

Ghost had told her about those monsters, too. About how they had appeared one day and started feeding on the trife, eating enough of them that humankind was able to staunch the bleeding, even if they still hadn't been able to stop it completely.

"This wall won't stop a goliath," Ghost said. "Other people. King's enemies."

"Does he have enemies?"

"Everyone has enemies."

"It seems counter-productive, doesn't it? For humans to be fighting with one another when the trife are out there trying to kill us all?"

Ghost shifted his eyes to look at her. Then he shrugged. "I don't make the decisions. I do as I'm told."

"Why?"

"Because it gets me what I want."

"Which is?"

"Respect." He paused a moment. "Four hundred years, Engineer," he said. "That's how long the trife have been here. We weren't able to win with the best military on the planet. How are we supposed to win with a few hundred thousand women and children?"

"There are fewer trife now."

"They still outnumber us ten to one. Why spend your life on a lost cause, when you can focus on enjoying the time you have? Believe me, Engineer. People tried. They failed. King is giving the common people something to work for. That's more than they've had in awhile."

"I don't want to work for King. I want to go back to the Pilgrim."

"I don't blame you. If I were you, I would want the same thing."

He turned his head away from her, indicating he was done talking. Natalia continued staring out the window, watching the first rows of worn and decayed buildings approaching. Most of the structures on the outskirts of Sanisco had been reduced to rubble, cleared and replaced with shanty houses of corrugated steel and plastic, cheap construction for the poorest of residents. She could see them there now, huddled together in worn and torn roughspun cloth, dirty and tired and too skinny. They stared at the car as it passed, and she could imagine them dreaming of one day being able to move around in such luxury.

The shanties gave way to buildings that were still occupiable, though they often had missing walls and large breaks, the frameworks that supported them exposed on the edges, worn and dirty from the years. There were families gathered in those spaces, some with old and tattered mattresses, some with nothing but the floor. A lot of the children she saw running around were naked, their parents unable to afford even meager clothes for them, or trying to preserve them while the weather was warm.

Even further in, the buildings became slightly more solid, the cracks diminishing. Some of them still had glass in the frames, cracked and broken panes that spared those residents from the wind. Most of the people there were Scrappers or the families of Scrappers. They were in better shape than the others, but not by a wide margin. Nobody here was living comfortably.

Nobody except King.

They made a few turns on their way toward the Fortress, crossing through Sanisco undisturbed. She heard shouting through the window as they passed one of the alleys between buildings, alleys that reminded her of the strands. She turned her head to see what the commotion was for, just in time to watch one Scrapper pull a gun on another, shooting him in the chest.

Civilization was gone. It had been for a long time.

Was there any way to bring it back?

If she did find a way to kill King, could she be the one to do it?

Hayden would have supported her in anything. These people were living like animals, and it was frightening and painful to see. Whether they could overcome the trife or not, they should be working together.

"The Fortress," Ghost said, as they turned one of the corners and King's castle came into view.

It towered over the other buildings in the town, a massive structure with a triangular point at the top, a beacon of power that had no right to be as intact as it was, considering the level of devastation around it. That wasn't to say it was in great condition. It was scuffed and scarred and beaten like every other building in the town, but it had held fast against the storm and weathered the worst. It was a fitting place to be the seat of the local warlord, as Natalia liked to think of King.

She stared at it but didn't respond.

The car continued toward it, approaching the front of the building. There were half a dozen soldiers stationed there, dressed in an odd looking armor of some kind and holding large, powerful looking guns. They barely moved as the car came to a stop a good fifty meters from the front of the structure, at the base of the street.

Ghost opened his door, sliding out and walking around to the other side. Natalia eyed the vacated exit when he did, momentarily considering trying to go out that side.

And then what? Run? She would be dead before she made it three meters.

The man in white opened the door for her, holding out his hand to help her out. She took it reluctantly, letting him bring her onto the street.

"Shall we?" he asked.

She didn't resist him. There was no point. They started toward the building.

She froze as the doors opened ahead of them, a large, metal contraption clearing the frame. It was bipedal, with two thick trunks holding up a large, rounded torso and flattened head. One of its arms ended in a barrel, like a gun. The other was composed of two fingers and a long thumb. It slumped forward, raising its hand to where its heart would be if it had one.

"What the hell is that?" she asked.

"We call them roids," he said. "They're old tech, left over from before the war. King's managed to get a few of them functional. He has a few other engineers on site."

"Roids? What do they do?"

"Whatever you ask them to if you've got their control transmitter."

They continued toward it. It remained stationary, waiting for them. As they drew closer, Natalia recognized the eagle and star logo etched into its side. It had a series of letters and numbers printed beside the logo. P1N-0CC-H10.

"H10," Ghost said. "Report."

The bucket head swiveled toward them. Natalia could see the cameras and other sensors attached to it, and her curiosity was immediately piqued.

"King welcomes you to the Fortress, Courier," it said in a stiff, echoing male voice. "He is waiting for you in his meeting chamber. I have been instructed to escort you."

The roid lifted itself on its legs and stomped ahead of them, back toward the door, which slid aside as it neared.

Ghost and Natalia followed behind it. She glanced back before passing through the doors, looking for a route to escape and noticing the soldiers had closed ranks behind her.

Damn.

14

THE LIFT STOPPED AT WHAT NATALIA ASSUMED WAS somewhere near the top of the structure. It was hard to know because the display was nonfunctional. The ride had been slightly jerky, the mechanism behind the elevator either slightly damaged or in desperate need of recalibration. She would have to look at the mechanics to know which.

She caught herself, dropping her eyes to the floor. It was second nature for her to want to fix things. It had been since the day she was born. As the doors to the lift slid aside and the roid stepped out, she noticed it had a slight limp in its gait, and she caught herself a second time, wondering if she could fix that, too.

Or maybe it was the stress. She was going to meet King, the man whose subordinates stole her from Metro, whose Scrappers killed her husband. Ghost carried knives tucked into the black belt that wrapped around his white pants. Could she grab one and stab it into King's heart before anyone could react?

She had seen Ghost fight. She doubted it.

Instead, she followed behind the roid, with Ghost a

couple of meters behind her. The lift had deposited them in a hallway similar to the one on the ground floor. Red paint, gold-framed images, and elegant carpeting. Where had he gotten it all? How many places had he plundered? How many lives had he upended so he could live in comfort, while there was nothing but squalor below?

She was familiar with Earth's history from the PASS. Did this part of it need to be repeated?

They made it close to the end of the hallway. All of the doors looked the same, but the roid stopped at one the third from the end, reaching out for the handle. It gripped it with its smaller hand, turning and pushing it open as it walked through. Its bulk blocked the inside of the room from sight.

"Your majesty," the roid said. "I present you with the Courier, Ghost, and his latest delivery."

Natalia still couldn't see him. Her heart was pounding, her face hot. She turned her head slightly to look for Ghost and his belt.

"I know what you're thinking," Ghost said. "Please, do not try."

She shifted her gaze forward again as the roid stepped heavily into the room.

"There she is," a scratchy voice said. "There is the treasure to end all treasures."

Then she saw him. An older man in a dark suit covered by a red velvet robe, a gold crown covering thinning white hair. He was short and stocky, his face wrinkled but well rested, his smile yellow, his missing teeth replaced with gold. He had bright, intelligent blue eyes, and she could almost sense his mind working as he held his hand out to her.

"And beautiful as well," he continued. "They didn't tell me you were beautiful." He smiled, stopping in front of her. She had to look down to meet his eyes. "Kneel before your King."

She continued staring at him. She was frozen by her fury.

"I said kneel!" he shouted.

Before Natalia knew what was happening, a stiff hand smacked against the side of her face, forcing it to the side and leaving a sharp sting behind.

He had hit her?

She turned her head back toward him, angrier than before, glaring down at him with contempt. He glared back, hardly afraid of her.

"Let me make one thing clear to you, Engineer," he hissed, pointing one of his stubby fingers at her. "Whatever you were, you are only what I make you now. You are property. My property. And you will do anything I say, or you will suffer. Your mind is what I need. Your body can be cut to ribbons for all I care, as long as you survive. Is that clear?"

She considered defying him again. From his voice, from his actions, it was obvious he would carry out any threat he made. She had to submit, for now at least.

She nodded slowly.

King took a step back. "Good. Then kneel." He said it slowly, emphasizing his command.

She fell to her knees in front of him. He held out his hand. He was wearing a large ring with a diamond set in the center.

"Kiss the ring," he said.

She leaned forward, kissing it. She could feel the guilt of her humiliation as a small pit in her stomach. She had to prevent it from growing, or he would be able to reduce her to the slave he wanted.

"Stand," King said.

She stood.

He backed away, retreating toward the other end of the room. A plush chair was waiting there for him, cracked brown leather on a base with wheels at the bottom. A pair of women were standing on either side of it, dressed in simple, low-cut white gowns. They were both very pretty. Neither looked particularly happy to be there.

Natalia turned her head slightly, noticing the wall of windows to her left. She gaped as she looked out over the city below, able to see the entire thing from the heights. It was brown and black and sharp, the destruction of Sanisco at the hands of the trife and the US Military trying to stop them still painfully visible despite the passage of time. Further out, she could see the water and the remains of a large bridge that had once spanned it. It was rusted and corroded and appeared to have collapsed at some point long ago. She could see hundreds of dark shapes moving around the base of it. Trife.

"Sit," King said, loudly enough to seize her attention.

She looked at him, and then at the plain, rectangular table in front of him. An assortment of mismatched chairs surrounded it.

"There," he said, pointing to one near the front, close to him.

She walked over to it and sat.

"Ghost, sit here," King said, pointing to the chair opposite her. "H10, wait outside."

"Yes, your Majesty," the roid replied, immediately removing itself from the room and closing the door.

King swiveled his chair slightly to look at her. He was silent for a few seconds before speaking.

"I don't want us to get off on the wrong foot, Engineer," he said.

"My name is Natalia," she replied. "Natalia Duke."

He bit his lower lip, his face turning slightly red. He swiveled the chair away from her, to face Ghost.

"Was she this much of a bitch to you?" he asked.

"No, sir," Ghost said. That was all he said.

King returned his attention to Natalia.

"I don't want us to get off on the wrong foot, Natalia," he said. "I'm not a hard man to please. You can ask my assistants if you don't believe me." He waved toward each of the two women beside him.

Natalia tried to make eye contact with them, but they lowered their heads submissively. She had no doubt King was a predatory cretin, or that he was harder to please than he was admitting.

"I got where I am because I have something too few people possess these days," he continued. "Do you know what that is?"

"No," Natalia said.

"No, what?" he replied.

She stared at him.

"I'll tell you this once. All statements addressed to me are to end in either 'your Majesty' or 'sir.' Do you understand?"

"Yes, sir," she said.

He smiled. "Perfect." He paused. "Vision," he said. "I have vision. Too many of us have learned to accept the status quo. They've learned to accept that this world belongs to the trife, and we're just trying to survive in it. I don't accept that, Natalia. Not at all. I believe we can rebuild. It won't be easy. It won't be quick. But I think we can make something of our society. Some people say I'm harsh. Do you think that makes me harsh?"

"No, sir," Natalia said.

"Good. The decisions I make aren't made solely for my benefit, but the benefit of all. My health and welfare is most important, of course, because I'm the driving force behind the recovery of our entire race. I have organized the Scrappers. I have started expanding our territory outward and recovering land once lost to the trife. I have brought back the production of common necessities, as well as arms and armament. I have restored old tech like H10, and sent expeditions to explore areas others believed overrun." His smile grew. "That's how we found you. Of course, I wasn't expecting them to find the Pilgrim still resting in her hangar. You can imagine my excitement. According to the data I've uncovered, your ship has an entire Marine Corp module installed in it, along with a full Space Force Deployment, a Research Module, and heavy equipment intended to assist with the construction of the colony. Not to mention all of the other items we can strip from her. She truly is the motherlode. The Jackpot. So are you."

"There are still colonists on board, sir," Natalia said. "Fifty-thousand of them. The Pilgrim is theirs. You can't just take it away."

King laughed. "No? Why not?"

"It doesn't belong to you."

He laughed harder. "To the victor goes the spoils, Natalia. The Pilgrim is mine, the same way you are mine. The colonists will be mine, too, once I'm able to reach them. Pig swore to me he knew a way in, but it seems his way in wasn't as agreeable as he thought. But don't worry, I will get through, I'm not worried about that. I'll find uses for most of them, and for the ones I don't need? I have no qualms about culling the weak from our midst."

A chill ran down Natalia's back at the statement. How many innocent people would he kill without a second thought?

"All of this time, and you thought you were on your way to a new home," King continued. "I can't imagine what that must be like for you, and for everyone still on board. I'm sorry you didn't make it. I truly am. Since you didn't, you will be of service to me instead."

"What kind of service?" Natalia asked. "Sir." She tacked it on when his face darkened.

"A simple request, to start," King said. "My Scrappers

recently recovered a machine they found buried deep in the woods to the north. A drone. My other engineers have already restored power to it, but it's still too damaged to operate. You have knowledge of the old technology few people, if any, in this society can match. I want you to repair it. A test of your skills, so to speak."

"And if I don't, sir?" she asked.

"If you aren't useful to me as an Engineer, I can make use of you somewhere else. I hate waste, and my Scrappers are always in need of companionship."

Natalia noticed how the woman to King's right blanched at the statement.

"There's no downside to helping me," King said. "I want to fight the trife, and the drone will bring me closer to doing that effectively."

"May I ask you a question, sir?" Natalia said.

"Go on."

"I see there are trife gathered near the remains of the bridge out there."

"Yes. What about them?"

"You say you want to bring the fight to the trife, but they're massing less than a dozen kilometers from this settlement. Are you certain your goals are as benevolent as you claim?"

King's smile faded. "What are you getting at?"

"Your man, Pig, was a cannibal, as were his Scrappers. I'm sure they aren't the only ones. In the short time they were holding me captive, I witnessed two of them get into an altercation. Only one of them survived it. I've only been in Sanisco for thirty minutes, and I've already seen the people out there are starving, and their children are going naked. Not to mention, there was a murder in the streets not two blocks from here, all while you sit high in your tower on your throne, surrounded by gilded paintings and fresh carpets. Are you really a King for the people? Or are you a King for yourself? If you own me, as you say, there's no reason for you to feed me bullshit about your true motives."

King's eyes darted from her to Ghost. For a moment, Natalia was certain one man was going to order the other to kill her. Then he stood, approaching her, his cheeks red with anger as he leaned on the table and put his face in hers.

"Engineer or not, if you ever dare question my motives again, I will bring you pain like you've never felt it before. This is my Kingdom, Natalia. This is my world for the taking. I have no use for the weak, and I have no care for those so far below me I can't even see them from here. My concerns are greater than they, or you, can even comprehend. I am the savior. The lord of light. The living god. You will honor and respect me. All will honor or respect me, or they will meet the fate they deserve."

He turned his back on her, fists clenched at his sides.

"Ghost, get her out of my sight before I do something I'll regret."

Then Ghost was at her side, gently holding her above the elbow and urging her from the chair.

"Take her north, to Ports. Show her the complex."

"Your Majesty, what about the drone?" Ghost asked.

He waved his hand. "Forget the drone. I was trying to be kind and ease her into her work, but this bitch doesn't want my compassion. She questions her King? Her Lord and Master? The complex, damn it. She fixes the mainframe, or she dies. I want you to stay with her."

"King, I'm a Courier, not one of your soldiers. The complex is no place for me. Or for her, for that matter. She's too valuable to risk-"

He spun around again, this time facing Ghost. "Are you questioning me?" he shouted. "Do you want to screw her? Is that why? You can screw her all you want, but don't you dare defy me."

Natalia thought Ghost might kill King for her. He was the one carrying the knives while the other man appeared defenseless.

He hardly reacted, his expression remaining flat and calm.

"I will do as you ask, your Majesty," he replied.

King's anger vanished, replaced with a smile.

"I knew I could count on you. Thank you."

Ghost gently squeezed Natalia's arm, tugging her gently toward the door. She could hear King return to his throne behind them, still muttering under his breath.

"It's not a good idea to provoke him," Ghost whispered as soon as they were back in the hallway.

"I don't know if you noticed," Natalia replied softly. "But he's fucking crazy. You could have killed him. Maybe I'm wrong about you, but you seem a hell of a lot saner than he is."

"That may be, but I'm not about to end his life."

"Why not?"

"He's my father."

Natalia turned her head to look at Ghost. He didn't look anything like King. "Are you sure?"

"He isn't my biological father. Thirty years ago, he was a nomad, like many people still are. Even then, he was different. He didn't run from the trife. He fought them. He killed them by the hundreds. I don't know how. I've never seen anything like it. That was how he found me. The trife came after my family. They killed my parents and had me cornered against a tree. He came from nowhere, carrying a heavy ax. He cut them down, one after another, and when they were all dead, he held out his hand to me. I took it, and I haven't questioned him since."

"Maybe you should start?"

"I'm not as quick to anger as King, but don't test me, Natalia. He's a hard man, and he can be cruel. But he does hate the trife, and he does want to see them destroyed."

"What about the people he's destroying in the meantime?"

"The trife have killed billions over the years. It's a fraction in comparison."

"And that makes it right?"

"It makes it the way it has always been."

"I've always hated that answer, no matter what context it's used in."

Ghost cracked a small smile. "I admire your compassion, Natalia. Help King get into the complex, and maybe he'll grant you a favor."

"What is this complex?"

"A former Space Force facility. We dug the rubble out of a garage and discovered a door, not unlike the hatch on the Pilgrim. It wasn't locked. It may have been scavenged at some point in the past because there was no equipment inside. Nothing except a large, inoperable mainframe. It's too big to move. Big enough that King is convinced there's valuable data stored on it."

"What kind of data?"

"That's what we want to find out."

"But you don't want me to go there?"

"The trife occupy the area in large numbers, and they move through the city often. It isn't safe enough for anyone to settle there. It took nearly four hundred Scrappers just to reach the complex and hold it long enough to dig it out."

"What about the goliaths? You said they go wherever the trife are to feed."

"They don't walk there. I don't know why."

"Your father sent you with me like he was sending you to pick up a food ration. Doesn't he care that you might die?"

"No."

"And you're okay with it?"

"I should have been dead a long time ago. He gave me years I wouldn't have had otherwise. Besides, I want to go."

"Why? Because you want to screw me?" She shuddered at the words and the meaning of them. "You have the power to take what you want."

"I'm not that kind of man. I care what happens to you."

"You hardly know me."

"I admire the strength of your spirit."

"My husband was the strength of my spirit, and you took me from him and left him for dead. Now that strength comes from my desire to kill your father. I don't know if you want to admire that."

"Regardless, I do."

"Enough to help me make good on it?"

He didn't respond, signaling the end of the conversation. They returned to the lift, entering and taking it back down.

"Can I ask you one thing?" Natalia said.

"I won't help you kill my father."

"That's not what I was going to ask you. King claims he's a living god. Do you believe it?"

Ghost glanced over at her, a strange look on his face. He was silent until the lift had reached its destination.

"It will take a few hours to assemble the soldiers for the trip to Ports," he said. "You'll be left under guard until we're ready to go. I'll have proper attire delivered to you. Is there anything else you need?"

"Yes. If I'm supposed to fix a mainframe, I'm going to need tools."

"I'll show you to our supply room before we leave, and you can select what you require."

"What if you don't have it?"

"That isn't likely."

He motioned with his fingers, and the guards at the door hurried over.

"This is Natalia Duke. She's an Engineer. King wants her brought to the complex in Ports. Put her in one of the guest rooms and make sure she stays there. Provide her with anything she needs. If any part of her is disturbed, you'll be held responsible, and the outcome will be painful."

"Yes, sir," one of the soldiers said. "This way, ma'am."

They both pointed her toward the lift. Before they could move, Ghost reached out and took her arm, leaning in close and whispering in her ear.

"My father is a god, Natalia. The Scrappers believe it. I believe it. Why wouldn't I? I'm a god, too."

Then he let her loose, heading off to arrange the expedition to the complex. Natalia was frozen in place, left shivering as she watched him go.

15

HAYDEN WAS PRETTY SURE WIZ HADN'T EXPECTED A DOOR TO keep him contained, not when she had recognized Hank's mechanical arm attached to his body, and not if she knew its capabilities.

The proprietor of Crossroads was counting on two things. One, that he wouldn't be stupid or desperate enough to try to escape at night when the world beyond the cold cement walls of the safe house was crawling with trife. Two, that her armed and armored guards would be sufficient to handle him, just in case he did.

Which might have been true if he had been alone. Wiz's mistake was that she had seen Chains as a uniquely pretty face, and instead of keeping them separate had decided to put them together.

"Are you ready?" Hayden asked, gripping the handle of the door with the mechanical hand.

"Let's party," Chains replied.

He squeezed the handle and pulled, ripping it, and the lock, right through the wood of the door, at the same time kicking it open with his foot.

There were two guards outside of their room, and they spun around at the first sound, halfway through their turn when Chains emerged, jumping and throwing a metal-wrapped fist into the first soldier's throat. Hayden could hear the wet thunk of the damage she caused as her body hit the guard, pushing him back.

The other guard already had a metal baton in his hand, and he swung it toward Chains' back, the thin rod whistling through the air on its approach.

Hayden reached out with the mechanical hand, putting it between Chains and the weapon and catching the brunt of the force. The baton clanged off the arm, leaving a slight dent in it. Hayden kept charging, throwing a punch into the armor and coming away with nothing more than pain.

It was a slight distraction, but it was enough. Chains had already reversed course, moving around Hayden and throwing her fist up and in at the guard's abdomen, taking an angle that found a soft spot in the armor, the metal cracking against bone. The guard grunted, swinging the baton again, and again finding it blocked.

Hayden threw his entire body weight into the man, shoving him back against the wall. They both bounced off and fell to the floor, with Hayden on top. He drew back the arm and threw it at the guard's faceplate, hitting it so hard it cracked and splintered, nearly puncturing the reinforced glass and making it to the man's face. He raised his hand to throw another punch when a familiar click brought him to an immediate stop.

"Don't move!" Sally shouted.

He looked up. She was standing at the end of the hallway, rifle trained on him. Chains was a few steps down the corridor, but she had frozen when the guard appeared.

"Wiz might have let you go after you brought her to your ship," Sally said. "There's no way that's happening now."

Hayden shifted his eyes to the guard beneath him, stunned and motionless. His rifle was on his back, all he had to do was grab it, aim, and shoot before Sally could put a bullet in him.

Was that all?

"Put your hands up!" Sally ordered, taking a few steps closer. "Both of you!"

Hayden complied. So did Chains.

Sally tilted her head slightly, talking softly into her transceiver. Calling for backup. That's what he would have done.

"Neither of you move," she repeated, coming to a stop.

Hayden stared at the woman. He couldn't let Wiz slow him down. It would take days to get back to the Pilgrim, and then what? She would spend days more trying to get in, and he already knew she wouldn't be able to. And then he would be stuck, the same way Natalia was stuck.

He had to risk it.

His hands dropped at the same time he rolled to the left, hoping Sally wouldn't track him that well. He reached for the rifle with his human hand, sliding it under the downed guard's back and grasping for the top of it. His grab missed, his fingers sliding off the edge but not getting a firm hold.

He clenched his eyes as he realized he was about to die.

The bullets never came. Not a single one. His head snapped up to find Sally, prepared to make another desperate attempt to grab the gun.

She was already on the ground. Jake was standing behind her, a baton in his hand.

"It was a good try," Chains said, looking back at him. "You get points for the effort."

"What are you doing here?" Hayden asked. He leaned over the guard, pushing his body sideways and taking the rifle. He found a pair of magazines attached to the armor.

"Trying to rescue you," Jake said. "I thought it would be easier to get you out at night."

"You're both crazy," Chains said. "In a good way."

"Grab their rifles," Hayden said. "We need to get to the armory."

"Does Wiz know you're out?" Jake asked.

"Yeah."

"Damn. We need to get to the stairs before-"

The stairwell door slammed open. Jake dove around the corner as the bullets started hitting the wall where he had been standing.

"Shit," he cried, pressing himself against the wall. He was fortunate the outer walls were all made of concrete, or he might have caught a bullet right through them.

Hayden ran to the corner, leaning the muzzle of the rifle out and firing a few rounds to keep the guards honest. Chains joined them there, having retrieved the other guard's weapon.

"I told you this wasn't going to work," she said. "I wasn't planning on dying when I took the damned job this morning."

The gunfire stopped.

"Come out with your hands up," one of the guards ordered sternly. "There's nowhere for you to go."

Hayden looked back down the corridor. The guard was right. There was only the one stairwell leading to the floor, and they hadn't reached it before backup arrived.

"What do you think, Sheriff?" Jake asked.

"I'm not ready to die yet, either," Hayden said. "I'm also not ready to surrender."

"Is there a third option?" Chains asked.

Hayden looked back at the downed guards. "I have an idea. Jake, Chains, get those guards out of their armor. I'll keep them honest."

They didn't question him, getting up and rushing to the unconscious guards. Hayden leaned out from the corner, taking a few random shots before ducking his head back. These guards were wearing Marine body armor, too. Where had Wiz gotten it?

"How do I open it?" Jake asked.

"There's a main clasp at the top, with a pull. Near the neck. You have to take the helmet off, first."

"Pozz," Jake said.

Hayden fired back at the guards a few more times, in short, four round bursts. It was enough to keep them near the stairwell instead of advancing on the corridor.

"Got it," Jake said. "Now what?"

"Put it on," Hayden replied.

"What?"

"I don't think it will fit over the arm," he said. "So you need to put it on. It's too big for Chains."

"And then what?" Jake asked.

"I'll tell you once you have it on. Grab the helmet, too."

It didn't take long for Jake to get into the armor. He approached Hayden in it, wearing the helmet. Hayden could see the kid's eyes through the faceplate. He was scared. For good reason.

"What do you see in the helmet?" Hayden asked.

"What do you mean?"

Hayden remembered trying the helmet on the Pilgrim, and how it seemed to have networking capabilities. They were all offline on the ship, but if Wiz were the kind of person he thought she was, that wouldn't be the case here.

"An image on the glass in front of your eyes. A targeting reticle. Anything?"

"No."

"Turn around."

Jake put his back to Hayden. The interface between the

16

THE BULLETS STARTED COMING THE MOMENT JAKE APPEARED in the hallway, even though he was stumbling and holding his arm out to brace himself against the wall.

Hayden hated to do it, but he was fairly sure the guards weren't great shots, especially with the somewhat rare and valuable rifles. They didn't have extra ammo to waste on target practice and likely carried the weapons more for show than for actual use. He knew from experience the armor could absorb most bullets, and he didn't intend to let them keep shooting for long.

He leaned out from the corner, following the targeting reticle on the rifle's display. He didn't try to aim too precisely, instead unleashing a heavy barrage at the upper quadrant of the first guard he saw, watching as most of the bullets hit the armor and stopped.

Most, but not all. One of them caught the area between helmet and neck, and a spray of blood and the falling guard told him he had gotten a clean hit. He didn't hesitate, moving to the next one, counting the passing of time with his rapid heartbeats. The first one had taken three.

He fired again, a stream of thirty rounds before the magazine clicked empty.

A second guard fell.

He drew back behind the wall to replace the magazine, finding that Chains was standing over him, continuing the barrage. Jake had recovered from the push and was trying to get back behind cover. There were dark marks all over the softer part of the armor, and scuffs on the heavier plates. Hayden didn't see any blood, but he was sure the kid was feeling the sting of the impacts.

He pressed a fresh magazine into the rifle, standing as the return volley suddenly stopped, the guards running out of ammunition. He broke down the corridor toward them, firing single rounds as he approached, watching them nervously trying to reload. They had probably never done it before.

He reached them while they were still pulling the magazines from the spaces on their armor. They lowered their rifles, trying to grab the batons attached to their hips. He didn't give them the chance, using the rifle to smack their arms away, driving into them and knocking them back into the stairwell. They hit the edge of the steps and lost their balance, falling to the second floor, the impact leaving them rattled.

"Let's go," Hayden shouted, looking back at Chains and Jake.

Chains was already on her way, but Jake was standing there, still confused about what had happened.

"Jake!" Hayden said. "Come on!"

He couldn't wait for him. He started up the stairs, with Chains right behind him. They made it to the third floor, bursting into the open space. Thankfully, Wiz wasn't there, and neither were any more of the guards.

Hayden ran to the area where Wiz had shown him the

weapons. He wasn't surprised to find the laser pistol wasn't there.

"Chains, check the cameras," he said.

"On it," she replied, retreating to the displays. "Oh shit, Sheriff. We have a problem."

"What is it?" he asked.

She didn't have to answer. He heard it a moment later. A high-pitched whine from the south side of the building.

The auto-turrets.

"Grepping trife," she said. "A lot of them. Of all the shitty luck."

He scanned the shelves in a hurry, skipping over the various weapons stocked there, pausing when he found a crate full of familiar magazines in the bottom corner. He pulled it out, checking them quickly. They were for the Marine Corps rifles. He thought he saw a couple of the secondary magazines with the explosives mixed in.

It was perfect, except he needed both hands to carry it. He tucked the rifle under his arm and lifted, carrying it out to the rugs, next to where Chains was watching the displays. He looked at it too, at the same instant the east turrets started to fire.

"Did you bring those greppers out of the starship with you, Sheriff?" Chains asked.

"Not that I know of," Hayden replied. "I've got the ammo; we need to get to your car."

"We can't go out there."

"We can't stay in here."

"Sheriff."

Hayden turned. Jake was standing there; rifle pointed at him.

"You tried to kill me," Jake said.

"Jake," Hayden said.

Chains stepped in front of him, grabbing the barrel of the

rifle and pulling it from Jake's hands. "Don't be stupid," she said. "You're still alive."

"It hurts," Jake said.

"Case in point," Chains replied. "Dead doesn't."

The bluntness seemed to penetrate the shock. He nodded.

"For what it's worth, I'm sorry," Hayden said. "But we have to move. Can you take the ammo?"

Jake handed Chains the rifle and then picked up the crate of ammunition. He followed behind them as they headed back toward the door, making it to the stairwell. The two guards he had knocked down were gone.

That didn't mean they were anywhere close to being safe. He could hear a storm of feet above them, beating a path down from the top floor of the building. He didn't know whether it was in response to their escape or the trife's attack, but either way, they didn't have a lot of time.

"My car's on the second floor," Chains said.

They bypassed the first underground level, escaping the stairwell to enter the second floor of the garage. There were a hundred or so travelers on this level as well, in even worse condition than the group above them. They had gathered together, sitting tensely as they listened to the barely audible thumping whine of the turrets firing round after round of heavy shells at the trife.

Chains' car was the only one down here, dark and menacing in the corner of the floor. A single traveler was sitting beside it, a rifle resting across his legs.

The people watched in silence as they crossed the dirty, garbage-strewn floor to the vehicle. The man stood, holding up the rifle.

"Relax, Gus," Chains said. "It's me." She reached into a tight pocket on her pants and retrieved a Note, handing it to the man. "Thanks for keeping her safe."

The man grumbled something as he made the Note

disappear. Chains ran around to the driver's side, pulling out another chain from the back of her pants. A single key rested on the end of it.

"Were you hiding that in-" Hayden started to ask.

"Safest place for it," Chains replied before he could finish. "Get in."

Hayden grabbed the back door and pulled it open. "Throw the ammo in here and then take the front," he said.

Jake tossed the crate onto the back seat. Hayden put his foot into the car, pausing to listen.

The turrets had stopped.

"The guns are quiet," he said.

"Maybe the trife changed their minds," Jake suggested.

"Or maybe Wiz ran out of bullets," Chains said. "I saw the display. There were hundreds of the buggers."

"It doesn't matter, we're leaving," Hayden said, finishing his entrance and pulling the door closed.

Chains turned the key, the vehicle roaring to life. Hayden's heart skipped at the sound. He had never been in a car before. He had seen them in old movies, but that wasn't the same thing.

"Hang on," Chains said.

Hayden was pushed into the seat as the car accelerated, charging toward the nearby ramp. They hit it hard, bouncing the heavy vehicle and jostling him, knocking him against the door. He winced at the spike of pain in his already bruised shoulder before steadying himself.

"I don't think I like this," he said, his stomach already getting queasy.

The tires squealed as the vehicle rounded the ramp, ascending toward the first level. The brakes screamed when Chains jammed down hard on them, throwing Hayden forward.

"What the hell?" he said, looking out the windshield.

One of the Scrappers was blocking their path; big revolver pointed at Chains through the glass.

"Where the grep do you think you're going, bitch?" he said.

Hayden slumped back in the seat. Chains turned her head toward him. "There's a seatbelt on your left side. Take the metal and click it into the small opening on the flat part on your right side."

He found the belt and pulled it across his body.

"Get out of the car, bitch," the Scrapper said. The others were approaching from the floor, their guns drawn. "Now!"

He clicked the belt into place.

"Are we getting out?" Jake asked.

"Not a grepping chance," Chains said. Her whole body shifted as she reached for the accelerator, gunning the engine and lunging toward the Scrapper.

He had just enough time to fire one round, which hit the glass and skipped away.

"It's bulletproof, asshole," she said at the same time the spikes on the front of the car slammed into him, puncturing his stomach and leaving him impaled.

He hung from the front of the car as it continued to accelerate, pointing his revolver at the windshield and firing wildly. The bullets scuffed the glass and ricocheted harmlessly away.

They rounded the ramp, and Chains slammed on the brakes again. Hayden's belt pulled tight against him, holding him in place. The Scrapper wasn't so lucky. The change in momentum pulled him from the spike and threw him to the floor.

"We forgot to open the gate," Chains said.

"I'll take care of it," Hayden replied. "Back up."

He leaned over, digging through the crate of ammunition until he found the shorter magazine. He pushed it into its place on the rifle before unbuckling his belt and opening the door. The roar of engines echoed from the garage behind him, the Scrappers preparing to give chase.

"Sheriff," Jake said, frightened.

Hayden brought the rifle to his shoulder and triggered the secondary munition. The small, silver ball launched from the smaller barrel with a thunk, hitting the bottom of the solid metal gate and sticking. He ducked behind the door as it detonated, the explosion blowing a huge hole in the barrier, and sending a wash of dirt and debris back toward them.

He climbed in, grabbing the door and pulling it, the car already starting to move again. He got it closed just in time, allowing them to pass through the hole without shearing it off.

"Sheriff," Chains said. "I think this was a bad idea."

He looked forward through the windshield. A sea of dark shapes was caught in the headlights, dozens of trife charging toward Crossroads.

And they had just given the demons a way in.

17

"We can't let them into the building," Hayden said as Chains drove the car through a group of the trife, spearing one and sending the others tumbling over the roof.

"Are you grepping kidding me?" Chains shouted in response. "You're the one who just blew open the door!"

"The guns had stopped firing. I thought they were gone. At the very least, I didn't expect there would be so many."

And now that they were out in the open, the many were giving them fresh attention. Chains turned the wheel, sending the car into a sliding spin and bringing it to a stop facing the doorway.

"How the hell are we supposed to seal it?" Jake asked.

Hayden started to open the door.

"What are you doing?" Chains said. "Close it."

"I can't shoot them from in here."

"Open the grepping window. The button on the handle."

Hayden found the button and pressed it. The window started to descend. As soon as it did, one of the trife jumped toward him, trying to stick its head through. He put the rifle to it and pulled the trigger, blowing its brains out.

The car rattled and shook as the trife climbed onto it, hissing as they tried to get through the armored exterior. More of the creatures were moving into the hole in the gate, making their way toward the innocent travelers inside.

They vanished a moment later, crushed or thrown aside when the first of the Scrapper Enforcer's vehicles rose out of the garage. They tore through the ranks of trife, the soldiers clinging to the frame opening fire on the creatures.

"We can't stay," Chains said, putting the car in motion again. Hayden fell back, barely avoiding a trife arm as it swept into the car. He put two rounds into it, and it disappeared.

"The people in there didn't do anything," Hayden said. "It was my mistake. We protect the innocent."

"Not this time," Chains said, jerking the wheel as one of the trife tried to jump onto the hood. Its body hit the spikes instead, tearing open against the metal before it fell off. "We've got company."

He motioned behind them with her hand. Hayden flipped over to look out the rear window. The Scrappers had altered their path, ignoring the trife and giving chase.

"Can they really be that mad about Orion?" Jake said, noticing their tail.

"Apparently," Chains said. "Or maybe they want the explosives I have in the trunk."

"Explosives?" Hayden said.

"Uh. Yeah. Maybe."

"What kind?"

"What do I look like? I don't know. The job was to transport the boomsticks to Haven for a buyer there. My contact told me not to stop until I reached Crossroads or Haven, no matter what. That's what I tried to do, but someone in the car with me cocked it up."

"How do I get to the trunk?" Hayden asked.

He watched the muzzle flashes from the Scrappers behind them and heard the pings of slugs against the back of the car. One of the shots hit the rear window, leaving a scuff on the glass.

"You can't without stopping, and I'm not stopping."

"You have to stop," Jake said. "You're on the south transverse. It doesn't go anywhere."

"Is that right? It goes away from here. That's good enough for me right now."

Something hit the car from the side, shaking it hard enough it skidded on the road. A trife head appeared in the windshield, blocking Chains' view. She slammed on the brakes again, throwing the creature off before accelerating into it. Its efforts to avoid the spikes failed, leaving it impaled by the leg and hanging in front of the car.

"Geez," Chains said.

They continued into the night, passing between the large guns on the south side of the Crossroads. Both guns had stopped firing, and smoke was pouring out of one of them, suggesting it had broken down. Dozens of dead trife were scattered in front of them, torn apart by the heavy slugs.

The path ahead of them was clear of the creatures, but that didn't mean they had escaped. The Scrappers stayed behind them, all three of their vehicles riding in a wedge formation at their backs. Bullets continued to ping against the metal, the Enforcers hoping they could score a solid hit. Chains tried to keep maneuver the car to keep their aim off, but as long as they were going south, they were going the wrong way.

"You're going to run out of road," Jake shouted, looking over at the woman. "Have you ever been this way before."

"West to Haven," Chains said. "North to Sanisco. Never south."

"I have, and since we aren't riding horses, you're driving us into a dead end."

"Shit," Chains cursed.

The headlights had captured what Jake was talking about. A pile of junk cars had materialized in the middle of the road, spilling across the entire thing. There was nothing but overgrown brush behind it.

"Stop the car!" Hayden shouted.

"No," Chains replied. She threw the car into another spin, slowing its momentum.

Hayden could tell how much the car was slowing. He couldn't stand by and let the trife kill all of those people. Not when he was responsible for them getting in.

He leaned back, kicking the door open.

"What the grep-"

He didn't hear the rest. He threw himself from the car, hitting the ground on his shoulder, the rifle cradled against his chest. He rolled away from the vehicle as it finished the spin, inertia pulling the door back closed. He came to his feet, the Scrapper vehicles approaching in a hurry.

He squeezed the secondary trigger, sending another silver ball their way. It hit nearby, exploding a moment later in a gout of dirt that sprayed across the open cars.

Bullets whizzed past him, hitting the ground nearby. Chains was starting to accelerate, swerving to get around the Enforcers.

"Come on, Jake," Hayden said, running to his left and firing the rifle at the oncoming Scrappers. He could see the bullets hitting the metal frames of the cars, sparking off and causing the shooters to turn aside. "Don't let her leave."

He kept running, the rifle clicking as the magazine ran dry. He pulled it out, grabbing the only one he had and pushing it in. The Scrappers were bearing down on him, changing direction to run him down.

Chains had passed them, headed back toward the north. The red lights on the back of the car brightened.

Hayden stopped running, turning to face the cars. He brought the rifle up again, using the reticle in the display this time. The roar of their engines was deafening, drowning out any other sound.

He pulled the secondary trigger, sending a silver ball into the ground only a half dozen meters in front of him.

The Scrappers kept coming without slowing. He could see the driver of the lead car, his lips split into a wild grin, his eyes wide with excitement at the thought of plowing into him.

The ball exploded.

The force of the blast threw up dirt from below the lead car, along with enough kinetic energy to lift the vehicle from the ground and throw it to the left. It hit the second Scrapper car there, slamming into it and throwing both of them violently to the side, the massive tires passing less than a meter from Hayden's face. The third car wobbled and skidded, sliding to a stop on his right.

He pivoted toward it, aiming for the Scrappers. Short bursts bypassed the frame, hitting the Enforcers as they tried to get a bead on him and dropping them off the car.

The ground started to shake.

"Hayden!" Jake shouted.

Hayden spun back toward Crossroads. Chains had stopped the car after all, and Jake was outside, pulling a box from the trunk.

"Come on!" he yelled.

The ground shook again. Hard.

Hayden turned in a quick circle, his eyes tracking closer to the sky. He could feel the goliaths steps, but he didn't see them.

He broke into a run, sprinting toward the car.

Guns cracked behind him, bullets digging up the ground at his back. The driver's side door swung open, and Chains climbed out, rifle in hand. She fired back at the Scrappers, cutting off their attack.

"Shit," Jake said. "Hurry."

Hayden looked back over his shoulder. Two goliaths had come into view behind the brush, their large eyes glistening in the moonlight. They were moving quickly, charging toward the source of the noise.

"Chains, get back in the car, let's go," Hayden said.

Jake slammed the trunk closed, carrying the case around to the side of the car.

A deep groan echoed behind them. The ground shuddered again. Hayden made it to the vehicle, yanking open the door and diving inside.

"Go, go, go," he said.

Chains shoved the pedal to the floor, the rear tires spinning without grip for a second before the car jerked ahead. The engine roared as they gained speed, heading back toward Crossroads.

"You're the craziest, luckiest son of a bitch I've ever met," Chains shouted back at him. "You should be dead."

"I'm not, and neither are you. Jake, open the box."

Jake did, revealing long, narrow cylinders with small wicks sticking out of them.

"How do you use these?" Jake asked.

Chains leaned over, pushing a small button on the dashboard. "When it pops back out, it's ready," she said.

"What?"

"Trust me."

They sped back toward Crossroads. The goliaths were behind them, following the sound of the engine. Hayden leaned between the two front seats, watching the button on the dashboard anxiously.

"How long does it take?" he asked.

"Not that long. It's an old car, okay? A grepping classic by almost five centuries."

They reached the dead turrets. The trife were still out there, massing near the entrance. Hayden could see the gunfire pouring out of the open garage door, Crossroads guards recovering and pushing the creatures back.

"Any time now," Hayden said.

"I know, it's slow, we get it." Chains growled as she spoke, slapping the dashboard. "Come on, you grepper!"

They waded back into the trife, the car powering through them and throwing them aside. The heaviest group was a dozen meters from the entrance, trying to make it through the hail of bullets.

The button popped up.

"About grepping time!" Chains shouted, pulling it out. The end of it was red with heat. "Put the fuse against it."

Jake did as she said, lighting the end of the wick.

"Now what?" he asked.

"Throw it out of the damn window, you idiot, or we're all going to die."

Jake hit the window control beside him.

"Into the middle, Jake," Hayden said.

He pushed himself up, climbing out of the window and sitting on the top of the door. He drew his arm back and threw the stick at the trife, the cylinder tumbling end over end and landing among them.

"Hold on," Chains shouted, throwing the car into another spin. Jake grabbed the side of the car and held tight as they reversed course yet again.

A howl split the air, the goliaths drawing close. The car accelerated away, toward the ramp that would get them back on the road to Haven.

The boomstick exploded, trife thrown into the air and

blown into pieces from the resulting force. The goliaths roared in response to it, reaching down and grabbing the demons, sweeping them into their massive mouths.

Hayden watched the scene as they sped away, the trife desperate to escape, the goliaths scooping them up and devouring them, the humans in Crossroads shrinking back and falling silent. The more distance they gained, the more his body relaxed, sinking into the plush rear seat of the car.

"Wooooooo," Chains shouted as they ascended the ramp to the highway and finally hit the open road. "We made it! I can't believe we made it!"

Jake looked back at Hayden, a huge smile on his face. "We did it, Sheriff."

Hayden smiled. "We did, didn't we?" He let his head rest on the seat. "Thanks for not leaving me behind, Chains."

"Like the Deputy would let me," Chains replied, turning her head to look back at him. "But you're welcome."

Hayden heaved out a tense sigh, his body finally starting to truly relax. Within seconds, he was as physically exhausted as he had ever been in his life.

"Wake me when we get to Haven or if we get in trouble," he said.

"Pozz that, Sheriff," Jake replied.

Hayden didn't hear him.

He was already asleep.

18

"STAY ALERT," OVERSERGEANT GRIMLY SAID. "WE LOSE OUR precious cargo; we might as well stay out here with the bugs."

The Scrappers surrounding the truck didn't respond. They kept their eyes on the landscape, their rifles at the ready.

Natalia watched them from inside the vehicle, a wide, low, heavily armored machine with big tires and a pair of rotating turrets jutting out from the top. The only visibility was through small slits in the metal that ran down each side of the transport, and a slightly larger windshield in the front.

The truck was a military design, loud and relatively slow, powered by a large combustion engine positioned in the front. It burned through fuel at a dizzying pace, fuel that Ghost had explained was a lot more limited in supply than the electricity that had powered the car they had taken from the Pilgrim's launch site to Sanisco. They had managed to uncover a stockpile of barrels of the petroleum that fed the beast, but they were also aware it couldn't last forever. Not like the wind, or the sun, or other older tech that had been salvaged and repurposed.

It wasn't a comfortable ride. The truck shuddered with every bump, and there was no shortage of bumps out here. The road ahead of them came and went, sometimes leaving them crossing rough and broken terrain or taking long routes around areas that had been destroyed either during the war or naturally over the ensuing centuries. There were areas of extreme growth and areas of flat nothingness, but no matter where they traveled there were always signs of former civilization.

A rusted pole with a faded sign on top that read "Speed Limit 65." A standing wall and pile of rubble in a flat central area advertising coffee, gas, or a recharge. The burned out husks of cars and military vehicles, and even the remains of a crashed fighter jet.

They had covered the first leg of the six hundred mile trip in four hours. But now the sun was going down, and the soldiers were getting nervous.

"We've got two miles to cover to the bunker," Grimly shouted to his crew. "We're going to make it, or nobody eats tonight."

Natalia felt a shiver run down her spine. She had the same reaction every time Grimly spoke. He was a frightening man, almost seven feet tall and all muscle, his arms covered in tattoos. Like many of the members of the Scrapper militia, he had the eagle and star logo on his cheek. Unlike the other members, he also had it on the backs of his hands, as well as the palms. He didn't display it as inked tattoos. Instead, the logo had been branded to him with a hot iron.

His appearance was the least scary thing about him. When Ghost had brought her out to the convoy that had been assembled, Grimly had been standing front and center, arms folded over his massive chest. He had looked at her like she wasn't even human, his eyes lingering on her body, which was covered head to toe in a fitted armor of some kind. It was lighter than the other type of armor she had seen, but she had been told it would stop trife claws and most calibers of bullets, depending on range. She hated the way it clung tightly to her breasts and hips and rear when she put it on, and she hated it more when Grimly ogled her.

"Now that's a piece of ass I'd like to eat in every way possible," she had heard him say to the man beside him, who he called Undersergeant Pine.

Ghost had heard him, threatening him in that cold way he had. The Sergeant had paled and offered a less than sincere apology. But the truth was out there, and she knew if the Courier were ever not at her side she wouldn't be safe from Grimly or his people. The Scrappers as a whole were composed of the worst kind of monsters. People that enjoyed inflicting violence and pain and using fear to keep the common people in line. Good people didn't become Scrappers. Even in the harshness of their reality, their consciences wouldn't allow it.

Instead, they became victims. That was how King had seized control of the area, and that was how he held it.

The terrain approaching their overnight checkpoint was more battered than anywhere else they had traveled so far. According to Ghost, the entire area had been hit with a tactical nuclear warhead almost four hundred years ago and had suffered a number of earthquakes since. The result was a rock-strewn wasteland, a hilly stretch of blight that was only beginning to recover. The bunker was a small, underground facility that had been excavated in the center of it, an armored garage just large enough for the four vehicles making the trip to squeeze into, and a ladder to guide the travelers down into hiding.

It was one of two checkpoints along the route to the area King called Ports, strategically positioned where the trife were the densest. For whatever reason, the goliaths didn't go as far to the north as the other aliens did. Having seen them, Natalia wondered if it was because the air cooled and the weather got more damp, and maybe the unclothed and sexless giants became cold. It seemed too simplistic to be the real answer, but maybe simpler was more accurate.

They had to pick their way through the area, the transport barely squeezing between scars in the earth in some areas. It forced them to move at a pace only slightly faster than walking, which was the reason the Scrappers had deployed from their more open vehicles to surround the truck. She was the precious cargo Grimly had mentioned.

"Mable, you getting anything?" Grimly shouted back to the woman driving the truck.

The military vehicle was equipped with all kinds of sensors, one of which Natalia had reluctantly helped repair. She wasn't that surprised to find the technology on the machine was nearly identical to the tech in Metro. While the city didn't have motion tracking, a burned out circuit was a burned out circuit, a soldering gun was a soldering gun, and she had a general understanding of what wire went where.

"Nothing yet, Grim," she replied in a hoarse, almost masculine voice.

"Good. Let's keep it that way."

Natalia turned her attention from the small viewport, back to where Ghost was sitting. She had barely spoken to him since they had left their audience with King after she had realized he was as crazy as his adoptive father. Maybe in a different way, but as far as she was concerned anyone who believed they were a living god was delusional.

He was already staring back at her. His gaze didn't make her uncomfortable the way Grimly's did. She didn't see lust or desire to use her in his eyes. In fact, she took the softness of his look as a gentle affection, a desire to protect her that she didn't quite understand. He said he admired her, but what was that worth out here? Was it simply because she was different? Fresh and new and holding onto naive hope that the world could be more than what it appeared to be? Or was it because he believed she could give King what he wanted? She still wasn't completely sure what that even was. He already lived more comfortably than anyone else. A crazy desire to be the ruler of the world? It was a simple answer, but maybe it was the right one.

"We'll reach the bunker soon," he said to her in his peaceful voice. "You'll be more comfortable there, in King's room."

"He has a room there?" she replied.

He nodded. "He has been to the complex in Ports twice already."

"Even though it's dangerous?"

"He doesn't fear the trife. He's killed more of them than you or I will ever see."

"And he can't be killed anyway, right? Because he's a god?"

"You mock what you don't understand. I've been with him almost my entire life. I've seen what he's capable of."

"Building an army of monsters," Natalia said. "People who would be in prison where I'm from. Metro's laws are the same laws that existed when the Pilgrim was supposed to have left Earth. The same laws this country used to have."

"The country doesn't exist; the laws don't exist. Things change, whether we want them to or not. The world changed against our will. We tried to resist, but couldn't. We survive the only way we know how."

"This isn't the only way to survive. Fear isn't the only answer."

"Don't you think that other ways have been tried? Maybe they have the old laws to the east? One day, we'll connect both sides of this land again, and then we'll find out." He smiled. "I hope you'll be here with us. With me."

"Why wouldn't I? Where am I going to go?"

"You aren't a prisoner, Natalia."

She couldn't stop herself from laughing. "I believe that about as much as I believe you're a god. If I'm not a prisoner, let's turn around. I can go back to the Pilgrim and bury my husband."

"You can't go back. There's no way to get inside, as much as King wants to. At least not yet."

"You haven't mentioned Hayden," she said. "Not one word. Not even an apology for leaving him to die. He was as good of a man as they come. You could learn something from his example."

A familiar pain in the pit of her stomach began to sprout again. She held her breath, choking it back, hoping her eyes would stay dry this time. She had cried over Hayden whenever she had been alone. She didn't want to cry in front of Ghost. She didn't want him to see her weak.

"He loved you, that much is clear. He was an enemy of King. I gave him the best chance he was going to get. If he's like us, if he's a god, he may have survived. That's what gods do."

Natalia stared at him for a moment, her sadness turning to anger. A god? Hayden was a great man, a wonderful husband, but he wasn't a god any more than Ghost was.

"Oversergeant!" Mable shouted from the driver's seat. "I've got something!"

19

"WHAT DO YOU SEE?" OVERSERGEANT GRIMLY SHOUTED BACK.

Natalia looked away from Ghost, back out the slit in the transport's armor. She caught the bottom of the huge soldier's feet as he hopped onto the top of their vehicle for a better look.

"I don't know exactly how to read this," the woman replied. "There's a blob coming from the north."

"Distance?"

"I don't know."

"Grepping hell, bitch, are you good for anything?"

"Go screw yourself, Grim, this piece of shit equipment has never been functional before."

"Natalia, can you read it?" Ghost asked.

She turned her head back to the front. She could see Mable's heavy shoulder jutting out from the driver's seat and the edge of the tracking display in front of it. She was tempted to say she couldn't, to refuse to help. What good would dying like this do?

She unbuckled herself from her seat, using the top of the

truck to maneuver to the cockpit. Mable looked over at her when she entered, scowling at her appearance.

"I don't need your help," she said.

"You're doing a great job," Natalia replied sarcastically, biting back as strongly as it was given. That was the only way to earn respect among the Scrappers. "Let me look."

She settled over the woman's shoulder, staring at the display. It showed a red blob ahead of them, with lines indicating the distance.

"Three kilo - miles." She had to stop herself from announcing the wrong measurement. While the Pilgrim had settled on the Metric system, these people were still using Imperial.

"Shit," Grim replied. "Any idea how fast they're moving, sweetie?"

Natalia clenched her fist at the word. She watched the speed of the blob, running the calculations in her head.

"They're going to get ahead of the bunker before we reach it," she shouted back.

There was an extended silence from outside.

"Okay, you meatsacks!" Grimly shouted. "All eyes and guns to the north. We've got incoming. Be ready to switch to lances; we don't want to burn up all our ammo on the first encounter."

The other Scrappers didn't reply. It was assumed that if Grimly was speaking, they were listening. If they didn't, they would die even if they made it through the trife's assault. The Oversergeant would see to that.

She knew they were listening when they all started moving forward, running up ahead of the truck.

"Haito, you on the turrets?" Grimly shouted.

"Affirmative," the Scrapper replied. She was the only other person in the transport, a wiry young girl who was in charge of the guns on top of the machine.

"Make sure you don't shoot any of us. Except for Goins. He's an asshole."

Haito smiled as if the statement was a joke, though with Grimly it was hard to tell if he was kidding or not.

Natalia kept her eyes on the tracker, watching as the blob of something drew closer and closer, their convoy staying on the move and heading right into it. There was no guarantee the mass was made up of trife - the tracker didn't differentiate. But what the hell else would be out here?

She could feel the tension growing as each second ticked by. Her heart began to pulse stronger and quicker, her body shivering with a surge of adrenaline. She glanced toward the back of the transport when she caught Ghost's movement out of the corner of her eye. He was removing his white jacket, revealing a belt of knives beneath. He reached up to open one of the hatches on the top of the vehicle, looking back at her and nodding before pulling himself up and out and sealing the door behind him. She was as safe inside the armored truck as she was going to get.

"It's trife all right," Grim shouted. "Shit, there's a lot of the bastards." He laughed. "I guess they've been holding some extra all-night orgies. Mable, all stop! Scrappers, three rounds each with the rifles, one blow through with the revolvers, and then switch to lances."

"Oversergeant, we can't lance that-"

The crack of a gunshot silenced the complaint.

"Haito, you don't have to worry about shooting Goins for me anymore," Grimly said. "Any of you other greppers want a guaranteed death?"

Natalia looked at the tracker, and then looked up. The truck was at rest in a small ravine between two splits in the ground, essentially protected from three sides. She could see a few Scrappers standing on the ground on both sides of them; rifles aimed and ready to fire, waiting for Grimly's permission to let loose. A cloud of dust was rising ahead of them, a dark splotch visible beneath it. The trife were charging toward them in a group a few hundred strong. They only had twenty soldiers in their group. How could those be good odds?

"Haito cut down the front line!" Grimly shouted.

It was followed by a whirring sound, and then the truck started to vibrate, a thumping rattle sounding from the top.

In front of them, the trife started to die.

They tumbled to the ground in a line, the rounds from the turrets cutting them to pieces. Natalia watched as they fell for a few seconds, and then gasped when they started breaking to the left and right, leaping into the air in a solid mass and covering nearly forty meters in one powerful jump.

Haito tried to track them, the two turrets able to rotate independently, but the sides of the ravine preventing the angle of fire from going too wide. They had seen where the destruction was coming from and had quickly determined how to avoid it.

"Get ready!" Grimly shouted.

The ground started to rumble. Not quaking from heavy pounding of the goliaths, but rippling with the lighter, more numerous footfalls of the demons.

"Fire!" Grimly said.

Twenty rifles triggered at once, an even number on both sides of the divided trife. A dozen creatures fell. A second crackle sounded, and more of them fell. A third and final volley from the rifles, and then silence as the Scrappers switched to revolvers and the trife continued to close.

"Here they come!" Grimly cried.

The trife were almost to their position, spreading apart as they drew near. A number of them jumped again, launching into the sky in powerful leaps that closed the gap in a hurry. Natalia shifted her head to the left, looking past Mable.

Bullets launched from revolvers, knocking down trife after trife. Six rounds, twenty guns. Even if every shot were a kill, it would still leave half of the creatures alive.

Not every shot was a kill. A third at most, the demons only a few meters away and closing fast.

"Lances!" Grimly said.

The trife arrived. One of them slammed hard into the front of the truck, hitting the windshield and punching at it with sharp claws. They bounced off the hardened glass, and then an electrified spear dropped from the top of the truck and pierced its skull, killing it instantly. A shout followed, and a Scrapper rolled down from the truck to the ground ahead of them, a trife biting hard into the soldier's neck.

"Come on you greppers," she heard Grimly shouting. "Come to daddy."

The sound of human and trife feet was loud on the top of the truck, the hissing of the creatures audible as they overwhelmed the Scrappers. She couldn't see the fighting, but she could hear the dying hisses of the demons, and the painful screams of the humans.

Ghost was out there. Was he still alive? As long as Grimly was still cursing, she hoped so. If the Oversergeant was killed? It would be better if none of her captors survived.

"Geez, what the hell is that?" she heard Mable say.

The statement drew her attention to where the driver was looking, a little further off and to the right. Natalia looked back at the tracker, her heart nearly stopping.

A second trife force was coming their way from the east.

"Ghost!" she shouted. "East!"

She didn't know if he heard her or not. She looked back up at the incoming creatures. They were larger than the first group. Larger than any trife she had seen. They were nearly three meters tall, wide and powerful. The lead creature left the ground, jumping toward them. She tracked it the entire way until it landed directly in front of the transport. It threw its long arm out at the windshield; thick claws bent into a semi-fist as it struck the glass.

A small crack appeared.

"Oh, shit," Mable said. "Grep me."

She threw the truck into reverse, starting to hit the pedal.

"What are you doing?" Natalia said as they began to shift backward.

"I'm getting the grep out of here. Screw this."

The large trife jumped onto the front of the truck, throwing its fist at the windshield again.

The crack got larger.

Then a large shape hit the creature, knocking it away. Grimly rolled to his feet in front of the truck, looking back into it.

"You stop grepping moving right now, or I will kill you!" the Oversergeant shouted.

Mable took her foot off the gas, putting up her hands. Grimly turned back to the trife, sidestepping its claws and jabbing his spear into its chest. It shuddered from the shock and crumpled to the ground.

"Get to your vehicles, now!" Grimly shouted. "We need to make a break for the bunker."

"We can't outrun them," one of the Scrappers said.

"Mable, go," Grimly said, sticking his face up to the cracked windshield as he climbed back on. "Haito, cover us once we're clear. Sweetie, you and me. One day." He licked the glass in front of Natalia before vanishing back on the roof.

The transport started moving forward again. They were still on rough terrain, and driving through it with any speed was going to be a major challenge. Mable did her best, the truck's engine roaring as it sped forward, crushing the dead trife beneath its wheels.

Natalia moved away from the front as they cleared the ravine, looking out the slits in the side of the transport, trying to find Ghost. There were trife all around them, large and small, and she was surprised to see the bigger ones were attacking both the Scrappers and the other trife. It was giving them the break they needed, reducing the pressure on the remaining soldiers. She had no idea how many were still alive, but she was sure it wasn't a lot.

The turrets on top of the truck started to thump again as they cleared the ditch, firing round after round, Haito rotating them in every direction. A stream of death met the demons, cutting them to ribbons and allowing the convoy to break free.

Mable continued to speed up, driving the truck wildly over the terrain. It bounced hard, rocking and rolling. Natalia saw one of the Scrappers fall off, rolling on the ground and getting up, running toward the truck before a trife jumped on his back and removed his head. She was thrown away from the side and to the floor as the vehicle skipped off a rock, shaking hard and heavy.

She got to her knees, looking back out of the windshield. She could see the glint of metal in the failing light, the bunker coming up ahead of them. They didn't have that much further to go.

The seconds passed like hours. Her heart hurt from pulsing so hard for so long. The sound of fighting lost its intensity, the trife falling behind or pausing to kill their competition. They made it to more steady ground and charged ahead, crossing the line where the first trife had fallen as though they had won a race.

The doors to the bunker began to slide aside as they neared, stopping at the halfway point. The transport entered first, rumbling onto a cement floor inside the steel building, pulling off to the side to allow the other vehicles in. She heard their engines echoing in the enclosed space, and then she heard more gunfire and the doors beginning to close.

She stood up, looking out the slits. She could see one of the other Scrapper cars right next to her, a trio of soldiers on it.

"I hate those buggers," Mable said, entering the rear from the cockpit. She was sweaty all over, but her clothes were especially damp near her groin. "Yeah, I pissed myself. So what?"

Natalia didn't answer. The big woman hit a switch on the side of the truck, and the hydraulics for the side door activated, moving the armor out of the way so they could disembark. She climbed out ahead of Natalia, leaning over and vomiting when she made it to the floor.

Natalia jumped out of the transport behind her, at the same time the entire building rattled with the shock of the heavy blast doors slamming together. She could still hear the movement outside, the trife swarming the bunker and trying to find a way in. There wasn't one.

She scanned the small enclosure. She only saw eight Scrappers at first. Where the hell was Ghost? The other side of the transport?

She started walking, around the side toward the back.

Grimly came around the back in front of her. He was bleeding from a cut on his head, and smiling like it was the most fun he'd ever had.

"Sweetie," he said, catching her in his arms before she could get around him.

"Let me go," she replied. "Where's Ghost?"

Grimly looked at her, and then quickly looked around.

"I don't see him," the Oversergeant said. "I guess it's just you and me."

20

"HAYDEN. SHERIFF. WAKE UP."

Hayden opened his eyes, shoving his head back further into the rear seat of the car when he saw Chains' face perched only a few inches above his.

She was leaning over him, straddling his waist. Her vest was hanging dangerously low, nearly giving him a full view of her breasts beneath. He turned his head to the side, looking away while the woman laughed.

"You're so cute," she said. "A lawman and a gentleman." She pushed herself back, off him and out of the car. She slapped the roof of it a few times. "We're here, Sheriff. Haven."

Hayden pushed himself to a seated position, looking out of the window. It was still dark, and he couldn't see much beyond the shapes of other vehicles parked around them.

"Huh?" he said, trying to recover from his grogginess.

"This is the Impound. King doesn't let cars go through the streets, not unless they're on official business, which we aren't. My ride's safe enough here for now."

"What about the trife?" he asked, still looking around.

They appeared to be inside again. Dim lights hung against a cement ceiling, revealing a number of cracks in the structure, some of which looked dangerously large. "Where's Jake?"

"Your friend is on his way to his shop. He asked me to let you rest a little longer, and then bring you over. Well, more like he paid me to do it. With your Notes." She laughed again. "Damn, I never thought I'd be so happy to make a nighttime run. That was something else. Come on, Sheriff. I still have another delivery to make."

"How long was I sleeping?" Hayden asked, dragging himself out of the car. He was becoming so used to being bruised and sore he barely noticed it anymore.

"An hour on the drive up, five hours after. The sun will be coming up soon."

He stretched his arms, his stomach letting out a loud growl. "I'm hungry."

"Tell me about it. Lucky for you, Haven has its own farm and good supply lines. You can buy me breakfast."

Hayden put his hand to his forehead. He had a splitting headache. "Thanks for getting me here."

"It's like you said, Sheriff. We were both heading this way anyhow." She reached out and took his hand. She was so tiny, she felt like a child in his grip. "This way."

She pulled him along, bypassing the other dozen vehicles in the Impound. Most of them looked newer than hers, but they all had various levels of armor plating and defensive spikes arranged strategically around them.

Like before, they had to go up a ramp to get out of the Impound. Unlike Crossroads, this garage had a reconstructed gate made of bars of iron that swung open from the center, held fast by a heavy chain and lock. A guard was standing outside, his back to them.

"Billy, I'm ready to go now."

Billy turned around. He was a child, no more than fourteen, and yet he already had the eagle and star logo marked on his arm in a pledge of allegiance to the Scrappers. He was carrying a revolver and a knife on his hips, and he looked at them with the hardened eyes of an adult. What had this kid seen or done already in his life?

"Sure thing, Chains," Billy said. He lifted a ring of keys and picked out the right one, unhitching the padlock and chain from the gate. He pulled it open enough for them to exit.

"Your boyfriend looks like he got beat to shit," Billy said as Hayden passed through.

"Doesn't he?" Chains replied. "Aww, don't get jealous, Billy. I don't really like him; he just pays well."

Billy smiled, his face flushing. They exited the Impound, moving out into the street.

"Do I need to worry about him?" Hayden asked.

"Not yet," she replied. "As near as I can tell, nobody knows you exist. I think we capped all of the Enforcers at Crossroads, so we don't need to worry about them, either. News doesn't travel all that fast around here."

"What about the other Scrappers already in town?"

"What about them? Stay out of trouble, stop trying to help everyone who crosses them, and you should be okay."

"That would be easier to do if crossing them didn't mean looking at them in a way they don't like."

"You learn to keep your head down, Sheriff. Watch the residents, you'll see."

Hayden looked around. It was hard for him to get a sense of bearing. The road was a mixture of broken pavement, dirt, and loose stone backed by once tall buildings in various states of destruction. Some were little more than piles of rubble and the hint of a wall. A few had stairs and intact surfaces. A couple of them bore evidence of inhabitants, flickering fires bouncing against the walls of raised floors, though he didn't see anyone.

"What residents?" he asked. They were the only ones outside.

"It's still dark," Chains said. "They'll show once the sun starts to come up."

"Where are they now?"

"Hiding."

"From the trife?"

"And from the Scrappers. They're bad enough sober. Those fires-" She motioned to the dancing reflections. "Those are all watchmen. They keep an eye out for the bad things and sound the alarm if they see anything. Again, if they're sober enough."

"You have alcohol?"

"Of course." She laughed. "It was probably the first thing we started making again once the war was over. I've been fortunate enough to get a sip of a bottle of bourbon that predates the trife. What we make now is more like warm piss in comparison. Not that I've tasted warm piss. Anyway, you'll see. This place was a city once. The number of people who lived here drew a mass of trife I've heard numbered close to a million. They figured the best way to take care of them was to blow the shit out of the city, so they did. They killed tons of trife, lots of people, and left this behind." She waved at the destruction. "For all the grepping good it did them. Now, most people stay underground once night comes, and they set up their marketplace during the day. That doesn't mean the trife never drop by, or they never need to evacuate for a goliath, but it's old hat for all of us."

"And there's nothing we can do about it?"

"It's been a long time, Sheriff. A really long time. Most people only know there was anything before because the evidence is still here. Otherwise, they're so accustomed to living among the aliens it isn't uncommon for them to get careless and wind up dead."

They were walking down the central road. Hayden could see the dim light coming up from beneath the buildings, revealing entrances to more underground areas.

"What about you?" Hayden asked. "Where did you come from?"

"I grew up in Lavega," Chains said. "Well, not in it. In a smaller town not too far from there called Carcity. I'll give you one guess why."

"Carcity?" Hayden said. "You have a lot of cars?"

"More than a lot. The place was a junkyard once. Cars by the thousands. It all got abandoned because of the war, forgotten for a long time until our founder stumbled over it and realized that shells of cars make great barriers against trife. You pile them up a certain way, even if the trife know you're in there they can't reach you, and they're smart enough to give up after a while, but not smart enough to wait nearby for you to come out. Or maybe that just isn't sporting enough for them. Most folks, they never leave the village where they're born. If it's safe enough to survive, it's safer than anywhere else. But I never had much of a mind to sit still. I didn't want to spend my life having babies and trying to repopulate the world. Especially in Carcity. Food is tight. Water is tighter. The founding family runs everything, and they're all a bunch of screwed up pedophiles."

She paused at the comment, her eyes dropping to the ground while she fought against some obvious past trauma.

"I needed to get out. King trades food and water to Carcity in exchange for parts. Sometimes he would send Scrappers to get new vehicles or have old ones repaired. I learned how to fix stuff, and then I started repairing my ride in secret." She motioned back toward the Impound. "That was five years ago. I've been making runs mainly between

Lavega, Haven, and Sanisco since then. I'm a Driver though, not a Courier. I'm not a killer, and I don't work for King or any of the other would-be rulers. I know how to fight because I had to know, and one thing we have a lot of in Carcity is chains."

Hayden glanced over at her again. He had originally thought she was older, but on second look maybe it was the dust and dirt that was aging her appearance. There was a softness to her face that he hadn't noticed before. "How old were you when you left?"

"Thirteen."

"You're eighteen?"

She nodded. "I had to get out when I started to bleed. There are a lot of children in Carcity if you know what I mean. A lot of them don't survive."

"I understand."

That didn't mean he liked it. Maybe people had to grow up faster in this reality than in Metro, but that was no excuse for what it sounded like the Mayor of Carcity was up to.

They had kept walking along the same main street. Chains came to a stop, pointing to a narrow alley between two of the buildings. A red light was illuminating a steel door on the right side, and a scrawl of graffiti that read "BORGER."

"Jake's shop," Chains said. "The light's on, which means he's in."

"You knew about Jake before Crossroads?" Hayden asked.

"Of his shop, sure," Chains said. "Borgers get a lot of attention because there aren't many of them left. I'd never met him or anything. I never needed his services. There are twenty-thousand or so living here in Haven; it's not like it's a small town."

"How many in Carcity?"

"About seven hundred, give or take. Pretty much all of us

are blood-related to the founders in one way or another. It's all relative in Carcity." She spat out the phrase with disgust.

She led him into the alley, to the door of Jake's shop. It had a small button beside it, which created a soft buzzing noise when she pressed it. A louder buzz followed a moment later, along with the sound of the door unlocking.

Hayden didn't notice the camera in the corner of the door frame until Chains had already started opening it, letting them inside.

21

The shop was larger than Hayden expected, and even more surprisingly wasn't underground. Instead, it was part of the bottom floor of the dilapidated building above it, which appeared to have all of its support walls and ceiling intact. As soon as they entered, he could hear a thumping sound vibrating through the room, a deep rumble that seemed to be coming from the wall opposite them, more than fifty meters away.

There was a seat in the center of the room, a chair of torn up leather, taped and stitched back together, resting on a pedestal that raised it closer to chest-height. A long arm reached up from it, and a single bulb was dangling from the end of a wire there, over the top of the chair. A rolling table sat next to it, some tools resting there. Hayden recognized a few of them from the farmhouse.

Four tables sat around the seat, showing off some of the available replacements Jake had available. Hands, arms, feet, and legs in various stages of quality and complexity. None of them looked anywhere close to as solid as the arm Hank had gifted to them, though he would have preferred any of them to the cauterized stump he had been left with. He was sure he wasn't the only one who felt that way.

Three of the walls were lined with old wooden shelves, which were stocked with faded boxes. More boxes lay on the floor around the shelves, additional supplies overflowing the space. The fourth wall had a large, white container against it, and a wire from it to a small, black device resting on the floor. Additional wires spread out from the device, connecting to the bulb over the chair and a pair of displays on a desk in the corner, which itself was next to an old mattress.

That's where Hayden found Jake. The Borger was slumped on an armchair whose upholstery had long been worn to individuals threads, looking up at them with tired eyes.

"Sheriff," he said. "What time is it?"

"Three," Chains said. "You came here to sleep?"

"No," Jake said.

He pushed himself straight up in the chair. Hayden noticed he had removed the body armor and taken his clothes off down to his underwear. He had deep bruises on his arms and legs, caused by the hits he had taken from the rifle.

"To be honest, I took a look at myself after I removed the armor, and I started thinking long and hard about turning you over to King."

"I told you I was sorry for pushing you out into the hallway," Hayden said.

"I know. It wasn't just that, Sheriff. Hell, it isn't that at all. You did what you had to do to get us out alive, and if I didn't want to get involved, I shouldn't have come to rescue you. We made it to Haven, and then I came here. Seeing this place again, I started thinking about what I was getting myself into, and wondering if I'm making a mistake. My Mom and

Dad are gone, but I still have the shop. I can live pretty comfortably here, maybe find a wife and settle down. Wherever you go, there's going to be trouble."

"Only for King and his Scrappers."

"That's not true. Look at me. This morning I was helping you recover from your injuries. Less than a day later I'm almost as bruised as you are. I know you want to find your wife, and I told you I would get you here. But now you're here, and I see two paths in my future."

He reached down to the floor beside the chair, picking up a square device. Hayden recognized it as one of the transceivers the Scrappers used to communicate.

"For all they did to my family, for what Pig did to my mother, I have an emergency radio with a direct line to the local militia. In case I get into trouble. Borgers are important to King. I help put his soldiers back together. The ones who are worth it, anyway. His man, Pig, killed my mother, and I still work for him. My father never knew. I couldn't bear to tell him who was paying for the farm, the horses, everything."

Hayden's eyes shifted to the radio. Could he kill Jake before he called for help if it came to that?

"Ironic, isn't it, Sheriff?" Jake said. "I can turn you in and be set for life. Or I can stay with you and head to Sanisco. I can help you try to find your wife and probably die along the way. One choice, my conscience is shit but I'm still alive. The other it's clear, but I'm probably dead. That's what I've been thinking about. I fell asleep thinking about it. Every breath has been unsettled since."

"It wouldn't be a hard choice for me," Chains said.

"What do you know about it?" Jake snapped. "Did the Scrappers kill your parents?"

"I wish," she replied. "Which is my point. How the hell can you even consider siding with the asshole who had your folks killed? If you were lucky enough to have good parents instead of monsters, you should appreciate that for all it's worth."

Jake glared at her in silence.

"You told me I was one of the good ones," Hayden said. "One of the good guys. That's why you saved me, isn't it? You could have let me die. I was at your mercy, and that's what you showed me. To collect a reward? Or to do the right thing? King has my wife, Jake. What do you think he's going to use her for? She's an Engineer, and she knows all about the tech he wants the most. Do you think she'll be repairing waste disposal systems, or helping him strengthen his army? Maybe you settle down and take a wife. And maybe in five years, ten years, a Scrapper comes along and takes her. Then what?"

"You're one person, Sheriff. Even if I help you, that makes two of us. How are we supposed to stand up against the Scrappers? There are hundreds of them, if not thousands. The more I think about it, the crazier it sounds. I'm trying to live the way Hank taught me, but damned if it's not scary as hell. I call the guards; the whole thing goes away. Maybe I'll even be able to live with it in time."

"Or maybe it'll eat you up from the inside out," Chains said. "That's what you would deserve."

"Don't you say a thing to me about it," Jake said. "I had to pay you to get you to bring Hayden over here. You don't have loyalty to anything but yourself."

"You don't even have that much," she replied. "You'll turn your back on what you know is the right thing to do because you're afraid?" She turned to Hayden. "Sheriff, whatever it is you're planning to do, I want in."

"What?" Hayden said, surprised.

"You heard me. The Borger's right that I've always been a loaner, and for a good reason. There's no hope in this world, Sheriff. No good men trying to make a difference. There wasn't anyway, until now. You helped me back at Crossroads despite what you had to lose. You jumped out of my car, and you didn't know if I was going to stop or not. You would have saved us even if I hadn't. Hell, you even looked away when I leaned over you to wake you up. I don't have any ties, and I'd rather die doing something I believe in than live in fear and guilt. Unlike some assholes in this room."

She looked back at Jake. He looked like someone had just punched him in the gut. His eyes drifted to Hayden. His hand was tight on the radio, his thumb on the button to send the transmission. His jaw was clenched, his whole face tense.

Then he breathed out, shuddering as he tossed the radio to Hayden, who reached out and caught it in his mechanical hand, crushing it as he did.

"Well,' Jake said. "I guess if there's going to be three of us, that isn't as bad."

"Welcome to the party," Chains said. She glanced at Hayden. "I have to finish making my delivery. I have a reputation to keep up, you know?"

"Why don't we come with you?" Hayden asked. "I'd like to meet the person who's buying explosives but doesn't want King to know about it."

She smiled mischievously. "Now that you mention it, that might not be a bad idea."

22

THE SUN WAS STARTING TO RISE BY THE TIME THE THREE OF them were ready to leave Jake's shop. They had each taken advantage of the small bathroom hidden behind one of the shelves of parts, really little more than a spray of water from a pipe coming out of the wall and a drain large enough to swallow any waste they dumped into it. Hayden was surprised to learn that Haven's sewer system was somewhat operational. The system designed for millions was able to handle the refuse of the thousands, thanks to power fed to it by solar cells which were surviving long beyond their expected lifespan.

Jake had a change of clothes waiting for him when he finished cleaning up, a plain white shirt and dark pants, along with a leather coat that went down to his knees, the sleeves long enough to cover his mechanical arm to the wrist. He also gave him a leather glove to wear over the metal fingers, enabling him to hide the replacement completely. A fresh pair of boots and a wide belt finished off the outfit.

"You look like a gunslinger," Jake said once he was finished dressing. The Borger had put himself back in the body armor, with an oversized shirt and robes covering it to keep its nature from being completely obvious. "Clint Eastwood."

"Who?" Chains asked. She had refused new clothes, preferring to stick with the vest and leather pants, which had been custom made to work around the many chains she wore.

"I've got a few of his videos on my mobile," Jake said, tapping the satchel that held his portable computer. "I can show you later. It needs to get a little sunlight to charge up a bit."

Jake's agreement to help them had cooled the tension between the two, at least enough that they weren't at one another's throats.

"Except I don't have a gun," Hayden said. "At least not one small enough to sling. We were in too much of a hurry to get out of Crossroads for me to grab a sidearm."

"You've got my dad's replacement," Jake said. "You'll never be unarmed."

Chains groaned. "Is that supposed to be a Borger joke?"

Jake shrugged. "It's true."

He moved to the chair at the center of the room, crouching down and pressing a button at its base. It slid back, revealing a small hole at the bottom. He reached in and pulled out a thick stack of Notes.

"I've been saving these for a long time," he said. "We should be able to get what we need with this."

Chains whistled. "You could probably buy Carcity with that many Notes."

"You're from Carcity? I should have guessed." He paused, his expression turning dark. "I've heard rumors about that place."

"They're all true," Chains said quickly, making it clear she didn't want to talk about it.

"I'm sorry," Jake said.

"I got out," Chains replied. "Who knows, maybe the Sheriff here can fix the place one day."

"Let's not get ahead of ourselves," Hayden said.

They made their way out of Jake's shop. He closed the door behind them, flipping open a hidden panel and entering a code there to lock it.

"What happens if the power goes out?" Hayden asked.

"The black box inside is a battery. It gets recharged from the main solar grid during the day and has enough storage to keep the place running for a week without external electrical. After that, the door won't stay closed, but if the power goes out for that long, we'll have other things to worry about."

"Metro is the same way," Hayden said.

"It must be nice, living in a self-sufficient city away from the trife," Chains said.

"For a long time, it was what it was. Now that I'm Outside, I realize how nice it was."

"There's an old saying," Jake said. "You can never go home again."

"I think that's especially true for us," Chains said.

They made their way out into the street. As Chains had promised, the entire area had been transformed with the emergence of the sun. Where there had been only a deserted street earlier, now there were dozens of people outside, walking up and down the main thoroughfare and making their way past a number of merchant stalls. The stalls were of varying shapes and sizes, from tiny homemade carts stocked with random items for sale or trade, to larger horse-drawn carts, to cars, to bigger trucks loaded with food. The largest crowd seemed to be around those stalls, and Hayden could see the Scrappers gathering there, too, keeping the people in line.

As they made their way toward it, Hayden realized that

the setup was all very deliberate. None of the stalls were very far from the garages where they had come out, and even the trucks were organized in a way that they could pack quickly and escape into the Impound. Scanning the buildings around them, he could see there were more Scrappers up on the dilapidated walls, as many facing out as in, watching for signs of trife or goliaths.

"Excuse me," someone said as they passed the line of smaller carts.

Hayden looked over and down, finding a young girl at his side. She was seven or eight, her hair tangled, her clothes dirty. She was clinging to a stuffed animal of some kind that had seen much brighter days.

"Can I help you, miss?" Hayden said.

She smiled at him. "Mama says we need to make some Notes or else we aren't going to eat this week. Come see what we have?"

"You don't have enough to eat?" Hayden asked.

"Hayden," Jake said. "They all say that to travelers."

"Is it true?"

"Sometimes it is, sometimes it isn't. King makes the people pay through the nose for the protection of the Scrappers, and these people don't have a lot as it is."

"We're in a hurry," Chains said.

"It will only take a minute," the girl said.

"So they go hungry?" Hayden asked. "What if there's extra food?"

"The Scrappers get what's left. That's where the name comes from. They get King's scraps. Anything they don't eat is discarded."

"Thrown away? When it could feed people?"

"King says he doesn't run a charity," Jake said. "Survival of the fittest. People who want to live will find a way to eat."

"Stealing?"

"Some try. They rarely succeed."

"Please?" the girl asked, reaching up and tugging on his hand.

Hayden smiled at her. "Show me."

Her return smile was massive, and she grabbed his hand and practically tugged him over to one of the carts, which was filled near to overflowing with an assortment of disorganized scraps. Paper, strips of cloth, writing instruments, empty bullet casings, even stones. A pair of old shoes was resting on top, and Hayden noticed the girl was barefoot.

"Make an offer on anything that catches your eye," the woman said. "Everything is for sale."

"Hayden, we have to go," Chains said. "We don't have time to wade through her crap."

"We have lots of pretty things," the girl said. She reached down and started spreading the collection. "Maybe one of the rocks looks like you? Or maybe you have a slingshot?"

The woman joined her daughter, helping her push their items around, trying to surface something he might be interested in. "This cloth is pretty, isn't it?" the woman said, lifting a faded red strip with a stain on the end. "You could give it to your girl as a gift." She held it out toward Chains.

"I don't need it. Sheriff, it's like this everywhere. All the time. You'll see. You stop for every little kid who says they can't eat; you'll never get where you're going."

"And then what?" Hayden asked, looking at her. "You learn to ignore the suffering? You begin to accept the world the way it is?"

Her face reddened with embarrassment. She looked away. "You can't help everybody, Sheriff," she said. "It's just not possible."

He looked back at the girl. "We'll see about that."

His eyes dropped to the cart again. A small piece of silver plastic was sticking out from under a stack of bottle caps. He reached for it, pulling it from the cart and holding it up with a smile.

It was a badge. It was dirty and made of plastic, and one of the points of the star had melted off, but it was still a badge. It even said 'SHERIFF' across the center, an engraving caked with dirt. It had a pin on the back to hold it in place.

"I'll take this," Hayden said. "How many Notes do you need to eat for a week?"

"Two," the girl said.

Hayden looked over at Jake. The Borger had to have pulled a few hundred notes from beneath the chair. He had at least fifty of them that he had pulled from the dead Scrappers.

"Jake."

He expected the younger man to protest, but he didn't. He dug out the Notes and handed them to the very excited little girl.

"Thank you, thank you," the girl said. She wrapped her arms around Hayden's leg, hugging it.

"Thank you, sir," the woman said at the same time.

It wasn't going to help them next week, but at least it was something.

"I have to go," Hayden said. "Thank you for this." He took the badge, pinning it to his coat over his chest.

They returned to the Impound without speaking. Hayden and Jake waited outside while Chains went in and grabbed the crate of boomsticks, carrying it out and leading them through the streets. They navigated off the main street, down an alley, and across three separate blocks. There were more people outside here, groups tired and dirty citizens organizing around better-dressed men and women who were waving colored scraps of paper. The residents were all carrying a variety of tools, from shovels to hammers to handmade scraps of metal tied to poles.

"What are they doing?" Hayden asked as they passed them by.

"They'll head out to the surrounding areas to dig," Jake said. "They look for stuff to sell or trade. There's a guy in town, Capaldi. He runs the digs, and makes sure the groups are compensated for their finds, not the individual."

"Isn't it dangerous to go out there unarmed?" Hayden asked.

"Everything is dangerous. That's why they go in groups."

Hayden wasn't sure how groups would help if none of them had weapons, but he didn't keep asking.

"I'm sure he takes a nice cut off the top, too," Chains said. "Probably gives them just enough so they can keep working for him."

"Do they ever find anything good?" Hayden asked.

"Every so often, but after all this time the area's been picked pretty clean," Jake replied. "The groups come back later and later because they have to keep ranging further out. Maybe one day Capaldi will let them have one of his trucks, but not yet."

"How do you know where you're bringing the explosives?" Hayden asked.

"I have an address," Chains said.

"An address? None of the buildings are marked."

"They're named," Jake said. "That one is 'Scar.'" He pointed to a building with a massive gash in its side. "That one is 'Drunken Monkey.'" He pointed to a line of rubble. "Once you know which building has which name, it's easier to find things."

"We're headed to 'Broken Sword,'" Chains said. She pointed to a building that looked like a sword that had been shattered near the hilt. "That one."

"Pozz that," Hayden said, getting the hang of the convention.

They crossed over two more blocks. As they moved closer to the building, an echoing rumble began to grow from further back.

"It sounds like an engine," Chains said, listening. "More than one. Probably some merchants or maybe more Enforcers coming into the city. It's normal. I don't think it's anything to worry about."

"Are you sure?" Hayden asked, looking back down one of the streets. The noise was echoing around them, getting closer with every second. "What if the Enforcers from Crossroads survived? They might have come here looking for us?"

"There's no way they made it," Chains said. "The goliaths had them, assuming they didn't die in the wreck."

"I don't like it," Hayden decided. He scanned the street, finding an alley nearby. "In there."

They hurried to the alley, ducking between the remains of two buildings, across the street from "Broken Sword." The noise continued to increase in volume until three vehicles pulled into the street in front of them, coming to a stop outside the building.

"Shit," Chains said. "I hate that you were right."

"Shh," Hayden replied. "Wait."

The doors of the cars opened. Twelve Scrappers poured out, led by a heavyset man in a dark suit.

"A Courier," Jake whispered.

"Ghost?"

"He's not wearing white."

The Scrappers grouped at the back of each car. The trunks opened, and one of them at each reached in and started retrieving shotguns and revolvers, distributing them to the group. Once they were armed, they headed en masse toward the front of the building, climbing broken stone steps up toward its mangled face.

"Where are they going?" Jake asked.

"My delivery address was on level 2," Chains replied. "I think whatever my mark was planning, King found out about it first." She turned to Hayden. "We should beat it, Sheriff. Keep the explosives and move on."

"I don't know," Hayden said. "Any enemy of King's is a friend of mine."

"If we start with the Scrappers here, we're starting with them everywhere," Chains said. "Plus we're outnumbered and outgunned."

"I've already started with the Scrappers," Hayden said. "It's way too late for that."

"There were still guns in the trunks," Jake said. "I saw them."

"I thought you were afraid to die?" Chains asked.

"I am, but I also said I'm all in. We're far enough outside the main run we might not get noticed, and if we can take them out, we might earn a new friend. At the very least, we'll get some more guns."

"Or dead," Chains said.

"Who's afraid of dying now?"

"Who's wearing bulletproof armor?" Chains retorted.

The Scrappers had reached the steps. They moved cautiously into the building.

"This isn't a good idea, Sheriff," Chains said.

Hayden watched the Scrappers, trying to decide what to do. A door in the building opened, a young woman stepping out. One of the soldiers turned and fired, three quick cracks that dropped the woman to the ground and caused the rest of the group to speed up their assault.

"She isn't even armed," Hayden said, a sudden, burning pit of anger in his gut.

They had murdered an innocent person for the crime of trying to get out of her home.

"I'm going in."

23

HAYDEN SPRINTED FROM THE ALLEY, TOWARD THE TRUNK OF the closest car. The Scrappers already in the building didn't notice him. They were organizing around the doors in the lobby, preparing to make their way deeper inside. There was no way whoever was in there hadn't heard the gunshots, giving them a chance to prepare for the assault. If Chains' contact wanted explosives, it stood to reason they had guns already.

He glanced back as he neared the trunk of the first car. Jake and Chains were behind him, heading for the other two vehicles. Jake had taken the explosives, carrying the crate with the enhanced strength of the armor and nearly keeping pace with the small woman.

As Hayden turned his head forward again, he could see the driver's side door of Chains' target swing open, and a Scrapper climb out. He already had a revolver in hand, and he was swinging it toward her.

Hayden changed direction, nearly slipping and falling when he tried to alter his course. The closer sound drew the gunman's attention, diverting him from her. Hayden dove between the cars, three bullets pinging off the metal of the car behind him, narrowly missing his body.

He rolled and bounced to his feet. The Scrapper was tracking him, revolver pivoting to where he was coming up.

A chain lashed out from the end of Chains' hand, slamming the Scrapper hard in the jaw. Hayden heard the crack, and then the man vanished beside his car.

"Sheriff!" Jake shouted.

Hayden turned to him in time to catch a shotgun and ammo belt the Borger had tossed his way. He balanced the ammo over his shoulder, getting the gun in position for use.

The Scrappers inside had heard the shots behind them, and a few of the soldiers had turned back. They were rushing toward the cars now, conserving their bullets until they had a better angle on the targets.

Hayden grabbed the door of the nearest car and swung it open, ducking behind it. He needed to get in closer to use the gun. Chains followed his lead, crouching beside him and pulling the passenger door of the adjacent car open.

"So much for a sneak attack," she said.

"Where's Jake?"

Hayden lifted his head, scanning for him. Where had he gone?

Bullets started to hit the car, pinging off the armor plating on the door, too close to his head. He ducked back down, waiting for the attack to stop.

He heard a shout to his left, looking over in time to see Jake emerge from behind one of the cars, firing the shotgun nearly point blank into one of the Scrappers. The shot tore a gash into the soldier's hip, pulling him to the ground.

The other Scrappers adjusted to retaliate, shotguns coming into line. Hayden cursed silently, unconvinced the armor could stop the rounds from penetrating at such close range. He grabbed the top of the car door with his mechanical hand, pushing himself over it in one hop and landing beside the Scrappers. He fired the shotgun, shot ripping through them and knocking two of them down. One of them got a shot of their own off, and Jake shouted when at least one of the fragments pierced the armor.

Hayden fired again, dropping another Scrapper. The last whirled around, leading with the shotgun. Hayden grabbed it with the mechanical hand, ripping it from the man's grip. Then Chains was there, and she slammed him in the side of the temple with a chain.

The group that had come back for them was down, but the fighting had only grown in intensity. Hayden found the Scrappers inside the building, having fallen back to cover when their opponents finally emerged, opening fire with simple guns of their own.

The sound of more engines rose in pitch, echoing through the street.

The Scrappers were sending reinforcements.

"We need to get inside," Hayden said. "Grab the boomsticks. Hopefully, they know we're on their side."

Jake retreated to where he had left the crate, picking it up and carrying it toward the steps. Hayden sprinted ahead of him, running toward the backs of the Scrappers pinned down in the lobby at the same time he pulled two shells from the ammo belt and shoved them in the shotgun.

The defense must have seen him because the bullets stopped coming as he approached from the rear. The Scrappers heard him then, rising to their feet and trying to turn around. He emptied the shells into them, killing his group. Then he ducked back behind the cover, reloading the weapon.

The reinforcements reached the building, brakes complaining as the heavy cars came to a quick stop. Two dozen Scrappers piled out of four armored vans, already armed.

"We need to get inside," Hayden repeated, loud enough that Chains and Jake could hear. They jumped away from the cover, the defenders ahead of them adjusting their aim to give them a path to one of the doors. A woman was crouched in it, a single-shot rifle on her shoulder. She fired, grabbed a shell from beside her and reloaded, fired and reloaded again, all in the space of a few seconds.

Hayden reached the door first, stopping to guide the others through.

"Let's go," the woman said once they were in, closing the door behind them. Hayden could hear the thunk of rounds striking the door, cracking into it and through.

They were already on the stairs by then, descending into the building's basement.

"Who are you?" the woman asked on the way down.

"Sheriff Hayden Duke," Hayden replied, twisting to show her the plastic badge. "No friend of King or the Scrappers."

"Then you're a friend of ours," the woman replied.

"And who are you?" Jake asked. "I don't recognize you."

"I recognize you, Borger," she said. "My name is Callie. I work for Huston."

"Huston?" Jake said. "You're kidding."

"Who's Huston?" Chains asked.

"The former Mayor of Haven," Jake said. "He disappeared when King took over."

"You would too if staying meant being executed," Callie said.

"We've got your explosives," Chains said. "I'm the Driver."

"I don't know if we'll have a chance to use them. Somebody ratted us out."

They reached the basement, coming up to another old door.

"It's Callie. Open up," the woman said.

The door swung open. Hayden could still hear the gunfire above them, getting closer. The Scrappers were closing in.

They piled into a dark, musty room. Equipment was piled along the walls. Guns, knives, ammunition, and more. There were old mattresses on the floor, garbage piled into the corner. The sharp smell of urine permeated the space.

A half-dozen men and women were gathered in the center, armed and ready to fight. Hayden didn't expect to know any of them, but Jake recognized the man at the rear immediately.

"Mayor Huston," he said.

The Mayor was a large, dark-skinned man. He smiled when he saw Jake. "I never thought I would see you down here, Jake, but I'm glad you decided to join us. Who recruited you?"

"I didn't decide anything," Jake said. "Chains was bringing your delivery; we just happened to come at the wrong time."

The door slammed closed behind them.

"That isn't going to hold them," Callie said. "Somebody ratted us out."

"Did we just lock ourselves in our tomb?" Chains asked.

"Not at all," Huston said. "Move the rug aside."

His soldiers stepped off a tattered old rug, grabbing it and rolling it up, revealing metal cover in the center of the floor. They returned to it, lifting it off a dark hole and dropping it to the side.

"My intention was to start sabotaging some of King's more valuable works. His smelter, for example," Huston said. "These explosives were supposed to do the trick. I don't think I'm going to get the chance." He looked at the woman. "Callie, take Jake and his friends with you and the others. I'll stay here and keep them from following."

"George," Callie said, trying to protest.

"Forget it. I had my chance, and it didn't work out. If you see that bastard son of mine, tell him he killed his father. Not that he probably gives a shit. I'm sure King's men paid him a small fortune for giving us up."

"It's more likely King put a bullet in his head," Chains said.

A slug hit the door, followed by a few more. Then something slammed into it, threatening to force it open.

"It isn't going to hold for long," Huston said. "Give me the explosives and go."

Jake dropped the crate in front of the older man.

"You've been down here all of this time?" he asked.

"Not the whole time," Huston replied. "Long enough."

"Come on," Callie shouted. "Grab your gear. Let's go."

There were half a dozen others with them. They scrambled to the wall, picking up the equipment resting there before returning to the center of the room. They heaved their packs into the hole and started climbing down after them.

"Where does this go?" Hayden asked.

"There's an old tunnel about ten meters down. It used to be part of a high-speed transportation system. We can use it to get out of the city."

"I can't leave the city," Chains said. "My car is still in Impound."

"It'll be safe enough there until you can come back for it," Jake said. "Unless you'd rather go ask if you can go out the front door?"

"Smart-ass," Chains said, smiling.

Something hit the door again, beginning to dent it in. Beside them, Mayor Huston was laying the explosives out on the ground and lighting a cylinder of paper. He put it to his lips, pulling on it and then breathing out the smoke.

"Come on, Sheriff," Chains said, at the edge of the hole. "Time to go."

Hayden looked back at the door, and then at the Mayor. He moved to the hole, dropping into it and getting his feet on the first rungs. It swung beneath him, the motion putting him off-balance. He caught himself, preparing to descend.

The door flew in, the force of a heavy blow ripping it from its hinges. Hayden expected to see a Scrapper there, but instead he was greeted with a large thing of metal, with thick legs and heavy arms attached to a steel torso. It walked toward him, into the room, the Scrapper soldiers moving in and opening fire behind it.

Hayden dropped his feet from the ladder, keeping himself connected to it with his hands and letting himself fall. Bullets sprayed overhead, hitting Callie and cutting her down. He slid along the rope, the material cutting into his human hand, burning it and tearing it open. He hit the ground hard, looking up as the machine reached the hole and leaned over to look down at them.

A sharp pop, and then the robot vanished in a wash of fire, the explosives going off. The ground shook above them, the backdraft flowing down the tunnel at Hayden's face.

"Shit," he said, diving out of the way as the fire reached out for him.

It was gone just as quickly, replaced with stone and dirt. The building and ground continued to shake, the Broken Sword collapsing further above them. A hand grabbed his shoulder, pulling him to his feet.

"Are you okay, Sheriff?" Jake asked.

"Okay enough," he replied. Now that the light from above was gone, he couldn't see a thing.

Someone ahead of them turned on a flashlight, revealing the area in a tight beam. They were in a small, perfectly round tunnel that stretched out of sight in both directions.

"Is everyone okay?" the man with the flashlight asked.

"Fine," Chains said, though she had a bleeding cut on her arm. "I've had worse."

"I'm okay," Hayden said, looking at his bleeding hand.

"We can't linger here. We need to go."

"We were supposed to head south," one of the others, a woman, said.

The flashlight shifted, showing the collapse above had come down the tunnel and blocked the passage heading that direction.

"It looks like we have to go north," the man said. "Come on."

Huston's people started moving. Hayden didn't hesitate to follow.

"Do you remember what I said about trying to help every person you came across, Sheriff?" Chains said.

"Yes," Hayden replied.

She waved her arms as if to say "this is all your fault."

"Don't forget who took the job to deliver the explosives. And don't forget who made you late. If Jake and I hadn't been here, you might be dead right now."

"Why do I have the feeling that might have been a more preferable option?"

24

NATALIA SAT ON THE EDGE OF THE BED, STARING STRAIGHT ahead, trying to think of some way out of her predicament.

Ghost was gone. He hadn't made it into the bunker with the rest of the Scrapper convoy, effectively proving with ultimate finality that his delusions of being a god were just that, and leaving her trapped alone with Oversergeant Grimly and his crew.

The Oversergeant hadn't done anything to her yet, but there was no part of her that felt comfortable he wouldn't. He had passed her off to Mable with orders to bring her to King's quarters. That's what the driver had done, and that's where Natalia had been for the last four hours.

A soldier had stopped by earlier, delivering a hot meal of stew with chunks of meat in it. Natalia had smelled it, remembered Pig's proclivity for human meat, and dumped it in the toilet, along with what little she was able to vomit up. Then she had put herself in her current position. Waiting for the moment she was sure would come.

She had no idea what was happening in the bunker beyond the suite. The walls were thick here, the door a heavy slab of steel that slammed open and closed after squealing on a track that desperately needed lubrication. Very little sound was able to penetrate, which she supposed was probably more to keep the inside in than the outside out. Judging by the overly plush nature of the suite and the hint of a smell that seemed to linger within it, the leader of the Scrappers used the space most often to sleep and have sex, though with who, what, or how many she had no idea. And she didn't want to know.

She drew in a strong breath and closed her eyes again. Every time she did, all she saw were the trife, charging toward the transport, killing soldiers. It didn't matter that they were Scrappers. They were still human. Watching them cut down by the aliens was hard for her to reconcile. She knew she needed to. She had to adjust to this world and all of its realities if she was going to survive long enough to assassinate King.

At least Ghost had been taken care of. If Grimly did attack her, she would survive, and despite his size, she was certain he was the less powerful of the two men. Ghost had gotten unlucky, Grimly the opposite. The outcome would benefit her in the long run.

It had to. It was the only way she could stay strong. The only way she could accept what she knew was coming. She had to stay alive. She had to keep fighting and not give in. For Hayden's sake. She owed him their revenge.

She opened her eyes when someone knocked on the door. The pounding only barely made it through the thick metal, but she heard it all the same. She stood up as the door started to slide open, howling along its dry tracks and pausing halfway.

Oversergeant Grimly entered, with Undersergeant Pine and Mable trailing behind him.

What was this?

"Hey, sweetie," Grimly said with a crooked smile. "Mind if we join you?"

"Do I have a choice?" Natalia replied.

"Not really."

The door screamed closed behind them. Pine vanished into the suite's pantry, while Grimly moved to stand in front of her.

"Me and my crew have been talking a bit about our situation," he said, looming over her. Maybe she was wrong about which man was the better killer?

"Situation?" she asked.

"We lost half our squad in that trife attack and all but the transport and one other vehicle in the convoy. Plus your hump-buddy, Ghost. To be honest, if I hadn't been here, I don't think anyone would have survived."

"You have a pretty high opinion of yourself."

"For good reason. Be that as it may, we're of a mind to head back to Sanisco and call it a massive failure. It wouldn't be the first time a convoy didn't make it out to Ports. Grepping King is out of his mind the way he keeps sending us out here to die."

Pine emerged from the pantry carrying a bottle and four glasses. He put them down on the table beside the bed, opening the bottle and pouring a deep red liquid out.

"That leaves us with an interesting choice," Grimly said as Pine handed him one of the glasses.

He offered it to Natalia, but she didn't move.

"Take it!" he screamed, right in her face. Her body started to shake on its own as she reached out for the glass. He smiled. "Thank you."

Pine handed him a second glass. Then the three Scrappers converged.

"Cheers," Grimly said.

He clinked glasses with them, and then with her. She

stood in one place, frightened and shocked, while they downed the liquid.

"You too, bitch," Mable said. "It'll make it all so much better for you."

"What do you mean by interesting choice?" Natalia asked, keeping her eyes on Grimly. Were they all planning on attacking her?

"One the one hand," he said, raising the empty glass while Pine refilled it. "We can do whatever we want to you, kill you, and leave you out near the scene of the attack, and King will never know what's what." He smiled like he had just offered her candy. "On the other hand, he might appreciate having you back enough that not hurting you will be worth it in the long run."

Natalia's heart thumped harder in her chest. She looked over at Mable. "How could you be part of this?" she asked.

"I don't like you," Mable said. "You made me look like an idiot back there. I want to humiliate you the way you humiliated me."

"We've spent time with King's Engineers before," Grimly said. "They're all so high and mighty. They think they know every little grepping thing about all the shit."

"You're just like them," Mable said. "And I don't care that much about the long run. Who's to say we'll even make it back to Sanisco alive?"

"Yeah," Pine said, downing another glass of wine. "I've never seen trife like those before. Big greppers, they were. Grepping evolution. Let's just get her clothes off. I've always wanted to put it to an Engineer."

"Now, now," Grimly said, putting up his free hand. "Let's not be too quick to make a decision. Let's give our guest a chance to convince us to let her go."

Natalia stared at him. She had prepared herself for the likelihood the Oversergeant would rape her. She hadn't been expecting them to decide to kill her and go back to King with the bad news. She closed her eyes, the tears welling up. She wasn't going to get the vengeance she wanted. She wasn't even going to survive the night.

"Aww, it's okay, sweetie," Grimly said. "We'll be gentle."

"No we won't," Mable said.

All three of them laughed.

Natalia couldn't breathe. She wanted to drop dead so she wouldn't have to experience whatever these monsters were planning. Why the hell did Ghost have to go and die?

"Does that mean we've made our decision?" Pine asked, putting the wine bottle down.

"I think it does," Mable said.

"I would have brought you back to King," Grimly said, leaning his face in close to hers. "But I guess I'm overruled."

He reached up, putting a rough hand on the side of her face.

She needed to stay calm. If she could get to the door, if she could hold out long enough for it to open...

Then what?

She would run right into the rest of Grimly's squad. Did she think they would help her? They'd probably prefer to watch.

If they were going to kill her, maybe she could make them kill her quickly.

She swung the arm holding the glass, hitting it against the footboard of the bed. It shattered in her hand, part of it cutting her palm but also leaving her with a sharp object. She lashed out at Grimly, but he caught her wrist easily.

"Oh, look at this," Grimly said, laughing. "She's got some real spirit."

He pulled her arm to his face, taking the glass out of her hand with his teeth, so much stronger than her she couldn't even move it to slice his lip. He spit it onto the floor, and then licked the blood from her wound.

"Mmmm," he said. "Delicious."

He shifted his grip, putting his arms under hers. He lifted her up and back, throwing her onto the bed like she was a doll. The tears sprang from her eyes, but she swore to herself she wouldn't beg, and she wouldn't make a sound.

Grimly climbed onto the bed after her, reaching for the clasps to her armor. He started unzipping it, spreading it aside. Pine got in her face, leaning in next to her and licking her cheek.

The tears rolled from her cheeks as Grimly's massive hands reached for her undershirt. She shifted her eyes to the ceiling, gazing up past them, refusing to watch what they were going to do to her.

The door began to squeal, sliding open on its rusted tracks. All three of the Scrappers froze, turning their heads toward it.

"I thought I said privacy!" Grimly shouted.

Natalia lifted her head, trying to see past him. He was too big to look around.

She had to settle for watching a knife blossom from Mable's throat.

"Shit," Grimly said, rolling off her.

She looked at the doorway. Ghost was standing in it. His suit was torn and bloody, his hair ragged, his face tired.

But he was alive.

"I don't remember giving you permission to touch her, Oversergeant," Ghost said calmly, entering the room.

Undersergeant Pine slid off the bed, standing next to it. Mable finally collapsed, unable to breathe past the blade in her neck.

"You weren't here," Grimly replied. "It was an executive decision."

"She's under my protection," Ghost said.

Pine's hand was working its way toward the revolver still on his hip. Did Ghost see him?

"Yeah, I guess she is. Why couldn't you just die out there like a good little bastard?"

"I was willing to believe you kicked me by accident," Ghost said.

"That's because you're an idiot," Grimly replied.

His hand moved for his hip, toward the gun there. Natalia barely saw Ghost move, but a moment later Grimly had a knife sticking through the palm of his hand. Pine made a similar move and suffered a worse fate. A blade sprouted in his chest, another in his stomach, and a third into his neck, sending blood spraying over Natalia and the bed.

She held back her nausea, watching as the big Over-sergeant charged Ghost, pulling the knife from his hand as he did. It looked like a toothpick in his grip, and he swung it at the other man, who ducked low, turning and kicking out, hitting Grimly in the knee with a heavy clang.

Ghost seemed surprised by the result. Grimly laughed, throwing a hard fist at the Courier that almost took his head off. He sidestepped again, throwing a round of punches into the huge man's ribs. Grimly ignored them, retaliating with another punch of his own.

Ghost ducked and backed away, maneuvering around the man. Natalia overcame her shock, looking to her right where Pine had fallen. His revolver was on the floor next to him.

She scrambled off the bed, landing beside it at the same time Grimly rushed Ghost, managing to catch him with his shoulder. He was so big and strong the glancing blow sent the smaller man into the wall, a tree trunk leg angling for his face. He ducked beneath it in a wide split, producing another knife from his belt. Grimly's leg hit the wall with enough force that it dented inward, dust spreading from the impact.

Ghost's knife went up and into the soldier's thigh, the tip breaking as it struck hard metal.

"Replacements," Grimly said, his next kick catching Ghost in the stomach and lifting him a meter into the air. Ghost landed face down; the breath knocked out of him. "Grepping trife cut off both my legs the last time I made a run to Ports. It's King's twisted sense of humor to fix me up and send me back out this way."

Ghost didn't move. The Sergeant had probably cracked his ribs.

Natalia picked up Pine's revolver. It was slick with his blood, but she managed to grip it in both hands, raising it in front of her face the way Hayden taught her.

Grimly noticed the motion, turning his head to look at her. He smiled.

"I'll be with you in one second, sweetie."

He reached down, grabbing Ghost by the neck and lifting, easily powering him up and off the ground.

"I didn't just lose my legs, asshole," Grimly said. "And they don't make replacement cocks. King cost me my manhood. I'm going to take his favorite Courier in payment."

Ghost's eyes shifted to Natalia. She held the gun steady. She should wait for the man to die and then shoot and be rid of both of them. Then again, how many of Grimly's squad were still outside.

"Grimly," Natalia said, getting his attention.

"What is it, sweetie?" Grimly asked, looking back at her again.

She pulled the trigger. The first round hit him square in the chest. So did the second, the third, and the fourth. Ghost fell from his grip, and he stumbled back. The fifth round hit in him the shoulder. The sixth and final shot took him in the head.

He bounced against the wall and crumpled to the ground.

"My husband was a fucking Sheriff," she said, dropping the weapon on the floor.

She reached down and closed her armor before rising and walking over to Ghost. Her whole body was shaking and weak, her legs like rubber. He looked at her as neared, a smile creasing his face.

"I was supposed to save you," he said.

She fell to her knees beside him, grabbing one of his knives from his belt. She held it up to her face, and then reached out, placing the blade against his neck.

"Wait," Ghost said. "Natalia, wait."

"I should kill you," she said, her shock rapidly shifting to a fresh round of anger.

"You need me," he said.

"For what?" she asked.

"To get us out of here. To keep you alive. Grimly's Scrappers are dead. All of them, between the trife and me. We're between Sanisco and Ports. You can't make it on your own." He coughed, spitting out blood. "Right now, neither can I."

"I'll take my chances with the trife," she said.

"Will you? You'll die for sure. You can't kill King if you're dead."

"You said you would stop me if I tried."

"A deal," he replied. "You spare my life, and I'll give you one chance. I won't help you, but I won't stop you."

"You can't be trusted. None of you can be trusted."

"You have my word. That's all I can offer."

Natalia stared at him. Into his eyes, searching for the truth. If he truly believed King was a god, then there was no way she could kill him anyway. What was the harm in letting her try? He was right, anyway. She couldn't survive out here alone. He had made it through the trife and into the bunker. He had proven he was a survivor.

"I can kill you right now," she said. "If you're a god, how is that possible?"

He tried to laugh but wound up coughing more. "Define god, Natalia."

"Can you walk?" she asked, instead.

"I'll be ready to go by daybreak. I need to bandage my ribs and get some rest. Those trife were mean."

"Are we safe here?"

He nodded. "Yes. I have no desire to harm you. If you want to clean up, there's a shower in the back."

"I saw it."

He nodded. "You're a deadly angel, Natalia Duke."

"Thank you for saving my life," she replied.

"Do we have a deal then?"

She had a feeling she would regret it, but she nodded.

"Yes. We have a deal."

She dropped the knife on the floor in front of him, stood up, and walked away.

25

NATALIA ONLY STAYED IN KING'S SUITE LONG ENOUGH TO shower, remaining under the heated water for a long time while she let her mind work through the experience of almost being attacked, and then killing a man. She didn't regret doing it. Grimly was rotten to the core. But Hayden had spoken to her multiple times about his emotions when he accidentally killed Frank Harris, and using the gun on the Oversergeant had given her new insight into how it made him feel.

She put the light armor back on after she finished the shower, finding a clean, oversized shirt in the room to wear beneath it. It took some time to smooth it out so it wouldn't chafe, but it was preferable to her torn and bloody undershirt. It was bad enough the armor had a blood stain on it from Pine's wound. A stain that would probably never come out.

After that, she gathered the belt from Pine's corpse, and the revolver from Grimly's hip. Ghost had every chance to take the weapon, but he had left it. Intentionally.

She found another three dozen or so bullets to feed the

weapon stuffed into the Scrapper's pockets, along with some scraps of paper with the eagle and star logo stamped on the side. She shoved all of it into storage areas on the armor, and then finally made her way out into the bunker.

The smell was bad, and it was getting worse by the minute. It was immediately obvious why. Dead Scrappers lined the corridor to the barracks, more in the garage, and a few more in the mess. There had to be fifteen in all. Not every Scrapper was dead. She passed five or six soldiers, the ones who had greeted them when they entered, carrying mops and working to collect the dead. They didn't even look up at her when she walked by, no doubt wanting to stay on Ghost's good side.

She could hardly believe one man had done this much damage, and that was after already having seen Ghost fight. It wasn't only the Scrappers inside. He had gotten through the mass of trife to enter the place. Why wouldn't he leave her a gun? It wasn't as though it gave her an edge over him. Besides, they had come to an understanding. For now.

Then she returned to the barracks. Each room had four bunks in it. The first one she opened was unoccupied, so she entered, pulling a storage crate in front of the door before laying down on one of the bunks. The mattresses and blankets were old and worn and had a musty smell she didn't like. It didn't matter. She was tired enough to sleep through anything.

She took the revolver out of its holster and placed it on the mattress beside her. The crate would give her early warning if someone tried to enter. She didn't think anyone would. Not with Ghost around.

It didn't take long for her to fall asleep.

Ghost was sitting on the bunk opposite her when she woke. He looked refreshed, his hair freshly cut, his suit mended. Or maybe he had a spare already stored here? He smiled when he saw her looking.

"Good morning, Natalia," he said. "Did you sleep well?"

"I guess so," she replied. "How long?"

"Six hours. It's daytime, though it's raining today."

She pushed herself up, collecting the revolver and putting it back in its holster. "You didn't trip over the crate," she said.

He smiled. "I don't rush into places without looking. But it was a good idea. Most people do. Are you hungry?"

She realized she was. She nodded.

"Good. I've got food waiting. There's a toilet down the hall if you need. Did you find the mess?"

She nodded again.

"I'll be waiting for you there."

He stood up, trying to hide the pain of the motion from her and almost managing. He took a few steps toward the door before stopping and looking back at her.

"I'm sorry about Grimly."

"It wasn't your fault. King's maybe, but not yours."

He didn't respond, leaving the room.

She got up and followed him out. She was immediately surprised to find the hallway had been cleared of corpses, scrubbed and cleaned. It even had a fresh scent to it that made it not feel like a military bunker at all.

She found the toilet before heading back to the mess. Like the barracks, the entire place had been cleaned, the bodies removed. To where? Did it matter? She entered the mess, immediately noticing the smell of cooking meat. Ghost was sitting at one of the tables. A plate had already been set out for her. She didn't recognize anything on it.

She sat down. "What is this?" she asked, pointing at the plate.

He smiled. "You really don't know, do you? What do you eat, on the Pilgrim?"

"Nutrient bars, mostly. Made from filtered waste, mixed with complex proteins, carbs, and minerals stored in huge vats near Engineering. We can grow meat from stem cells, but it's a delicacy reserved for the upper class."

"I imagine being an Engineer makes you upper class?"

"Yes. Being the wife of a Sheriff does the same."

"All of this must be quite a change for you."

"You have no idea."

"There are some benefits to being part of the world again." He motioned to the plate. "Fresh eggs laid this morning. Bacon. Bread. Eat it slowly. I'm not sure how your system will handle real food."

She picked up her fork and stabbed the eggs, lifting them to her nose. "The smell is interesting." She put them in her mouth. The taste was interesting, too. She was so used to bland, the amount of flavor was nearly overwhelming.

"It's always intrigued me," Ghost said. "The trife kill humans by the thousands, but they don't go after anything else. Chickens, cows, horses, you name it. None of them are targets to the creatures. But, they also don't eat us. They kill for fun, or maybe because it's what they were made to do."

"Made by who?" Natalia asked, after swallowing the eggs. She didn't like them, but she needed to eat. She forced herself to take another forkful.

"The question of the millennium," Ghost said. "Sent from the stars. Apparently designed to wipe out humankind. To feed the goliaths? Or was there another purpose? A war that was started, but could never be finished?"

"What do you mean?"

"What if an alien race sent the trife to destroy us, but then were destroyed themselves before they could come and claim the planet? What if the universe is teeming with alien species all battling one another for survival, a macrocosm of our existence here?"

"You don't think the goliaths are the master aliens?"

"They don't seem intelligent enough, do they? Maybe the master group is somewhere else, sending the goliaths out. I don't know. It's an interesting thought exercise, but we're in no position to discover the truth."

"We could be if King would unite people instead of ruling over them with violence and fear. There's an old saying, you-"

"Catch more flies with honey," Ghost finished. "Yes, I've heard it. We've had four hundred years. We've learned it doesn't work. Not for long. As long as there's one person out there who wants to do violence and can get others to join them, there can never be true peace. You have to become the biggest and baddest."

"Maybe the trife were sent to keep us preoccupied?" Natalia said. "Maybe their whole goal was to set us back and keep us from reaching the stars? Was it a coincidence they arrived around the same time the Generation ships were being made?"

Ghost stared at her, his brow lowering as he considered the statement. "Nobody has ever made that connection before," he said. "Interesting. What do you think of the bacon?"

Natalia picked up a piece and put it in her mouth. She started to chew. The flavor was similar to the steak, but different. It was delicious.

"Now, that is good," she said after swallowing.

"I'll leave you with your meal. If you need anything else, Sergeant Nil is waiting to serve you. I'm going to prep the transport. We still have a long way to travel, and without the convoy, we'll need to move fast."

"We aren't going back to Sanisco?" Natalia asked, surprised.

"No. King gave me a mission. It is my responsibility to

complete it. The complex is important. It may be a key to everything we hope to accomplish. I'll get you there safely. You have my word."

He smiled and tried to look confident, but she could tell he was in pain as he turned and headed for the door.

Had she survived the prior night, only to die today?

26

Hayden and the others spent the next four hours walking. There were nine of them in all, including the six members of Kilambe Huston's failed guerrilla rebellion. He had tried to speak to them, to introduce himself, Chains, and Jake to the group, but they didn't want any part of it. The rebels were blaming him for the failure, despite the fact that the explosives had saved their lives.

In the end, they let Huston's people range ahead, staying just close enough to them that they could still take advantage of the light from the flashlights they carried. Not that much light was necessary in the tunnel. It was straight, perfectly straight, with no turns, no rises, no dips. It seemed to go on forever, as though they were falling horizontally into Hell.

They didn't say anything to one another. The other group was being quiet, just in case, so they had fallen into the pattern as well. It had left Hayden alone with his thoughts, which wasn't a place he wanted to be.

Winding up down here was a setback to reaching Sanisco, but at least now he had time to think about what to do once they arrived. If they arrived. Ghost and Natalia had a three-day head-start on him, meaning she had been in the capital city for more than forty-eight hours already. He had to assume that whatever work King wanted her for, she had already been put on it. He was sure she was doing a great job of it, too. Somehow, he would have to find out what that work was and where it was located. He was thankful to have Chains and Jake along with him for that. They could steer him in the right direction, get him talking to the right people.

Once he found her and got her back, then what?

He wasn't sure. It was hard for him to see the way the people suffered under King, and a large part of him wanted to bring the man down. But how was he supposed to get through all of the Scrappers to reach him? Besides, he would have to do more than that. If he killed King, someone would take his place. Another Scrapper, who was probably more of a monster than their current leader. He would have to start a rebellion of his own, and having seen what happened to Huston's efforts; he didn't have much confidence in that.

What were the other options? Head off to the east, get out of the Scrapper's territory and try to make a new start with Natalia? Return to the Pilgrim and clear it of trife. Get Malcolm to let them back in? Or tell Malcolm the truth and try to lead them to a new home on Earth? A home filled with demonic aliens who wanted nothing more than to kill them, and even larger monsters that wanted to eat them?

Was there a good option? As much as he would love to head off into the sunset with his wife like John Wayne, he couldn't leave the citizens of the Pilgrim behind knowing there were people like King or Wiz trying to get into Metro. People he knew would use and abuse them. He also couldn't just abandon the people of Haven, or the others he was sure occupied the other cities and towns. He had been raised to believe in law and order and justice. The plastic badge on his coat was proof he couldn't stop being a Sheriff just because he left his jurisdiction behind.

He fell deep into the thoughts, the monotony of the tunnel and their travel through it making it easy to become outwardly lethargic. His mind worked in circles, trying to plot and plan and figure out how he was going to succeed.

It hit a rough spot when he remembered the trife disease.

Three months, and then he might not be alive. Worse, Natalia might not be alive. If they both died of the contagion, he could handle that. If only one of them went?

One thing at a time. He had to find Natalia before he could worry about their ultimate fate.

"Sheriff."

The word dragged him out of his head. He noticed a light shining toward him, and one of Huston's people approaching.

"Sheriff," he repeated in a whisper. He reached Hayden, stopping in front of him.

"What is it?" Hayden asked, looking past the man. The other rebels had stopped and backed up.

"We have a problem. We'll need to work together to solve it."

"I tried to tell you that before," Hayden said.

"I know. I'm sorry for being an asshole, but I figured we would come out in the countryside and go our separate ways. It looks like fate has other plans."

"What kind of other plans?" Hayden asked.

"Come take a look." He paused, and then put out his hand. "I'm Hollis, by the way."

Hayden took it. "Nice to meet you."

"You might want to take that back in a minute."

Hollis led them forward, back to the other rebels. There were three other men and two women.

"This is Sia, Lily, Bruce, Aman, and Abjit." He pointed to

each of them in turn. Hayden nodded toward them. "We're going up ahead. Stay here. Stay silent. Stay ready."

The other rebels put their fingers to their foreheads in acknowledgment.

"You two wait here," Hayden said.

Chains opened her mouth to protest but thought better of it. She gave him a silent thumbs up.

He looked at Hollis, who started forward, keeping his flashlight aimed at the ground only a dozen centimeters ahead of his feet. They walked down the tunnel that way, a hundred meters or so.

Hollis came to a stop. As soon as there was complete silence, Hayden could hear it. The friction. The hissing. He could smell it, too.

"A trife nest?" he said.

Hollis nodded before slowly raising the flashlight off the floor, toward the blackness ahead of them. The beam exposed an opening in the tunnel, an expansion of the space into a larger area. It crossed over the trife, a thick pile of them slithering around one another, so far oblivious to the intruders.

"I think it's a station," Hollis whispered. "There are a few to the south, leading out to the fringe of Haven. This is probably the same, but this one has these guys in it."

"We have to get around them," Hayden said. "There's no other way out."

"I know. I wanted your opinion. Should we try to sneak around, or should we blow them away while they're preoccupied?"

Hayden had already counted his remaining shells. He had ten, plus the two already loaded into the shotgun. Chains had six rounds. Jake had a revolver with a full cylinder.

"How many rounds do your people have?" he asked.

"About seventy, all told," he said. "But our rifles are single-shot, and our sidearms are discarded pieces that failed inspection. They could blow up in our hands at any time."

"You're saying it's better if we try to sneak around."

"That depends on what you can bring to the fight."

"Not enough," Hayden decided. "We need to take our chances getting past them."

"Okay."

They retreated to the others.

"What is it?" Chains asked.

"Trife nest," Hayden replied. "Not the biggest I've seen, but big enough. One hundred trife, maybe."

"Too bad we don't have any boomsticks left."

"We'd just as likely collapse the tunnel on ourselves if we did. We've decided we're going to sneak past them."

"Are you kidding?" Jake said.

"They're pretty distracted when they're reproducing," Hayden said. "We should be able to make it by without drawing their attention."

Jake's expression showed he was terrified, but he didn't say anything else.

"How do you want to do this?" Hayden asked.

"We'll mix ranks," Hollis replied. "That way neither of us has any cause to do anything that would screw the others."

"I wouldn't do that, regardless," Hayden said.

"Yeah, right. You must not be from around here. Huston's own son turned us in."

Hayden shrugged. He couldn't change the man's mind in an instant when it had been conditioned his whole life. "We'll do it your way. Jake, take point. Chains, between Aman and Sia. Make sure you keep your decorations quiet. I'll take the rear."

"Sounds like a plan," Hollis said.

The entire group organized into a single line, with Hollis at the head. They moved together, one slow step at a time, barely lifting their feet to keep from making any noise, approaching cautiously.

It took almost an hour to reach the station. The bulk of the trife nest was on the left side, on a platform next to the tunnel. There were stairs behind them, but they were covered over by the remains of a collapsed building. An old vehicle rested awkwardly tilted in the station, a corroding, bullet-like shaped craft with a rusted 'T' icon still visible on its front.

Hayden tapped Bruce on the shoulder. "Tell Hollis to try to get us around that wreck," he whispered as softly as he could. Bruce tapped his forehead, and then tapped Abjit, sending the message forward.

It reached Hollis, and he turned back and tapped his forehead, changing direction slightly to get behind the old vehicle.

They kept going, inching out beyond the tunnel and into the station. Aman kept his flashlight aimed near the nest, just enough so they could see the motion of the trife within it.

Another hour passed in tense silence, the group working their way deliberately across the station. Hollis reached the old craft, passing behind it and out of sight of the trife. Soon enough, all of them were in its relative safety.

Hollis turned his flashlight, pointing it into the next segment of the tunnel.

Hayden's heart started to thump harder in his chest. The others in the group looked at one another, and then between Hollis and him, the sudden fear obvious.

The corridor ahead of them was littered with trife, apparently asleep on the ground.

27

He didn't even know the damn things slept. Why weren't they part of the nest?

Hollis backed up toward him, the group pulling tightly together.

"What the hell?" Sia said.

"Seconded," Chains said. "I've never seen them sleep before."

"Maybe they're dead?" Aman said.

"How many nests have any of you seen?" Hayden asked.

"One," Hollis replied. "Besides this one."

The rest of them shook their heads. They had never seen a trife nest before.

"I don't think we know enough about them to know if they do or don't sleep," Jake said. "Most of us have never been this close to a nest before."

They all turned to look when they heard a slight shifting in the group. Hollis put his finger to his lips, and they all remained still and silent for a minute.

"We have to go past them," Hayden said. "There's no other option. Go slow. Stay quiet. Hope they don't wake up."

None of the group looked happy, but they all nodded their agreement. Hollis returned to the front of the line, beginning the long walk through the organic minefield.

He stopped as he neared the first trife, pointing his rifle down toward it as he approached. He made it to the creature, putting his foot right next to it. The demon didn't move. He stepped carefully over its legs, and then continued, looking back at them with a relieved expression.

Until the legs suddenly moved, snapping out, sharp claws catching his ankles and ripping through them, pulling him to the ground.

Hollis cried out in pain as the trife pounced on him, silencing him with a quick slash from its razor hands.

It was already too late. The sound of the scream echoed in the tunnel, the other trife rising from their slumber. Behind them, Hayden heard the rising pitch of the hissing, the trife in the nest realizing they weren't alone.

"Grep me," Chains said, bringing up her shotgun.

"Run," Hayden barked.

They did, all eight of them, charging headlong into the trife. The creatures rose to meet them, claws ready, mouths open wide. They hissed joyfully at the challenge.

The rebels fired their single shots, two of the trife falling to the rounds. Then they switched to their poorly made revolvers, unloading slugs one after another, filling the lead trife with holes.

The nest was stirring behind them, the activity increasing as the creatures pulled themselves away.

Hayden aimed his shotgun and fired, the blast nearly ripping one trife in half. He whirled on a second, using his other shell to drop it, too. He scanned the area while he reloaded, watching as Chains shot two more of the demons.

Another scream pierced the tunnel. Hayden saw Bruce on the ground, his left arm missing, a trife at his throat. Jake fired into the creature, killing it before it could kill the rebel. He should have let it finish the job.

A trife jumped from the top of the tunnel, heading toward Hayden upside down. He gripped the shotgun in his right hand, swinging his left, squeezing his fist to extend the metal claws of his replacement as he did. The trife looked surprised by the attack, and it rolled in the air in an effort to escape the sudden blades, failing miserably. The claws impaled the creature's head, and Hayden turned with it, redirecting its momentum and throwing into another demon at his side.

"No. Nooo!"

Hayden had just enough time to see Lily die, a trife's claws piercing her chest. He swung the shotgun and fired, hitting two more of them before looking back at the nest.

They were out of time.

"Go!" he shouted, sprinting forward. "Keep moving!"

They had nearly cleared the path ahead, but the trife behind were on their way, dragging themselves out of the serumen and scurrying along the floor. Hayden caught up to Chains, urging her forward.

A trife dove toward her, claws flashing. She grunted, putting her arm up in defense, the sharp fingertips getting stuck in her chains. The trife dragged her back and onto the ground, preparing to pounce.

Hayden kicked out at it, the force knocking it aside. It hissed and jumped at him, meeting his claws with its forehead and dying.

They kept running, breaking away from the trife, putting a little bit of distance between them. Distance that wouldn't last long. The trife were too fast.

Hayden reloaded the shotgun while he moved, realizing he was nearly out of shells. Chains had already dropped her weapon, and Abjit and Sia had also left their guns behind.

The seconds passed like hours, each step feeling like it was coming in slow motion. Hayden looked back over his shoulder, searching for the creatures. Hollis' flashlight was resting on the ground beside his eviscerated body, shining just enough light to see them gaining, a mass of chaotic limbs flailing their way.

He twisted to fire the shotgun, the shot catching the lead row of trife and causing them to stumble and hiss. The others climbed over them, barely slowing.

"I see light up ahead!" Sia shouted from the front of the line.

Hayden looked forward, barely able to make out the pinpoint of daylight in front of them. The demons were nearly nipping at his heels, only seconds from cutting him down.

He wasn't going to make it.

He took two more steps and then turned to face them, firing the remaining round in the shotgun point blank into the face of one of the creatures. Its head exploded, splattering viscera across his body. He ignored it, claws angling toward the first trife to reach him, slicing through its face as he ducked below its grab.

Another trife moved in. Hayden took a step back, swinging his mechanical hand as hard as he could and slamming it into the creature, bouncing it into another. He backpedaled, getting closer to the apparent escape while still facing off with the trife.

One of them jumped up, turning over and hitting the ceiling, using it to spring off and dive toward him, at the same time another came in from his left in a synchronized attack. He dove to the side, barely avoiding the claws of the first creature as he hit the ground, scrambling to get back to his feet as quickly as possible.

The second trife jumped on him, claws digging into his leg. He cried out in pain, throwing a metal fist into the side of the demon's head and knocking it away. He pushed himself up, on his knees when another trife slashed out at his neck. He barely got his metal hand up in time to block it, falling onto his back as he did.

The trife were hissing at one another, communicating their excitement and urging the first trife on. It approached Hayden slowly at first, and then darting forward with its face, teeth leading in for the kill.

A large chain hit it dead on, shattering its teeth and snapping its head to the side. Chains cried out in time to the blow, covering Hayden. "Get up, Sheriff."

He didn't need another invitation. He dragged himself to his feet, facing the trife. They had fallen back a few steps, lining up in the tunnel while they tried to judge the best method of attack.

A sharp series of cracks sounded behind them, and then a line of chipped cement kicked out from the tunnel between Hayden and the trife. The creatures dropped back a few more steps; their attention turned to the source of the assault. Hayden turned his head around again, too, finding the muzzle of a rifle jutting out from an open hatch in the ceiling. It flashed as the shooter opened up again, dropping four of the trife in a strong barrage.

A dark hand reached down from the hatch, at the same time Sia reached up. It took hold of her, pulling her up and through the hole. It returned a few seconds later, taking Abjit out of the tunnel.

"It's like the grepping hand of fate," Chains said.

"Let's hope it's the hand of an ally," Hayden replied.

The continued backing to the hatch as the dark hand reached down and took them out, one at a time until only he was left.

He stared at the trife. They stared back at him. As the

hand came down one final time and he reached up to take it, the creature in the front bowed its head.

Respect?

Hayden began to rise up and through the hatch.

The trife hissed once at him and then began to walk away.

The hand kept lifting him, its other one grabbing him beneath the shoulders as he cleared the twenty centimeters of cement between the tunnel and the space above it. He was facing outward, away from his savior, looking directly into a graffiti-covered wall.

He swung his legs to the side, finding purchase on the ground. As soon as he was clear, a metal lid was dropped over the hole, the access point sealed and locked. The hands pulled away from his body.

He turned around.

He recognized the robot in front of him immediately. It was the same one, or the same version of the one that they had encountered in Huston's hideout. It was rusted and dented and looked like it had seen better days, but then what didn't?

Beside it, a man in dark fatigues extruding from a rough-spun robe, the eagle and star logo printed on his cheek. He eyed Hayden like a predator, his face tight.

There were four more Scrappers behind him, holding Jake and Chains at gunpoint. Abjit and Sia were laying on the floor in separate pools of blood, their throats cut.

"I'm Commander Nathan Ales," the leader said, his eyes dropping to the plastic star on Hayden's coat, and then to his mechanical hand. The blades were still extended beyond the cuff. "A stranger missing a hand escaped from one of our excavation sites a few days ago. Your features match the description I received from one of Oversergeant Pig's subordinates." The Commander smiled. "He isn't referring to you by any chance, is he?"

28

"HOW DID YOU FIND US?" CHAINS ASKED. SHE WAS POSITIONED behind Commander Ales, held roughly by one of the Scrappers.

"Broken Sword is going to be known as Crumbled Sword from now on," Ales said. "Whatever Huston detonated in there, it took out the entire building."

"That's not an answer," Chains said.

The Commander nodded slightly, and one of the other Scrappers slammed the butt of his rifle into Chains' stomach. She grunted, wincing in pain.

"I don't owe you an explanation," Ales said. He looked back at Hayden. "You should be glad we found you. You should be thankful I'm in command of King's resources in Haven. Most of the Oversergeants here wouldn't have the moxie to have come looking for you. First I heard that you escaped and that you killed Oversergeant Pig, an enviable accomplishment. Then I heard there was some trouble at Crossroads last night. Then Broken Sword collapsed." He looked back at Chains. "I'm not an idiot."

"No comment," Chains said, earning another shot to the gut. She refused to make a sound the second time.

"I knew the old tunnels were down here. The south side has been blocked off for a long time, so if you made it out of the building, you would have had to go north, through the trife. I've been hesitant to clean their nest because it keeps people out of the tunnels. Once the shooting started, you were easy to locate." His smile somehow managed to get a little wider, a little more malevolent. "The trife would have killed you, pilgrim," he said, his use of the ship's name surely intentional. "I saved your life. All of your lives."

"Not theirs," Hayden said, motioning to Abjit and Sia. The Commander thought the south side was blocked? Well, it was now.

"They were plotting a rebellion against King."

"I was with them."

"A fact I'm willing to overlook. As I said, I'm not an idiot. I can smell the value you would be to King. You escaped from the site. You came from Inside. I still can't completely believe the colony is intact. King knows what treasure is there. He has records of the asset deployments. The damage to the upper structure is going to make retrieving it a bit more difficult, but then you can't control the goliath, can you?"

He paused as if he was waiting for Hayden to answer the question. When Hayden remained silent, he continued.

"We recovered one of the trucks at the site and the equipment that was abandoned during the rush to escape the planet. It will be sent to Sanisco, to the Fortress, as a gift to King. So will the three of you."

Hayden still didn't speak. He glanced over at Jake and Chains. Ales was sparing their lives when he didn't have to. Why? Maybe Jake would be valuable as a Borger. What about the Driver?

"Take them out to the transport," Ales said to one of his underlings. "We'll wait here for the rest of the convoy to arrive."

"Yes, sir," the Scrapper said. "You heard the Commander. Move your asses."

The Scrappers were anything but gentle, holding Jake and Chains by the arms and pulling them from the room, out into a graffiti-covered hallway. The exodus left him alone with Ales and the robot.

"My wife," Hayden said. "Ghost has her. Do you know what happened to them?"

Ales was amused. "The Engineer is your wife? Is that why you're out here? I have a wife, too. She'd love it if I did something like that for her." He motioned to the robot. "Take him." Then he looked back at Hayden. "I wouldn't."

The robot reached out and took Hayden by his mechanical arm, holding it tight and lifting him to his feet.

"You didn't answer my question," Hayden said.

Ales shook his head, and then punched Hayden in the gut. Hayden winced, the bruises there throbbing from the blow, but he didn't cry out. He kept his head up, eyes on the Commander.

"You think you're strong, do you?" Ales said. "We'll see. King sent the Engineer north to Ports with Ghost. If the Scrappers don't kill her, the trife will. Get him out of here."

The robot dragged Hayden forward, past the still amused Ales. Hayden turned his head, looking back at the Commander. He could see in the man's eyes that he wasn't joking about Ports. He really did expect Natalia to die there.

He was led down a long, worn corridor, around the corner and out the door of an old utility substation of some kind. There were four Scrapper vehicles already waiting outside. Three were large, big-wheeled cars that had been pieced together from other salvage, open-framed vehicles with large engines and placements for soldiers to ride and defend the convoy. The fourth vehicle was ten meters long, a rectangular shape, with barred windows lining each side, and extra metal plates added along the flanks and down over the wheels. A pair of metal turrets had been added to the rooftop, and a pair of Scrappers were already positioned there, rifles in hand.

The robot led him to the transport, its heavy feet thudding with every step, its worn servos and hydraulics hissing and grinding. It didn't speak. Hayden didn't know if it could speak. He had never seen anything like it before. An ancient creation, yet completely new to him. It was frightening and amazing at the same time, and he could imagine how much Natalia would love to get a look at its inner workings.

It released him from its grip at the edge of a doorway leading into the vehicle. He considered trying to run, but only for a second. The Oversergeant inside stuck a revolver in his face.

"Come on in, Insider," he said. "We've got a great party going in here."

Hayden entered climbing a few steps into the transport. He found Chains and Jake already tethered to the vehicle, heavy chains binding their hands and locking them in. The four Scrappers were standing around them, sticking their clothed groins into their faces, laughing and leering and doing their best to make them uncomfortable.

"Have a seat," the Scrapper said, waving him to a seat across from Chains.

He went to it and sat. As soon as he did, they produced another heavy chain and wrapped it around his wrists before locking it to a pole in the center of the transport.

"Wait here," the Oversergeant said.

All of the Scrappers filed out of the vehicle.

"Well, this sucks," Chains said, looking at him.

"It's your fault we're here," Jake said to her. "If you hadn't insisted on making the delivery-"

"Nobody told you to come," Chains replied, interrupting his accusation. "You could have waited for me and avoided the whole situation."

"It's my fault," Hayden said, speaking over them both. "I shouldn't have let either one of you get involved."

"Bullshit," Chains said. "I wanted to be here. I'm so sick of the grepping Scrappers and the way they get to do whatever the hell they want. They grepping eat people!" Her face paled as she wrinkled it in disgust. "I know why they didn't kill me. I'm a hell of a lot prettier than Sia was."

"So much for modesty," Jake said.

"Screw you, Borger. I've been through this shit before. It's the reason I left Carcity."

She looked back at Hayden. It was the first time he had seen her afraid.

"We'll find a way out of this," Hayden said.

"Are you kidding, Sheriff?" Jake replied, holding up his bound hands. "How are we going to get out of this?"

Hayden looked at his own hands. He pulled against the chains, yanking them tight against his wrists. He kept straining with the replacement, testing to see if the added strength of the metal limb could weaken the links.

It couldn't.

He gave up, leaning back against the seat, quickly losing hope.

"Damn," Chains said. "If you could get a piece of metal out of that thing, I could probably pick the lock."

Hayden raised an eyebrow and looked over at Jake.

"There are a few pieces you might be able to dislodge," he said. "But you'll have to do it with one hand, and without the Scrappers noticing. And then you'll have to pass it to Chains without them noticing. And then she'll have to pick the lock without them noticing."

Hayden considered for a moment.

"Have either of you heard of Ports?" he asked.

They were both silent. Staring at him.

"What about it?" Jake said after a few tense seconds.

"Ales told me King sent Natalia there with Ghost."

"Geez," Chains said. "He's out of his damn mind."

"Why?"

"Ports is in the middle of trife central. At least, trife central in this neck of the woods. The goliaths don't walk up there, so the buggers multiply out of control."

"I heard he had managed to get a line going through to the old city," Jake said. "But it costs a lot of soldiers to keep it going. If he sent your wife that way, there has to be something valuable up there. Something he needs an Engineer to retrieve or fix."

"Not just any Engineer," Chains said. "If he's willing to risk your wife on it with what she knows, he has to be pretty sure it's going to pay off in a big way."

"If she makes it," Jake said.

"King sent Ghost with her."

"That might help. I don't know. I'm sorry to say this, Sheriff, but I want to be completely honest with you. It's more likely Ghost will wind up dead, too."

Hayden eyed them both. He wouldn't give up hope. He shook his mechanical hand in the chains.

"Tell me how to break this thing."

29

IT DIDN'T SURPRISE NATALIA ALL THAT MUCH WHEN THE transport broke down. They had been on the trail north to Ports for most of the day, and some piece of the machinery had started clanging and thumping from the bottom of the vehicle, signaling that it needed some sort of repair.

Ghost kept it going for an hour after the first sign of trouble, pushing them through an area of thick growth, certain that it would be a bad place to be ambushed by the trife. Not that there had been any sign of them all day. They liked to reproduce during daylight hours, and only the sentries and scouts were out in force when the others were copulating and feeding.

Natalia quizzed him further on the subject, and he explained that the trife were fueled by energy, like the radiation of the sun, not matter. In many places, they would gather in the thousands in a sunny place for an hour each day, and afterward retreat to often subterranean nests to reproduce. Where there wasn't enough sun, they could often be found near old reactors that were still giving off heat and radiation, or massed around the few that continued to function, year after year, despite the fact that there was no one to tend to them.

They finally did stop when they reached a more open section of the trail, a clearing in the growth where a makeshift bridge had been constructed to allow the transport to clear a stream. Natalia spent minutes peering out of the slit in the side of the machine, watching the water flow freely along its course. She had never seen so much water.

That was the hardest thing. Experiencing this world, their homeworld, which they thought they had left behind. So much of it was so beautiful, even after the trife and the goliaths. And at the same time, so much of it was so ugly. She missed Hayden. If she had to be alive in this world, she wanted to share it with him. She wanted him to be alive, too.

"Do you think you can fix it?" Ghost asked, leaving the driver's seat and coming to the back of the transport.

"I don't know. It's probably not all that different from the Medical transports in Metro. Wheels and a motor, right? Are there tools on board?"

"There have to be, somewhere." There were compartments under the seats. He started opening them, looking for the tools.

Things had changed between them after they had left the bunker. Natalia wasn't sure why. Maybe because Ghost knew she needed him, and so he felt more comfortable around her. Maybe because his infatuation was growing stronger. He was more relaxed. More talkative. Less restricted. He was treating her like a partner instead of a captive, a friend instead of a prisoner.

The level of humanity within him had surprised her. He had admitted he didn't believe in everything King was doing, though he would in never question or disobey his father. He told her stories of kindness, and ways he had helped the people of Sanisco and Haven, and in some instances had spared them the violent abuse of the Scrappers. He had never eaten human meat, and he claimed it was a practice he abhorred. The whole thing had started for King's soldiers to prove they weren't afraid of anything, and to show dominion over their enemies. That there were no taboos that could stop them from claiming what they wanted. No rules to bind them to anything beyond their conscience, which many didn't seem to have. It had become a rite of passage for the soldiers, and any recruit who refused to taste was beaten or killed. Of course, some of them found they enjoyed it and added it as a regular part of their diet.

Whatever the reason for Ghost's change, Natalia could feel the shift.

Now she had to decide out how best to use it to her advantage.

In the back of her mind, she already knew. If she could get Ghost to turn against King, she would have a much easier time getting close to him. If she could get close to him, she would have a much easier time killing him. While the Courier had already said he wouldn't help her, maybe she could change his mind if she could finish changing his heart? The idea of it was sickening to her, and she had spent half the ride in turmoil with the decision. Even now, it was twisting her stomach in knots.

"I think this is it," Ghost said, pulling out a solid box and unlatching the front. He flipped the top open, revealing multiple levels of tools. "It is." He looked at her and smiled. The smile started to fade when she saw her nervous expression. "What's wrong?"

Natalia shook her head. "I think I'm just motion sick," she replied. "We've been cooped up in here all day."

"I was starting to feel the same way. Some fresh air will help."

"Is it safe?"

He glanced at the front of the transport. "The sensors are clear. I'll keep a lookout while you work."

He moved to the back of the transport, where he had stowed the gear he had taken from the bunker. Two rifles were resting among the smaller arms. They were bigger and meaner than the others she had seen so far. They almost looked too big to carry. He picked one of them up, checking the magazine and switching it on. He looked at something on the display and then put it back down. He picked up another sidearm, a small, rectangular weapon with a magazine, checked it the same way, and then handed it out to her.

"Just in case," he said. "You already know how to shoot. This one has twenty rounds."

She took the weapon. He didn't wait for her to attach it to her armor before turning away. She could have shot him in the back. He trusted her not to. They were dependent on one another out here.

He picked up the rifle again.

"I thought you don't like guns?" she said.

"I don't. But I like dying less." He turned the weapon so she could see the display. "The N80 has a one hundred times zoom scope built-in, with an automatic barrel adjustment to account for wind. I can hit a target from over a mile with it, two if the conditions are right. That's why we stopped in the open. The woods help them more than it helps us."

"And there are no goliaths here?"

"No. It's early fall, so it isn't too cold yet, but they still don't come."

"Are you sure it's temperature that keeps them away?"

"Not at all. We'll go out the top. The side hatch closes too slowly and is too hard to defend. If I spot any trife, I want you to head inside straight away. They can't penetrate the armor."

Natalia raised her eyebrow and then pointed to the

cracked glass up front. "I don't think that's an accurate assessment."

Ghost smiled nervously. "I've never seen them do that before. They're still evolving. Let's go."

She followed him as he opened the top hatch and climbed out. She could see his face twist as he did, still in pain from the damage Grimly inflicted on him. He hadn't complained about it at all. He was like Hayden in that way.

The air outside was crisp, but not cold. The sky was darkened by clouds, a light mist coating the area. Natalia gave herself a moment to savor the real atmosphere while Ghost moved to the front of the transport's roof, bringing the rifle to his face, the display at eye level. He turned a full revolution, sweeping the landscape.

"You're clear," he said.

She responded by climbing off the low-slung transport. The noise had been coming from the forward left wheel. She set herself beside it, opening the toolbox and digging through it until she found a flashlight. She turned it on and moved to her back, sliding under the vehicle. She was relatively slim, and she still hardly fit.

She adjusted the flashlight to the well. It was filthy with blood and gore, and she turned her head away and clenched her mouth closed as a small bit of vomit worked its way up her throat. She swallowed it, looking back. She stopped the flashlight on the axle, noting the way the rod was bent. Unsure if that was the right position on this specific vehicle, she slid out and circled to the other side, repeating the scan. The axle on the driver's side was bent, but not like that.

She came back out, returning to the toolbox and closing it. She looked up at Ghost. He was still scanning the area, paying her no mind.

"The axle is damaged," she said.

He looked down at her. "That sounds bad."

"It is. I can't fix it out here. If we had a lift, a blowtorch, some other materials, I could probably do something. How far are we from Ports?"

"Too far," he replied. "Thirty miles at least, and it's going to be dark soon. Let's get back inside, and we can decide what to do."

Natalia passed the toolbox up to him, and then let him help her onto the roof of the transport. He tugged her up in front of him, their faces drawing near as he did. Her instinct was to pull away, but she didn't. She forced herself to linger there and look into his eyes.

"Thank you," she said softly.

He remained in position, his expression soft. "You're welcome."

It was enough to steel her resolve. As much as she hated the idea, she could do this.

She leaned forward, brushing her lips lightly against his. He responded gently. Softly. Easing ahead to meet her, but not pushing back with lust.

Then she moved past him, back to the hatch into the transport, her heart pounding, her stomach nauseous, her decision made.

30

The convoy moved out two hours later. Six more vehicles had joined it while Hayden, Jake, and Chains were waiting, sitting alone in the back of the transport while the Scrappers organized the group. Jake had given Hayden clear instructions on how to dislodge two of the small, narrow pins that helped stabilize the synthetic musculature inside the hand, and he had spent that time doing his best to get it out and over to Chains before they got underway.

The work was delicate, and his hand was sore and swollen. He had only gotten one of the pins out and over to Chains when the Oversergeant had climbed back on board along with two guards and a driver.

He had quickly tucked the mechanical arm under his other hand, covering the open compartment to the inner workings of the prosthetic. He kept his head down, staring at the floor as the Oversergeant approached.

"Are we all tucked in back here?" the man said, grabbing Jake's chains and pulling on them. The motion jerked him forward, proving he was still locked in.

He took Chains' chain next, tugging it to ensure it was all

connected. Then he stood in front of Hayden. The Scrapper reached down, putting his hand under Hayden's chin and lifting his head until they were looking each other in the eye.

"I hated Pig, but he was still one of ours." He leaned back, and then punched Hayden in the side of the head. The blow knocked him sideways, but he managed to hold his hand over the compartment. "That's for him."

Then the Oversergeant pulled on his binds, checking them. Again, Hayden managed to keep the replacement covered.

"Take a look out the window there, Insider," the man said, pointing at one of the trucks that had joined them.

Hayden recognized it from the upper level of the Pilgrim's hangar. It had a long bed in the rear, covered by old canvas long spared from the elements.

"Grepping trife had a huge nest down there, hiding a damn treasure. We cleaned up that mess and loaded her up."

"You took the weapons from the Marine module?" Hayden asked.

"Damn right," the Oversergeant replied, wiping his nose on the back of his hand, and then wiping his hand on Hayden's leg. "This ain't all of them, but it's a good haul. The first of many. Personally, I can't wait to get into the colony. The women in there must be mmmmm, delicious!"

Hayden clenched his teeth. He knew the man was trying to get under his skin. He couldn't let him.

"I'm glad you have them," he said.

"You are?"

Hayden nodded. "I'm going to kill you with them."

The Oversergeant roared with laughter, at the same time he punched Hayden in the head again.

"You keep telling yourself that, Insider. Maybe if you wish hard enough it'll even come true."

He kept laughing on his way to the front of the transport.

The other two Scrappers remained in the back, keeping an eye on them.

Hayden left his gaze on the truck, watching as the large robot climbed into the back, vanishing into the shadows. He shifted his eyes to the guards. They were paying close attention to the three of them right now, but would it last once they started moving? He glanced at Jake and Chains. Jake looked terrified, Chains more confident in their ability to escape.

She was more confident than he was.

Three engines roared to life as Commander Ales appeared from the substation, flanked by a smaller man with a large backpack connected to a transceiver of some kind. They said something to one another as they made their way to one of the later arriving vehicles. That one had the USMC logo on its side, along with a series of letters and numbers. It was heavily armored, ran on treads, and had a massive gun turret resting on top of it. Both men climbed to the top of it, and then pulled open a manual hatch leading inside. Hayden watched them disappear into the machine.

"What is that?" he asked, looking back at Chains.

"Did anyone tell you that you could talk?" one of the guards asked, circling to him. "One more word, and this goes in your face. Do you copy?" He raised the butt of his rifle threateningly.

"Pozz," Hayden said.

"Huh?"

"He said 'pozz,' dimwit," Chains said. "As in, yes."

"Shut your mouth, bitch," the guard said, turning and getting in her face. "I'll show you how dim I am when we get to Sanisco."

"What does that even mean?" Chains said, laughing.

It earned her a shot to the gut. She took it and kept laughing.

"SHUT THE GREP UP, I SAID!" the guard shouted.

"Helks, shut the hell up and move away from the prisoners," the Oversergeant shouted from the front of the transport. "If they want to talk, let them talk. It ain't going to do them any good."

"Yes, sir!" Helks said. He glanced at Chains, lowering his voice. "You're lucky he likes you right now. You won't be so lucky he likes you when he brings you to his bed later. If he even bothers to take you anywhere first."

Chains made a face as Helks went back to his place behind them. Then she leaned toward Hayden as much as she could. "It's called a tank. It's pretty much immune to the trife as long as the occupants stay inside. But nobody can stay inside forever."

"Are they expecting a problem?"

"On the way to Sanisco? Probably not, but you never know. They ambush the convoys every once in awhile. My theory is that Commander Ales is a pansy."

The guard behind them that wasn't Helks laughed softly at the comment.

The transport jerked a couple of times, making an awful noise before starting to move. The engine was mounted in the rear, and it roared loudly as it worked to bring them up to speed. The other vehicles began to get underway, too, maneuvering around one another to get into position, with the tank in front, the transport in the center, and the old USSF truck in the back. The other Scrapper cars rode on either side of the trio, protecting it from potential attack.

"How long is the trip to Sanisco?" Hayden asked. What he wanted to know was how much time he had to get the other pin out of the arm and into Chains' hands.

"About nine hours," Chains replied. "We should get there shortly after nightfall."

"After nightfall?" Hayden said, surprised.

"Yes. I wouldn't worry though; we'll be close enough to the city it shouldn't be a problem."

Hayden started shifting his fingers, moving his hand slowly to reach into the compartment and feel for the second pin.

"I don't know," he said. "I'm hoping it will."

31

As Hayden suspected, the two guards standing behind them got more lazy with each passing mile, becoming distracted with the landscape as they made the trip from Haven to Sanisco. He barely noticed the outside of the transport himself, glancing down every few seconds to get an eye on the work he was doing in trying to get the pin loose.

When he did look beyond the barred windows, he saw a landscape hued in brown and orange, cracked and swollen and dirty. The road between the former cities had once been littered with cars, the oxidation of rust followed by rains staining the area around it. The cars had all been moved over the many ensuing years, pushed to the side of the road or reclaimed as salvage, but the impact on the earth had remained.

They stopped once about two hours into the trip, the convoy pulling off the side of the road and into nearby vegetation, taking cover and falling silent. The Scrappers had spent the time ignoring him completely, staring out the window and waiting while a goliath crossed over their path. Hayden was tempted to look for the thing with each rattling step it took, but he had to take advantage of the distraction to keep working.

By the time the group felt safe enough to get back on the road, he had nearly gotten the pin free.

They had been on the road for four hours when Hayden finally felt the small snap of the strip of metal dislodge from the arm. He coughed lightly to cover up the noise, quickly shifting the piece into his hand and tucking it up into his cuff with his thumb. He glanced up at the guards. Helks was biting his fingernails, his rifle resting against the back of the seat. The other one, O'Dell, was looking right at him.

"You need something?" O'Dell asked. He was the more reserved of the two, and he seemed more kind. As kind as any Scrapper could be, at least.

"No," Hayden said. "Thank you."

He looked away, to Chains. She had her head back, her eyes closed. He was managing to keep his anxiety under control and stay focused on the situation, but how could she sleep through this? He shifted his attention to Jake. He was clenching his hands together, probably doing his best not to look nervous. It wasn't working.

He put his head back on the seat. He wouldn't be able to pass the scrap to Chains until O'Dell decided to stop doing his job. It would happen sooner or later, he was sure. It was the interruption by the goliath that had renewed his attention to them.

Another dozen minutes had passed when O'Dell finally looked away, his head turning and his body dipping so he could see out the window opposite them. He reached out and rubbed the smudged glass, clearing it off and squinting his eyes. Then he turned back toward Helks.

"Hey, Helks. Helks."

The other guard broke out of whatever thought process he was lost in. "What the hell do you want?"

"Take a look outside. Over there." He pointed through the glass.

Helks leaned over, joining O'Dell at the window. He stayed there for a few seconds before standing up again.

"Sarge, we have a problem!" he shouted.

"What is it, Helks?" the Oversergeant said. He had been resting at the front of the transport, eyes closed and feet up. He stood now, angry to be disturbed.

"Looks like someone's coming," Helks said.

The statement caused Chains to open her eyes, and Hayden to sit up straight. He looked at her, asking her who it could be with his body language. She shook her head. She didn't know. He looked at Jake, who was equally confused.

The Oversergeant banged on the top of the transport. "Hey, you assholes see that? Or are you bastards sleeping up there?"

The roof thudded as feet pounded, turning inside the turrets.

"Shit, Sarge," someone shouted back from outside. "Motorcycles."

"Who the grep could that be?" the Oversergeant said. He leaned over the driver. "Tell the Commander."

The driver picked up his transceiver to radio the tank.

"They look friendly?" the Oversergeant shouted up to the lookouts.

"Can't say for sure. They're ar-"

Hayden could see the flash of light in the distance, even through the grimy glass. A half-second later, the world started spinning.

The impact felt like it picked the heavy transport up and turned it ninety degrees before throwing the vehicle roughly onto its side. One moment, Hayden was looking out the window, the next he was being jerked hard against his restraints, the rest of his body hanging in the air. He grunted at the sudden pain in his human hand, turning his wrist in a desperate attempt to keep the pin from sliding out of his cuff. Chains and Jake were equally dislodged, rolling on their binds, bodies flopping back to the seat, then to the side, the roof, and the seat again as they flipped.

The Scrappers weren't so fortunate. Nothing was tethering them to the vehicle, and they were thrown independently from it, inertia and force slamming them into the hard surfaces. Hayden heard the wet crack of O'Dell's neck as his body was tossed into the roof at an awkward angle, his face planting into the metal. Helks' body was equally battered, arm shattering as it hit the metal bars on the windows, nose breaking when his face crashed into the back of the seat.

It seemed like it took minutes for the transport to come to a rest, settling on its side. Hayden turned his body in his chains, getting his feet under him though he wasn't able to fully stand up. Chains was beside him, still gathering herself, while Jake was up and alert, the body armor protecting him from the worst of the blows.

"What the hell was that?" the Borger said.

"I don't know, but we need to get out of these chains," Hayden replied. He picked the pin out of his shirt, holding it out to Chains. "I hope you can do this fast."

She took the pin from him, producing the other one from her mouth. "Damn thing cut my mouth up pretty bad," she said, spitting out some blood. "Give me a few minutes."

The sudden sound of gunfire interrupted the silence of the crash's aftermath. Shouting joined it a moment later, along with the increased pitch and variance of engines.

"Whoever's on those bikes, they don't like the Scrappers," Jake said.

"That doesn't mean they'll like us," Chains replied. "Anyone with the balls to ambush a convoy like this probably doesn't give a shit about prisoners."

"Unless they know who the prisoner is," Jake suggested. "Or what was in the convoy."

"How would they know that?" Chains said.

"I don't know, but that doesn't mean they don't."

"We can't risk it either way," Hayden said. "Get us out of these."

"I'm on it. Give me your wrists."

Hayden put his hands out, spreading the chain so the lock holding it together was easy to reach. Chains took one strip of metal in each hand, sliding it into the hole.

"How'd you learn to pick locks?" Jake asked.

A motorcycle passed close by, the thump of its motor drowning out her answer. Someone shouted, and the gunfire increased, some of the rounds finding the more vulnerable roof of the transport. The slugs pierced the metal, digging into the floor nearby.

"Shit," Jake said.

"What the grep are you worried about?" Chains said. "You have the grepping armor."

She kept her hands working, manipulating the pins inside the lock. The shouting, engines, and gunfire continued to swirl around them, a chaotic maelstrom of violence that threatened to swallow them at any second.

"I thought you knew what you were doing?" Jake said, his nerves frayed.

"Does this look easy to you?" she snapped back. "Shit. Just give me one. More. Second." She turned one of the pins, and the lock clicked open, the chains falling out of it and setting Hayden free. "Hell yeah!"

Hayden shrugged out of the bonds, trying out the mechanical hand. It was still functional, but he could tell he didn't have the same fine motor control over it. He looked over the downed transport, finding Helks' revolver on the floor. He picked it up and turned back to the others.

"Put the chains against the pole and put your heads down," he said.

"How's your aim, Sheriff?" Jake asked.

"Good enough. Do it."

Chains and Jake did as he said. He took a moment to steady his hand and then fired, the first round snapping Chains' restraints. She smiled as she rubbed her wrists.

Then something else exploded.

The force of the blast shook the transport, sliding it back a meter on its side and knocking them off-balance. They all tumbled to the ground, scurrying to get back up as a wave of heat washed over them.

"They're going to bring a damned goliath coming with all the grepping noise," Chains said.

A pair of feet landing on the side of the transport. Then a head appeared near the dirty glass, looking in at them. It was wearing a USSF helmet, the owner barely visible through the tinted faceplate.

"Seriously?" Hayden said, recognizing her.

Wiz knocked on the glass and waved.

32

"You have to be kidding me," Chains said, looking up at the owner of Crossroads.

Hayden didn't say anything. He aimed the revolver and pulled the trigger, the bullet punching through the window and hitting the edge of Wiz's helmet with enough force to back her off the vehicle.

"Jake, hold up your wrists," Hayden said. "Chains, grab Helks' rifle."

She was already reaching for it, leaning over the Scrapper's corpse.

Jake put his hands up against the pole. Hayden fired, missing the lock but snapping the chain holding the restraints to the transport. He cursed softly, shifting his aim to try again.

Something hit the top of the vehicle, small and dark and shaped like a projectile.

"Get down!" Hayden shouted, throwing himself to the ground. He put his hands over his head, covering his ears as the device detonated, the explosion peeling away part of the transport's roof.

He couldn't see anything through the smoke. Wiz and her soldiers were out there. He knew that much.

"Shoot at anything that moves," he said to Chains, quickly checking the cylinder of his revolver.

Three rounds.

Not enough.

Not even close.

He stayed low, moving along the side of the bus to where the Oversergeant's body had landed. The man was a mess of broken bones; his face smashed, his arm twisted awkwardly. His revolver was still in its holster, and Hayden grabbed it as Chains started to shoot.

Wiz didn't shoot back. She had come all the way out here to get him. She wanted him alive. Then again, if that were true then why the hell had she blown up the transport?

Three soldiers in Marine body armor moved into the smoke-filled space. They had abandoned their rifles for batons, and they charged toward Jake. Hayden aimed for the weak spot near the neck and fired a single round, hitting the shoulder of the soldier instead. At this range, it was enough to hurt, but not enough to pierce the shell.

Jake fell back from the attackers, swinging the loose chains of his captivity at them. They raised their batons to block, splitting up as they got a clearer view of the transport's innards.

Hayden fired again, missing a second time, the smoke burning his eyes and messing up his aim. The round hit the soldier's faceplate, scuffing the transparency as it ricocheted off. He lowered the weapon, squeezing his mechanical arm to extend the claws.

Nothing happened.

He squeezed again, but the claws remained retracted. The pins he had removed helped control the mechanism, and now it was broken.

The soldier reached him. Hayden threw a heavy punch instead, surprising the man and hitting him on the side of the helmet, the force knocking him away. He saw Chains coming under attack, her defense useless against the superiorly outfitted enemy. She put up her arm to block the baton, the weapon striking the chains and sparking. The strike must have hurt because her arm fell dead at her side.

Wiz's soldier grabbed her by the throat, holding her and raising the baton again. He didn't see what happened next, forced to duck away from his attacker, barely avoiding getting hit in the head. He fell backward, tripping over the bars in the windows, rolling to the side to dodge the baton. He raised the revolver to fire, in hopes of distracting the soldier, but the baton hit his hand, a shock coursing through it and making it numb, causing him to drop the weapon.

He put his mechanical hand up, blocking the next blow with it. The soldier straddled him, raining strike after strike down with the weapon, a spark flying between it and his hand with every hit.

Suddenly, almost miraculously, the attack stopped. Hayden watched a large, metal hand wrap around the soldier's helmet and twist, the motion snapping his neck and killing him instantly. Hayden could see the robot as the body fell beside him. It was turning back to the other soldiers, bullets uselessly hitting its armored shell from outside.

Hayden pushed himself to his feet, grabbing the rifle attached to the soldier's back. He moved behind the robot as it reached the soldier holding Chains. He dropped her to face it, trying to back away. Its arm shot forward, a heavy blow slamming into the soldier's chest and knocking him hard into the floor of the vehicle. It turned away, to where the last soldier was pulling an unconscious Jake from the wreck.

More rounds were pinging off its shell, most of them concentrated around its head. They were trying to shoot out its camera eyes. Hayden shot back at them past the machine, not expecting to hit anything but managing to diminish the incoming fire.

He remained behind the robot as it cleared the destroyed transport, moving out into the open in a swirl of smoke and ash. Hayden scanned the area, finding the Scrapper cars all tipped over, and in pieces, the riders and drivers left as corpses on the ground. There were wrecks of motorcycles around the area, too, the battle not winding up completely one-sided.

Some of the Scrappers were still alive, hunkered down near the tank and firing from its heavily armored flanks. Wiz's soldiers had them pinned there, their superior armor and weapons giving smaller numbers the upper hand. The truck filled with spoils from the Pilgrim was sitting behind it, almost daring the Collector and her people to try to reach it.

The robot moved across the battlefield, taking a path that made it clear it was aware of his presence, and it was leading him toward safety. Only there was nothing safe about where it was going. The machine was taking him from one captor to another, the two sides fighting over him to open a hatch he had no way of opening.

He broke away from the robot, rushing back toward the transport to where Jake was still lying prone on the ground. Neither side fired a shot at him, but he caught motion out of the corner of his eye and saw two of Wiz's soldiers running his way.

The machine saw them, too. It sped up its movements to intercede, getting between them and him. He backed away, returning to Jake as Chains joined him.

"At least they don't want to kill you," Chains said.

"We need to steal that truck," Hayden replied, motioning to it.

"Screw the truck," Chains said. "We need that tank. Leave him here."

"I'm not leaving him."

"We won't. Trust me."

Hayden only spared an instant to think about it, and then he nodded. The two of them broke from their position, rushing toward the line of Scrappers next to the tank. The robot charged along with them, trying to keep up and block Wiz's soldiers from a clear line of sight on them.

The Scrappers held their fire when they saw Hayden and Chains approaching, assuming he preferred them to Wiz.

Assuming wrong.

He opened fire on them at close range, the Marine rifle spitting out rounds in a hurry, the force of the shots nearly tearing the unarmored Scrappers apart. They went down in a line, one after another, the last few doing their best to run but not making it very far.

Hayden spun back toward the robot. Had his ambush changed its decision not to hurt him? It was coming toward him, but without facial expression, it was impossible to know what it would do.

"Sheriff," Chains said.

She was already on the side of the tank, climbing toward the hatch on the top. Wiz must have guessed what they were planning, because her soldiers changed their aim, firing on the small woman instead. She cursed and ducked behind the turret, the bullets bouncing off the other side.

The robot was getting closer, and showing no sign of slowing as it neared Hayden. He aimed the rifle at its head and pulled the trigger, only then noticing the display's announcement that the magazine was empty.

He threw the weapon aside, diving away from the robot as it stretched out its hand to grab his arm. He rolled on the ground, to the corpse of one of the Scrappers. A revolver was resting beside the man's dead hand, and Hayden grabbed it, rolling to a knee and facing the robot.

It lunged at him again, and he fired, two rounds in quick succession. The first pierced its left camera eye. The second, its right.

He jumped away from it as it came to a sudden stop, suddenly unable to process the world around it. A light in the center of its head flashed a few times and then became a solid blue.

It started moving again.

What?

Hayden didn't waste more time. He started scaling the tank. Wiz's soldiers were moving in, getting more daring now that he had taken out so much of the Scrapper's defense. He met Chains near the top of the tank, staying low as they inched to the hatch.

"How do we get in?" he asked.

"We can't unless someone comes out."

"Don't you think you should have mentioned that before? Why the hell would anyone come out?"

She smiled as the lock on the hatch clanged open.

"To pull you in and save your life," she said.

The large lid swung up and open, and Commander Ales emerged, holding his gun right in Hayden's face.

"Don't think of doing anything-"

Ales was cut off as Chains punched him in the side of the head with a metal-wrapped fist. He crumpled beneath the blow, falling off the ladder and into the tank.

"Idiot," she said. "Armed Sheriffs first."

Hayden dropped over the edge of the hatch, bypassing the ladder and landing on the floor. There were three more Scrappers inside, and two of them shot at him as he landed, their bullets coming dangerously close but missing. He shot back, his aim vastly superior to theirs, each slug catching one of them in the chest.

He rushed to the front of the tank as the driver pulled his weapon and turned to shoot.

"Don't," Hayden said, holding his weapon out at the Scrapper.

The man let his gun fall to the ground and slowly started raising his hands.

"Good choice," Hayden said.

The Scrapper lunged at him, reaching down and grabbing a knife. He slid it across Hayden's forearm, cutting into his coat but not through. Hayden pressed the revolver to his gut and pulled the trigger, the Scrapper going limp in his grip.

"You shot the driver?" Chains said, catching up with him.

"He tried to stab me," Hayden replied, showing her the cut on his coat. "You're a Driver. Can't you steer this thing?"

"It's a tank, not a car. Shit." She settled into the driver's seat. "I'll see if I can figure it out. Go close the hatch."

Hayden rushed back through the tank, hitting the ladder and starting to climb.

A soldier appeared above him, preparing to climb down while he was going up. Hayden grabbed them, pulling them roughly into the tank and tackling them, falling on top of them as he dragged them to the floor.

The soldier struggled beneath him, trying to pry him off. Fists flew up at his face, one of them hitting his jaw and knocking him off-balance. He recovered quickly, reaching out with his replacement and wrapping it around the soldier's neck.

They stopped moving instantly, the stillness allowing Hayden to get a look at the face. Her face.

Wiz.

"I think I've got it!" Chains cried, the tank jerking forward. "Did you close the hatch?"

Hayden looked up at the hatch above him, at the same time something heavy connected with the side of the tank, its weight enough to bounce the machine on its treads.

However it was still able to see, the robot was coming to get him.

"I need to close that hatch or the machine is going to kill all three of us," he said to Wiz. "Do you understand?"

She stared back at him, considering her next move.

"It's a roid, Sheriff," she said. "It doesn't think on its own." She motioned toward Ales with her eyes. "Commander Ales has its control transceiver."

Hayden looked over at the unconscious Commander.

"What does it look like?"

"Get off me, and I'll find it for you."

"You were trying to kill me."

"No, I was trying to capture you. I lost, you won. Like you said, either we close the hatch or tell the Butcher to stop, or we're all going to be trapped in here until we die. Either way, you have to get off me."

"Butcher?"

"Late model. Early twenty-second century, produced probably ten years before the Space Force finally fell apart. They were supposed to be our best hope to fighting the trife because they're damn near unstoppable."

"So what happened?"

"We lost the infrastructure to maintain them. It doesn't matter if it can kill a million trife if its batteries die and nobody is there to charge them. Do we have to talk about this now?"

The Butcher was on the top of the tank, each lumbering step vibrating the thick shell. It would be at the hatch in seconds.

Hayden rolled off Wiz, watching as she scrambled to Ales

and started patting down his clothes. She reached into a pocket, producing a small black box with a dim display.

The Butcher made it to the opening. It was too big to fit through, but it had picked up a gun from somewhere, and it stuck its arm into the hole.

Wiz and Hayden stared at one another. They both knew she could order the Butcher to kill him.

She raised the device toward her helmet, opening her mouth.

Chains grabbed the box from her hand, sneaking around her and yanking it away.

"Stop," she said. "Cancel all orders."

The Butcher stopped moving above them.

Hayden and Wiz both looked at her. The tank was still moving, but nobody was at the controls.

She tossed the box to Hayden. "I knew you couldn't trust her," she said, before rushing back to the front of the vehicle.

Hayden held the transceiver and the revolver.

"What do you say we negotiate the details of your surrender?" he said.

33

THE WORLD OUTSIDE HAD FALLEN INTO SILENCE WHEN Hayden, Chains, and Wiz emerged from the tank. The battle was over, the Scrappers all dead or otherwise incapacitated. Commander Ales was still out cold, but that hadn't stopped them from restraining him inside the armored vehicle, tied to the metal post of one of the seats with the shoelaces from his boots.

Chains went to find Jake, while Hayden and Wiz stood together on the turret, looking out at the destruction. The area around them was a scorched mess of slagged metal, destroyed vehicles, and bodies. Even the Marine body armor hadn't been enough to save all of Wiz's soldiers.

"I already told you, I can't get you in," Hayden said. "Was it worth it?"

She stared out at the destruction and shrugged. "Nothing ventured, nothing gained."

"King isn't going to be happy with what you did here."

"He'll never know it was me."

"Who else has so much old military equipment?"

"True. It looks like we're both on the wrong side of King's favor now, doesn't it?"

Hayden raised an eyebrow, turning to face her. "Are you talking about a truce or an alliance?"

"I don't know," she replied. "I'm starting to wish I hadn't locked you up. You came back to Crossroads. You didn't have to."

"I did. There's no reason innocent people should die because of us."

"That's not a very smart way to look at things out here, Sheriff."

"No? From what I've seen, your way doesn't work all that well. Maybe injecting a little bit of honor and responsibility back into the world is the shot in the arm it needs?"

"There have been other people like you, who thought they could change the way of things by will alone. They all died."

"Maybe I will, too. Maybe in less than three months. I can't stand here and watch people get taken advantage of. I wasn't made that way."

"So what are you going to do now?"

"I'm still looking for Natalia. According to Ales, she and Ghost are on their way to Ports."

Wiz's face darkened. "Ports?" She shook her head. "Sheriff, you can't go there. It's death."

"I've heard. If that's where Nat is, then that's where I'm going. I don't expect you to understand. You know about you. You care about you. I'm the least of my concerns."

He stared at her, waiting for a rebuttal. She stayed silent.

"What are you going to do now?" Hayden asked.

"That depends on you. You're right that King won't be happy once he finds out what happened here. He won't try to attack Crossroads, at least as long as he doesn't know half the guns are out of ammo, and the other half are broken. He'll probably send a Courier for me. At least it won't be Ghost."

"Why do you want to get into the Pilgrim so bad, anyway?"

"I told you before; I want what's on it."

Hayden pointed at the truck. "There's some of it. You want it? Let me take what I need, and you can have the rest."

"A truce?" she asked.

"An alliance," he replied.

"After what I did to you?"

"It ended well. I'm free of King's assholes."

"Are you always so generous?"

"You might not call it generous later. I don't need you right now. If I die, I'll never need you. If I don't? You might regret accepting the terms."

"How do you know you can trust me?"

He looked down at her, their eyes meeting. "Can I trust you?"

She smirked. "Yes. I don't make dirty deals."

"It seems like everything is dirty out here."

"We learned the hard way. You will too. I still believe that." She paused, scanning the horizon. "We shouldn't stay here long. We're lucky we didn't attract the trife or the goliaths. Better not to tempt fate."

Hayden looked back out to the remnants of the battleground. Wiz's people were gathering their dead. "How many soldiers do you have left?"

"Good soldiers? A dozen or so. Lousy soldiers? I can always hire more. The body armor can be mended. It won't be as good as it was before, but it's better than nothing. The Butcher is worth a hundred soldiers if you'd consider giving it to me."

"I think I might need it where I'm going."

"Who needs a Butcher when you have a tank?"

"It can't go everywhere. Do we have a deal?"

Wiz glanced back at the truck. "Yeah. We have a deal."

She put her hand out. Hayden took it.

"Deal."

34

THE TRANSPORT MADE IT NEARLY TWENTY MILES BEFORE THE axle gave way completely, snapping without warning and causing the vehicle to lean to the side as the wheel came out from under it.

"Damn," Ghost said, grabbing the seat to keep his balance.

"We made it pretty far," Natalia replied.

"Not far enough. Ten miles to go, and we'll have to do it on foot." He pointed out through the cracked windshield, to a line of broken skyscrapers in the distance. "That's it up there."

"Was it nuked?" she asked.

"No. The USSF had a base there. It was too important to nuke. They bombed the hell out of it, though. Napalm, too. They burned thousands of the trife. They needed to burn thousands more."

"I take it the trife are still active there?"

"Very. Our base is well fortified, so once we get inside, we'll be safe. The hard part is getting inside."

"Can you radio them and have them come out to meet us?"

"Not from here. The transceiver is only good for a mile or two."

He moved past her, into the back by the equipment. He started organizing it, putting extra magazines and guns into a pair of backpacks.

"We're inside the active zone," he said. "We need to make as much progress as we can before nightfall. There's a town few miles from here. Once it gets dark, we find an empty building and we hide there until morning."

"Okay," she replied. "I'm ready when you are."

He helped her put one of the packs on. It was heavy, and it pulled against her. She shifted a few times to get it sitting more comfortably.

"I know it's not light," he said. "But part of this is to bring supplies to the base. The people there have to be sick of eating trife by now. If we get into trouble, we'll ditch the packs first."

"Understood."

He put his pack on and then hefted one of the N80 rifles. She didn't try to take the other. She knew she couldn't carry it and the pack, and she had never shot anything larger than a handgun before.

He moved to the side hatch and pressed the release. It slid open, and he hopped down, turning and offering her a hand. She took it and climbed out of the transport, and then he entered the code on the side of it to close the hatch from the outside.

"This way," he said.

He led her along the road for nearly a kilometer, before peeling away from it and moving into some brush. There was a light footpath here, and he followed along it, pausing every hundred meters or so to listen for activity. He kept the rifle ready to fire, glancing into the scope every so often.

Thirty minutes passed without incident, allowing them to

begin drawing closer to the remains of the city ahead. The brush started thinning out a little bit, revealing the remains of the town Ghost had mentioned. Structures dotted the landscape around lines of cracked cement, dislodged by vegetation but still holding its own. Most were damaged in one way or another, the windows long gone, the contents claimed centuries before. They were empty husks, dark and ugly and imposing in their size and condition. Any one of them could have trife hiding inside, waiting for someone to happen by.

Ghost must have been thinking the same thing, because he proceeded more cautiously, keeping his eyes locked on the N80's scope. He swept it back and forth along the street, squinting slightly to get a little bit more resolution in his vision. He didn't speak, waving her ahead with his hand.

They crossed the street, heading toward a large building that looked as though it had been cut in half, the debris of the levels that had collapsed surrounding it. The bottom floors were still relatively intact, offering a small measure of shelter. A long-dormant sign rested against the side of the wall:

Holiday Inn.

Ghost continued to scan the area with the rifle, maintaining his alertness. They were a few dozen meters from the building when he froze, the weapon shifting ever so lightly in his grip. He used his other hand to stop her, holding out his palm.

He was tracking something.

She stood behind him, the sudden tension nearly choking her. Her heart pulsed, counting the seconds with every two beats. She leaned to the side, peeking over his shoulder at the display.

She could see the trife in it. Three of them moving slowly across the scope. The creatures hadn't seen them yet. If they stayed silent, maybe they wouldn't.

She watched them over Ghost's shoulder, a fresh sense of dread bubbling up when the three were joined by a dozen more. They gathered together, standing with their arms at their sides, communicating something to one another.

Then the trife turned in unison.

Then the demons started to run.

Right toward them.

A split second and a shot echoed. The first trife on the display went down. A second shot and another fell. Natalia looked past the weapon to the area ahead of them. She couldn't see the trife yet. They were still too far away.

Ghost fired three more times, and then reached out and grabbed Natalia's hand, pulling her toward the building. They sprinted over to it before Ghost sighted the creatures again, firing twice more.

Natalia pressed herself against the wall, lifting her sidearm. Her body was shaking, and she tried to convince it to calm.

Something thudded inside the building, a loud crash too close. Ghost spun toward it with the rifle, just as a trife burst out of the open doorway and grabbed at the front of the weapon. He pulled the trigger, and its head exploded.

He shoved his body into her, knocking her away as more of the creatures emerged from the space. He shot one, and then lowered the weapon, grabbing a knife from his belt and throwing it into the trife's neck. It collapsed with a weak hiss, and he brought the weapon up again, aiming it down the street.

The first group was coming in fast, their numbers diminished but the remainder eager for the fight. Ghost squeezed off two more rounds, dropping one of them.

Another trife came out of the building, rushing toward him. He didn't see it.

Natalia did. She brought her pistol up and fired, needing

half the magazine to drop the creature before it reached Ghost.

"This way," he shouted, breaking away from the building, toward the other side of the street.

She followed, getting past him as he slowed to keep an eye on the rear. She charged toward another building, a much smaller structure with a mix of wood and aluminum planks nailed in over the windows. She didn't see a door.

"Around the side," Ghost said, recognizing her confusion.

She changed direction, angling for the west end.

A dark shape hurtled out of the sky, hitting her from the side. She felt sharp claws scrape against the side of her armor, trying to dig through the tough fiber to find her skin. An ugly face hissed in hers before momentum carried it away. Natalia rolled to her knees while the trife scrambled on the ground, finding purchase to pounce on her again. She raised the pistol and fired, three rounds in the chest that brought it down for good.

Ghost's hand grabbed her by the arm, pulling her up. They made it around the corner, to a handmade door that had replaced the original. Ghost grabbed it and yanked it open, urging her inside. A trife came off the roof, only to be shot a moment later.

Then the Courier ducked into the building, grabbing the door and pulling it closed. A metal bar was resting beside it, and he seized it and shoved it through matching loops on the door and both sides of the frame.

The first trife hit it, knocking it in slightly. It hit the door again, and again. It hissed, sounding annoyed. More of them joined it, jumping onto the roof, their feet pounding above them. Natalia scanned the top of the structure, making sure it was intact.

Ghost heaved out a heavy breath and wiped his forehead. "That was close," he said, smiling.

"Are you even afraid of them?" Natalia asked, trying to catch her breath.

"Very. That's why I'm still alive."

They continued to pound at the door, and then the windows. It had all been installed and reinforced by somebody at some time, well enough to keep the creatures out.

"You're bleeding," Ghost said, looking down at her side. He put his rifle on the ground and unslung his pack, kneeling in front of her and examining the wound.

Natalia looked down at it, too. She didn't think the claws had gotten through the body armor.

"Is it bad?" she asked.

"It's hard to say," he replied. "You need to take off the armor so we can clean it up. I have a kit in the pack."

"What about the trife?"

"They can't get in here. Whoever used to live here made sure of that."

He motioned to the corner, where old blankets and debris proved someone used to call the place home, but not anywhere near recently.

"Why didn't we come here, first?"

"I didn't see it. It's my fault. I was too focused on the distance, watching for trife. They'll get bored in a while and go back to whatever it was they were doing."

"They won't wait for us to come out?"

"They might, but probably not. They prefer the sport of the hunt over waiting patiently."

"Good thing for us, I guess."

"It is. Now, take off your clothes."

"What?"

He smiled. "So I can clean the wound."

She unclasped the armor and unzipped it, pulling it off her upper half, and then shrugging out of it completely. She was still wearing a shirt and a pair of underwear beneath, but the shirt had been torn and was stained with her blood.

She started to feel the pain of the wound once she saw the damage it had caused.

Ghost turned around, opening his pack and rummaging through it, pulling out a small metal box and placing it on the ground.

"Lie down," he said.

It was chilly without the armor on. She shivered as she lowered herself to the ground, lying prone on the old blankets. They had a sickly sweet smell to them.

Ghost leaned over her, looking down at her body. She suddenly felt exposed, and had an urge to tuck herself in, get up, and put the armor back on. She had to remind herself that if he wanted to hurt her, he had already had ample opportunity.

"I need to move your shirt, okay?" he said.

She nodded, and he pulled her shirt up, folding it below her breasts. Then he opened the metal box and took out a container of liquid.

"This is going to sting," he said.

"Okay," she replied.

He poured the liquid onto the wound. It hurt, but she didn't make a sound. Then he took a clean pad and wiped it down.

"I don't think you need stitches," he said. "It will probably scar."

"It could have been worse."

"Much."

He finished cleaning the wound and then spread a thick gel all over it before bandaging it. When he was done, he leaned back on his heels, looking over his work.

"I think you'll live," he said.

She lifted her head, looking down at the patch, and then up at him. "You're a man of many talents."

"When you're a Courier, you learn how to survive, or you die. Are you hungry? I have some food in my-"

He stopped speaking when she reached up and took hold of his arm.

"Come here," she said.

He stared at her, confused.

Her heart was pounding, her body weak. She had to make her move now, or risk losing the moment.

"Fine," she said when he didn't move. "I'll come to you."

She pushed herself up, despite the pain in her side, wrapping an arm around his neck and using it to balance as she brought her mouth to his. He was hesitant at first, his lips moving but unsure. She stayed with the kiss, ignoring the part of her that was telling her not to go through with it. She would always love Hayden, but she had to learn to survive, too.

He overcame his initial surprise, putting more effort into his response, returning her affection with his own desire, and letting her pull him down on top of her.

She closed her eyes at the same time she opened her mouth, imagining Ghost's hand was Hayden's as it explored her body. She pretended that Ghost's tongue was Hayden's as it explored her mouth.

It was the only way she could follow through with her plan. She had to do more than survive. She had to get back at the man that had cost her husband his life.

She would do whatever it took to get Ghost to love her, and then they would go back to King.

Then they would kill him.

Together.

35

"I THINK THEY'RE GONE," GHOST SAID, PEERING OUT THROUGH a crack he had opened in the doorway. "They didn't want to wait for us."

He looked back at Natalia with a smile. His eyes traveled her body, unclothed as she used a clean, wet rag to wipe the blood and sweat away. She was thankful they had found the supply of water in the back of the old fueling station, hoarded there along with hundreds of cans of food by someone who had never made it back.

"That means we can be on our way?" she said.

She was trying to keep her mind off the guilt she felt. She had to stay focused on her goals. This was an important first step.

"As soon as you're ready," he replied.

He had risen early to search the station, cleaning and dressing before going to take a look outside. The trife were nearby then, but it had also been dark. Now that the sun was rising, they were returning to their group to feed.

She grabbed her panties and shirt, quickly pulling them on. Then she started slipping into the body armor. Ghost returned to her then, helping her dress, kissing her neck as he zipped the front of it and clasped it closed.

"I hope we have a chance to do this again under better conditions," he said.

"Me too," she lied. She smiled at him. "Now that we've been together, I think it's only fair that you tell me your name. Your real name."

"Charles," he said, laughing. "Charles Danforth."

She put out her hand. "Pleased to meet you, Chuck."

He laughed harder, taking her hand and shaking.

"We should go," he said. "We have another eight miles to travel, and just because it's light doesn't mean it's safe."

She responded by walking over to her pack and picking it up. She felt a tug at the wound in her side but ignored it, getting the bag balanced on her back. Then she picked up the pistol, attaching it to the armor.

"I put a fresh magazine in for you," Ghost said.

"Are you flirting with me?" Natalia replied.

"Always."

He lifted his pack, getting it settled before hefting the N80. Then he pushed the door to the station open, bringing the rifle's display up to his eyes and sweeping the area as he held it for her.

She stepped outside, into the sunlight. The landscape looked different in the daytime. It was eerie, and at the same time possessed a certain beauty that amazed and frightened her. It was too natural. Too raw.

There were dead trife on the ground nearby, the remnants of the prior night's attack. Natalia noticed one of them had an open gash in its side, and it looked like its entrails had been pulled out.

"An animal probably happened by and saw an easy meal," Ghost said.

"The other trife would let it feed like that?"

He nodded. "They only attack humans and each other."

She looked away from the corpse, following Ghost back through the town. He was especially cautious as they passed the Holiday Inn, keeping the rifle trained on the doorway. Nothing came out.

They passed through the town, taking a much more open approach to Ports than they had the night before. Ghost seemed confident that the route was clear, though that didn't mean he let his guard down. He was intense in his focus because he knew he had to be.

Two hours of walking found them closing in on the outskirts of the city, where the remains of larger buildings started to fill in the world around them, intermingled with random vegetation. The ground was wet from rain, the broken cement at their feet holding intermittent puddles that Ghost navigated them around, to keep the splashing from drawing attention. The air was cool, and she felt it more through the tears in her armor, biting at her wound beneath its bandage. She accepted the stinging pain as penance.

Ghost put his hand up, motioning her to wait against the ragged wall of a damaged building. Then he sprinted across the street, vanishing into the doorway of a building on the other side. She could see him climb a set of exposed stairs to the next level, and then crouch in the corner, the barrel of the rifle resting on a break in the cement. She leaned out from her spot to look in the same direction, ducking back behind the wall when she spotted a group of trife. There had to be a hundred of them or more, hissing at one another in an indecipherable conversation.

She looked back at Ghost. He had his hand up toward her, telling her to wait.

She heard a soft whine in the distance. She peeked around the corner again. The trife had heard it, too. They raised their heads in unison, turning to the east before splitting apart, racing to the buildings on either side and scaling them with ease.

What was going on?

She found Ghost again. The barrel of the N80 had vanished from the wall. He was tucked back and out of sight. Or had he abandoned her?

The whine didn't get much louder, but soon after a vehicle appeared in the streets. It reminded her of the car Ghost had pulled her into, only it was open on top, and had a pair of guns mounted to makeshift turrets. Two Scrappers were manning them, while a third drove the car. It slowed to a stop where the trife had been a minute before.

The soldiers at the turrets turned left and right, looking for the trife, swiveling their guns in the same direction. The weapons were crude, eight barrels sticking out from the main cylinder, and what looked like a hand crank dropping down and to the left, a feed of bullets vanishing into the vehicle.

She heard a high pitched noise that seemed to come from all around her. An instant later, the trife launched their attack.

They poured from their hiding places, rushing toward the car, spreading apart and taking different routes to attack it. The Scrapper facing her smiled, rotating the gun on its mount and turning the crank.

Slugs began to launch from the weapon, one after another after another, tearing through the first line of trife coming their direction. The same thing happened on the other side, cutting down a dozen of the creatures within seconds.

The trife spread apart more, making a wide line, the second row getting closer before it too went down in a hail of projectiles, the Scrapper assault too much for them to take.

Something cast a shadow over her then, and she looked

up. More trife were crossing between buildings over her head, leaping and spreading their arms, revealing what looked like fleshy wings beneath. They didn't notice her standing there, or if they did, they ignored her. They hit the stable part of the debris and vaulted again, a line of them ready to attack the car from the sky.

The Scrappers saw them coming, turning and trying to swivel their guns upward to attack. Only the mounts didn't adjust high enough, the rounds spitting below the creatures.

Natalia heard a loud crack nearby and caught the muzzle flash from the N80 out of the corner of her eye. One of the airborne trife tumbled from the sky, crashing to the ground and rolling to a stop. A fresh series of shots followed, sending more of the demons to the earth.

Ghost hit a lot of them, but not all of them. The driver of the car decided to move, the car lurching forward while the shooters held onto their guns to stay upright.

Three of the trife reached out, their claws scraping the armor plating of the car and sliding off, sending them rolling on the ground, bones breaking from the force. One of them managed to find purchase, springing from the back toward one of the soldiers, claws extended.

Another crack and its head exploded sideways, the momentum carrying its body away as the car turned and accelerated up the street toward them.

The guns adjusted to the rear, firing back at the trife, who were increasing in number, drawn in by the noise. Natalia looked back up to Ghost, finding him standing in the open, waving toward the car.

It came to a hard stop beside the building. Natalia didn't wait for Ghost to urge her to it, breaking from her hiding spot and running toward the vehicle. The driver looked her way, not reacting much to her presence other than to give a curt nod as she reached the car and vaulted over the door.

Ghost joined her there an instant later, jumping down from his perch into the vehicle between the two gunners. The noise of the firing weapons was deafening, the back seat of the converted vehicle littered with both spent and unused shells.

"You're wasting a lot of ammo!" Ghost shouted at the men, at the same time he brought the N80 back to his shoulder and resumed firing single rounds, at the same time the car accelerated away again.

They kept shooting for a few more seconds until the speed of the car was outpacing the speed of the trife. They bounced through roughly cleared streets, slowing to corner and making their way deeper inside, leaving the creatures behind.

Once they were clear, one of the shooters dropped the weapon, letting it hang from its mount. She turned to Ghost, offering him a big smile. "Hey baby," she said. "I heard you were on your way with a new bitch." She glanced over at Natalia. She couldn't have been more than eighteen. "So," she said, still staring at her. "Did you screw her yet?"

Ghost shifted his eyes toward Natalia, offering her an expression that froze her to the bone. It wasn't the look of a man falling in love with her.

It was the look of a predator.

The biggest and the baddest.

"You know me," he replied. "I'd say she's been completely screwed."

It took every bit of her will for her to keep herself from falling apart.

How could she have been so fucking stupid?

What the hell had she done?

36

THE CAR ENTERED THE SCRAPPER BASE THROUGH A HEAVILY reinforced gate that led into an underground garage. It had been a short ride from the scene of the trife attack to the location, the vehicle passing through heavier devastation before entering what Ghost had called "The Clean Zone" because it hadn't been bombarded or napalmed.

That didn't make it clean. The buildings were still grimy and old, overgrown and breaking down from the passage of time. But they were mostly intact, standing ten to twenty stories high. Some of them even had a few window panes left.

Natalia was sitting in the passenger seat, facing forward. She hadn't been able to look at Ghost since he had revealed his true nature to her, and shown her that he had known what her game was the entire time. She was an idiot to have ever thought she could get through to him. Not out here, where attachment was a word and not a deed. Where close bonds were a detriment, not a strength. Where there were only predators and prey.

She had let herself be one of the prey. She had set herself

up for it. He had never been interested in her beyond the conquest. Beyond the dominion. He had used kindness to keep her under control, to earn her trust against the dangers outside of their circle. He had done it convincingly enough that she had forgotten he was a Scrapper. King's son. A monster, like the rest of them.

Like everything else in this fucking world.

Her heart ached to be back in Metro. To be back behind the sealed doors. It wasn't an easy life, but it was better than being out here. At least there was still a human civilization on the Inside. There was nothing civilized about any of this.

The car eased through the gate, passing between guards stationed on either side. They saluted Ghost as they entered, thumb and two fingers in the shape of a gun, pressed over their hearts. He saluted them back, his smile huge as he reveled in their adoration.

Natalia would have never expected such a greeting, especially considering the way Grimly had treated him. The way the Oversergeant had nearly killed him. She had guessed the Courier was a relative outsider, and the things he had said to her had only reinforced it.

She had guessed wrong. Completely wrong.

They drove down one level, out into a garage that was already home to nearly two dozen other vehicles. Cars with gatling guns like the one she was riding in, as well as supply trucks and a couple of old USMC armored transports. There were crates scattered around the vehicles, boxes of guns and ammunition and other supplies. What they were carrying in their packs seemed a pittance compared to what they already had.

She blanched when she saw what else they had in the garage. Corpses. Trife corpses, at least fifty of them in a pile. Two Scrappers were standing beside it, taking them out and cutting off the skin with knives, stripping them down to claim their meat. They looked up at the car as it passed, and then returned to their work.

At least she didn't see the same operation with human bodies.

"What the hell happened out there?" the female shooter asked. "Where's Grimly and the rest of the convoy?"

"Grep Grimly," Ghost said. "That asshole tried to take what was mine." He motioned his head toward Natalia. "Then he tried to grepping kill me. He damn near broke my ribs before I stuck him and his goons good."

He didn't mention that she had saved his life, changing the facts to make himself look stronger.

"The convoy got attacked on the way up, before we reached the bunker," he continued. "Two competing groups of trife. One of the groups, the trife were bigger. Stronger."

"And now they're grepping flying," the other shooter said. "I ain't never seen that shit before."

"Grimly kicked me off the transport," Ghost said. "Grepping coward. Right in the back. He left me out there for dead. He forgot who I am."

"Ghost," the girl said. "God of Death."

Natalia's skin crawled again, hearing the way the Scrapper referred to him. She believed his godly claims.

"Corvan, take our guest to her quarters," Ghost said. "It's on level nine, right above the server room."

"Yes, sir," the other gunner said.

Ghost looked at her and smiled again. "And make sure you disarm her first. She isn't afraid to use that thing."

Natalia still had the pistol in her hand, though she had forgotten about it in her shock. Not that she could have used it unless she wanted to kill herself. As upset as she was, she wasn't ready for that.

She started raising it, to point it at Ghost. Corvan's hand came down, grabbing the barrel and pulling it from her grip.

"I'll take that," he said.

"Liv, why don't you go and find your sister?" Ghost said to the other gunner. "I haven't had a bath in ages, and I could use a little extra attention."

The girl smiled. "Of course. We'd be happy to help you with that."

She jumped out of the car, looking back at him once as she hurried away.

Corvan climbed over the side of the car and then opened the passenger door for Natalia. "Let's go," he said gruffly.

She started to climb out, her whole body numb. She couldn't believe this was happening. She swung her feet out before freezing, looking back at Ghost.

"One way or another, I'm going to find a way to kill you, you son of a bitch," she said.

Ghost smiled. "That's one of the things I love about you, Natalia. Your tenacity. Your passion." He leaned forward, lowering his voice. "You have a choice now. Be a part of the team. A valuable part of the team, and you'll be rewarded as such. We don't have to be enemies. We can be more than friends. I truly do like you, Natalia. But you need to learn important lessons about the real world. About your real future. The sooner you learn, the better off we'll all be. You have potential. Don't waste it."

He waved his hand, dismissing her. Corvan grabbed her arm, pulling her out of the car and leading her away. She could feel the eyes of the other Scrappers on her as they crossed the garage, heading toward a stairwell.

She had done her best to hold onto something, some reason to have hope despite her situation. Despite Hayden's death.

Now that hope was slipping away.

37

CORVAN LED HER TO A LIFT, WHICH CARRIED HER FIFTEEN floors down beneath the five levels of the garage, deep below the Earth where both trife and bombs couldn't reach. He didn't speak to her. He didn't even look at her. He acted like if he did he would wind up doing something he would regret. Something Ghost would make him pay for.

They stopped at the floor one up from the bottom, the lift opening up into a long corridor that wrapped around the shaft and spread out in every direction. They took the northern fork to a wing marked as "barracks," which turned out to be a cluster of thirty small rooms organized around a central common area, where tables and couches that must have been centuries old were organized for both recreation and communication. They had held up well to the passing of time, the only indication of their age a slight smell that rose from the fibers.

Corvan led her to one of the rooms. Six of the doors were closed, and she assumed that meant there were six other Engineers inside with her. Not Engineers from starships like the Pilgrim, but whatever passed for it in today's world.

People who had learned only from manuals and books, or who were skilled at tinkering and reverse-engineering. Smart survivors with an aptitude for machines, not people who had gone to school, taken classes, mentored under a senior Engineer, passed countless grueling exams, and then worked their way up to Lead with time, experience, and skill.

There was only one of her, maybe in the whole world. At least for as long as the colonists of the Pilgrim remained locked inside the Pilgrim. King thought enough of this place to risk her life, and his son's life, to get her here. Whatever information was hidden in those black boxes, he wanted it that badly.

The other doors were open, and she could see immediately that they were all identical. Corvan gave her a quick tour, entering the room and pointing.

"There's a bathroom back there. The shower might not work, maybe you can fix it. The toilet only has enough pressure to flush some of the time, so it might be better to shit into a napkin and toss it in the trash. Work uniforms are in there if you want one. You can sleep on the cot, eat and work at the desk. If you need anything else, there's a comm system on the wall here." He tapped a plastic square near the door. "Just ask for it, and it'll probably be brought to you."

Then he stepped out of the room.

"I'm going to lock you in for now. You'll get some food soon. Try to relax and get adjusted. Nobody's going to hurt you down here. Not with you under Ghost's protection."

He turned to leave.

"Corvan," she said.

He looked back. "Yeah? What?"

"Thank you."

The Scrapper looked confused by the kindness. He shrugged and closed the door. She heard it lock a moment later.

She paced for a minute, trying to calm her mind. She had made a fool of herself, thinking she could turn the Courier against King. She had been naive to the point it was embarrassing. He had used her. Or maybe he had just let her try to use him without revealing he knew what she was doing until he had gotten what he wanted. It wasn't about feelings or even sex. It was about domination. Conquest. Control.

It made everything worse.

And now he wanted her to fix the mainframe for him? Why should she? What was her incentive? She couldn't get him to help her kill King. She couldn't touch the leader of the Scrappers from down here. Could she get out? How? There were at least a hundred of the assholes between her door and the gate to the outside, and who knew how many trife waiting in the city.

There was no way out. No escape. She had tried. Futilely, maybe, but at least she had tried.

She had also failed.

She moved to the cot and sat down on the edge, burying her head in her hands. She started to cry. She wanted to be stronger than that, but her strength had fled with her hope. She missed Hayden. She missed the Pilgrim. She missed the simplicity of the life she had before. It was measured and consistent, and it was a lot of work, but at least everyone was working together, not fighting one another or struggling to survive against monsters both human and inhuman.

She wasn't going to help them. She wasn't going to help King bring his version of rule over the survivors of this apocalypse.

If she were dead, at least she would be in the same state as Hayden.

She stood up, walking to the small closet and opening it, searching for something she could use to harm herself. There was nothing in it save for a single white lab coat, still clean and pure after all of these years. She took it out, held it up. Tears burned her eyes again. She turned around, looking for something she could drape it over. Maybe she could hang herself?

The strength to do that fled her. She collapsed to the floor, the sobs coming again. How the hell had she wound up here? Why couldn't they have just left the fucking planet like they were supposed to?

It took a few minutes for her to calm again. She stopped crying, picking herself up and putting on the lab coat. She settled onto the cot and closed her eyes. She didn't fall asleep. Instead, she thought of Hayden. His face. His smile. His laugh. His awkwardness the day they met. The day he was elected Sheriff. The pride on his face.

Some time passed. The door to the room clicked open. Her eyes opened with it. She turned her head as Ghost entered, carrying a plate of vegetables.

"Natalia," he said simply. He had showered and changed, replacing his filthy suit with a fresh one.

She almost laughed at the idea he kept an identical change of clothes all the way out here. She was in no mood to laugh.

"Charles," she said. "If that's your real name."

"It is," he replied, smiling.

Someone else entered behind him. A woman. Not Liv. She was older, with gray hair and scarred hands. She had the USSF logo tattooed on her cheek. A soldier.

"This is Bones," he said.

Bones stared at her but didn't speak.

Ghost held the plate out to her. "Vegetables. Don't worry. They're hydroponically grown. No concerns about radiation. You can't eat the trife meat because you haven't built up an immunity."

"We have vegetables on the Pilgrim," Natalia said, taking the plate.

There were no utensils. She wasn't hungry, but she started eating anyway. She wasn't going to let him see her upset.

"I want to make sure we're clear on things, Natalia," he said, taking a seat beside her. "I brought you here for a reason."

"Because King told you to. You're a good little boy."

Ghost flinched, anger filling his eyes. Bones took a step toward her. He held up his hand to stop her.

"This facility was once called the United States Space Force Datalink Bunker Portland," he said. "I know it's a mouthful. It was a repository for the intel being passed between the Space Force bases after the war began, a home base if you will. There were some engineers and scientists down here, collecting, collating, and parsing the data. Trying to find patterns. Trying to solve riddles. Directly below us, there's a room. It's filled with computers. Over two hundred large machines, with who knows how much information on them. The problem is that the room is dead. The power goes on, but the computers won't start. We've had our people looking at it, and they've made some limited progress, but they aren't you. Do you understand?"

Natalia nodded. "What are you hoping to find down there?"

"Directions. We know the Space Force had bunkers and caches all across the country. We know they were stockpiling munitions in the hopes they would be able to make a final push against the trife at some time in the future. I've seen the videos. This whole city was being bombarded, thousands of trife were dying, while the scientists hid down here and continued their work. They talked about their plans. How they were trying to prepare for a future that might not come in the final months before it all ended. King wants those munitions. He wants those resources. With them, we'll be able to unite the scattered remains of civilization under his order."

"What order?" Natalia said. "His soldiers are murderers and rapists. They follow nothing but fear and pain. The innocent people are naked and hungry. How is that world better than this one?"

Ghost glanced over at Bones. She came toward Natalia, her hand moving so fast she barely saw it before it slapped the side of her face.

Her cheek burned. She looked back at the woman.

"Unlike my father, I don't believe in hitting women," Ghost said. "So I brought a woman to do it for me. Do you know why she's called Bones?"

Natalia could guess. She nodded.

"Good. The Scrappers are the biggest and the baddest. That's what the world needs right now. Now, you're going to fix the servers. You're going to get us into the data stores. That's why you're here. That's the only reason you're here, and your value is tied directly to that outcome. Do you understand?"

Natalia nodded again. "You should kill me. I'm not going to help you."

Ghost smiled. "Yes, you are."

"You can't force me."

"Yes, I can. I'm not going to kill you, Natalia. Bones is quite skilled at inflicting pain without causing death. Do you want a demonstration?"

Natalia looked at the woman. She wanted to say no, to give in, but she couldn't bring herself to do it.

Bones reached for her. She tried to struggle, but it only took a few seconds for the woman to subdue her, grabbing her in a choke hold and pulling her off the cot. She removed a small blade from her pocket, maneuvering it to Natalia's hand. She shoved it beneath one of her fingernails.

Natalia cried out in pain. She couldn't believe how much it hurt. Tears sprang fresh to her eyes.

The blade was removed an instant later.

"How much of that can you take, Natalia?" Ghost said. "That was two seconds. Imagine it for two hours. Imagine torture worse than that."

She shook in Bones' arms until the woman let her go. She fell back onto the cot beside Ghost. He turned toward her.

"I don't want to hurt you. I do respect you, and care for you. You're a valuable asset and an excellent lover."

She clenched her teeth. He threw that in to sting her again.

"Bones will stay with you while you work. If she thinks you're stalling, if she thinks you're breaking things instead of fixing them, she will cause you pain. Do you understand?"

Natalia glanced at him and nodded.

"The coat comes off when you return to your room. Everything comes off when you return to your room. I won't have you killing yourself while I'm sleeping." He pointed over the door, to a small hole there. "There's a camera up there. I saw you in it. I saw you thinking about it. Someone will be keeping an eye on you."

"You're going to leave me in here naked? With someone watching me?"

"Whatever freedom you had ended when Pig pulled you out of the Inside. You can get it back, but you have to earn it. Do you understand?"

Her whole body was shaking. She was angry at herself. She had a chance, one chance, to kill herself, and she hadn't taken it. She couldn't bear the thought of sitting in here, knowing she had failed. She didn't want to be naked. She didn't want someone watching her. If she had to earn his trust, she would earn his trust. If that was the only way she could survive in this hellhole of a planet, then that's how she would survive.

She had no strength left to resist.

"I want to get to work," she said. "I want to earn your trust."

Ghost smiled. He leaned over, kissing her on the cheek. She didn't try to escape from it. She leaned in toward it.

It was better than the pain.

38

They never went to Sanisco.

They never even came within a hundred kilometers of it.

There was no reason to go there. Hayden already knew where King had brought Natalia, and after an hour of driving Chains had stopped the armored vehicle, declaring they didn't have enough fuel to take the already beaten path north to Ports.

That was fine with him. He could deal with King later. Natalia always had been and still was, his goal. Once she was back in his arms, they would figure it all out together.

There was no specific course for them to plot. They didn't have a definitive path to follow. Chains had driven the route between Haven and Sanisco multiple times, so she had a general idea of the landscape heading toward the north, including the mountains and valleys in their way. She had set a vector she guessed would bring them to the road King had cleared toward the city fifty kilometers from the Fortress, hopefully bypassing notice.

With a little bit of pressure, Commander Ales had agreed with her overall approach, claiming the maneuver would put them at least ten kilometers past where Sanisco's Enforcers typically ranged.

Not that they could count on anything the Scrapper Commander said, but he wasn't in the best position to lead them astray. If they came under attack, he would come under attack, too.

Her decision turned out to be the right one. Darkness was falling by the time they rumbled up a slight incline, crushing the light vegetation around the road beneath the tank's powerful treads. They had bashed their way through countless bushes along the way, the heavy machine able to shove aside or climb over everything that had been in their path. They had been forced to stop a couple of times while a goliath roamed past, and they had driven directly through a group of trife that attempted an attack before the Butcher crushed a few and scared the rest off, but otherwise, it had been easy-going.

Hayden was confident, and he had reason to be. The vehicle they were riding in was invulnerable to the trife, and the Butcher sitting on top of it was deadly to them. They had claimed a raft of gear from the Pilgrim's spoils, not only weapons and ammunition but armor and food as well. Maybe the Scrappers in Ports would have superior numbers, but he would have superior firepower.

He was going to get her back.

He looked over at Jake. The Borger had been quiet since Wiz's attack. Withdrawn. Hayden had put him to work finding a way to modify the USSF body armor so he could wear it either over his mechanical hand or in spite of his mechanical hand since the wider profile of the metal prosthetic made the default sizing impossible. Feeling useful seemed to be helping. Jake was completely focused on the task, and his work bag had fortunately contained what he needed to start making the alterations.

Alterations that had required disconnecting the replacement and the band that kept it synchronized with his organic musculature. It had taken nearly two hours to get it off and had come along with no small amount of pain. It was impressive that the Borger was able to do the work while the tank was in motion, the unsteady ground keeping it shivering the entire time.

He knew his work, and he did it well.

Jake noticed Hayden looking at him. He raised his eyes from the armor. "It's almost finished, Sheriff," he said. "I could have just cut the whole sleeve off, but that would have left your entire arm exposed." He held up the band that coordinated the signals from his brain to the hand. "I put some connectors on here, with matching pairs on the suit. You're lucky it stretches. Oh, and I repaired the pins."

He pushed on part of the hand, and the claws extended outward. He opened the hand, and they sank back in.

"Good as new," Hayden said.

"Just about. Give me another hour, and I'll be finished."

"I appreciate all you're doing for me."

"Kill a lot of Scrappers, and we'll be even."

"This isn't about killing Scrappers. This is about what's right."

"Killing Scrappers is right," Chains shouted, listening in from the driver's seat. "Sheriff, I think we should stop here for the night. I'm getting wonkers, and could use a little shut-eye."

Hayden stood and made his way to the front of the tank. Chains was using the vehicle's external cameras to see beyond the armor. Only six of the eight displays were intact, leaving the right rear corner of the tank invisible to them.

"Where are we?" he asked.

"King's road, north of Sanisco," she replied. "If we opened

the hatch, killed the engine, and listened hard enough, we might even be able to hear the ocean."

"I've never seen an ocean," Hayden said.

"It's something else; I'll give you that. I never saw the ocean either. Not until I left Carcity. It's incredible." She smiled. "But if you're going to see it, best to see it with your wife."

Hayden smiled. Chains was still a bit of an enigma to him, but she seemed to have a truly righteous heart. The kind it seemed the world needed many, many more of. "Pozz that. Are we safe out here?"

"We're in a tank. We have a Butcher. So long as a goliath doesn't step on us while we're sleeping, I think we'll be fine."

"Thank you for making the trip with me. I don't think I could have figured out how to steer this thing."

"I'm sure you could have, Sheriff. But, you're welcome. You know, I left home to run away from something. Thanks to you, I feel like I'm running toward something."

"Pick a spot to settle us in, and then come on back."

"Pozz that," Chains said, copying him.

Hayden returned to the rear of the tank. He looked over at the stump of his arm as he did. It was hard for him to adjust to the sight of a blank space where his hand had been.

He positioned himself in front of Commander Ales. They had shifted the Scrapper from the floor to one of the seats, binding him tightly to it. He had been silent for most of the trip, except when they had spoken to him directly, observing their actions with a quiet smugness that Hayden didn't quite understand. Now he looked into Hayden's eyes, exhibiting the same smugness.

"What can you tell me about Ports?" Hayden asked.

"You're going to die there," Ales replied.

"Then so will you."

"Most likely, but I'm sure I can't convince you not to go."

"No."

"Can I convince you to set me loose?"

"That depends on how much you have to say. Do you have any idea where we are?"

"There aren't any windows in here, Insider. Maybe you're accustomed to that, but we like to be able to see outside."

"Being a belligerent asshole isn't going to get you anywhere, Commander."

"What I'm saying is that if you want to know where we are, I need to see the road."

Chains made her way back, joining him there. "We don't need anything from him, Sheriff," she said. "We should have tossed him out of the hatch when the trife showed up."

"I can't kill a man in cold blood," Hayden said. "Not even a Scrapper. Do you have a knife?"

Chains shook her head. "I don't like knives."

"She prefers punching people in the head with steel knuckles," Jake said. "Here."

Hayden turned toward the Borger, who was offering a knife. Hayden took it, holding it out toward Commander Ales. Then he knelt down, reaching behind the chair and beginning to cut through the laces that were holding him.

"You're letting him up?" Chains said.

"I want him to take a look at the displays and try to tell us where we are."

The ropes fell free.

"Don't do anything stupid." Chains said, warning the Scrapper.

"I know you have a low opinion of King's soldiers," Ales said. "And rightly so. I'm an educated man, and I'm certainly not about to try to get away."

"If you're so educated," Jake said. "Why are you working for King?"

"There are two reasons why anyone works for King. One,

because he offers the most for the least. Food. Shelter. Freedom. His Officers get even more. Whatever we want, really. Two, because I believe in the fate of my eternal soul."

"What the hell does that mean?" Chains asked.

"When a god comes to walk the Earth with you, the wise man follows wherever he leads."

Chains looked back at Hayden, her eyebrows twisted.

"You think King is a god?" Hayden said.

"I don't think it, Insider. I know it. I've been with King for many years. A disciple of his, if you will. He was sent by the divinity to re-unite humankind against the trife. He came down from Heaven to save us."

"Does he walk on water?" Jake asked, mockingly.

Ales ignored him, keeping his eyes on Hayden. "There's a story about King whereby he wads into a group of a hundred trife and comes out unscathed on the other side. I know sometimes legends get exaggerated, but I was there. I saw it with my own eyes. He is the hand of justice, come to cleanse the world. I guarantee it."

"And it doesn't matter how many innocent people suffer at the hands of his followers?" Chains asked. "It doesn't matter how many people go hungry, or naked, or without shelter?"

"No. Why would it? This existence is nothing. A waypoint on a longer journey. The sacrifices the people make to King's Scrappers guarantee them a place by his side when the true end comes."

"Forget this, Sheriff," Chains said. "He's clearly out of his grepping mind. Show him the displays and shut him up."

"What you call insanity, I call faith," Ales said. "I don't need you to believe what I believe."

"Come on," Hayden said, taking him by the arm. Ales didn't resist, heading to the front of the vehicle to examine the displays.

"Hmm," Ales said, staring at them.

"What is it?" Hayden asked.

"You're further north than I expected. You're getting close to the bunker."

"Bunker?" Chains said.

"A waypoint on the trail to Ports," Ales said. He leaned forward a little more, getting a closer look at the screens. "Do you see that?" He put his finger on the display, beneath a small, dark lump. "If I'm not mistaken, that's a trife." He moved his finger. "So is that. And that. And that."

Chains leaned in behind him. "They're dead."

"Yes. It looks like there might be more of them further up. If I had to guess, I would say they attacked the convoy King sent out this way."

Hayden's body shook at the statement. An attack? What if?

"Chains, we have to keep going. I need to know what happened. I need to know if-"

"I understand," she said. "I'm on it, Sheriff."

She pushed past Ales, dropping back into the driver's seat. Hayden grabbed the Scrapper's arm again, quickly guiding him back toward his seat.

"How do you think your god is going to get you out of this?" he asked as he led Ales back.

"Oh, I can get out of this one myself, Sheriff," Ales replied. "My King will honor me in the next life for my sacrifice in this one."

Hayden started to react, but he was too slow and unaccustomed to working with one hand. The Commander lunged toward him, reaching beneath his coat and grabbing the revolver holstered at his hip. Hayden turned, trying to get his good hand on the weapon and turn it aside before the Scrapper could shoot him.

But Ales wasn't trying to shoot him. He lifted the

revolver, turning the barrel on himself, sticking it against his left eye and pulling the trigger. The back of his head exploded outward an instant later, and his corpse toppled to the floor.

"Shit," Jake said, some of the blood splattering against his face. "What the hell?" He saw Ales on the ground, the revolver in his hand beside him.

Hayden looked down at the dead Scrapper. He believed he would be rewarded for killing himself? For an educated man, he sure was an idiot.

Hayden bent down and picked up his gun, putting it back on his hip before turning to Jake.

"Give me a hand, will you? I need to find out what happened to my wife."

39

THE TANK RUMBLED ACROSS THE STAINED AND DIRTY landscape. Each passing second brought another loud snap or crunch from beneath its treads, as they overtook another corpse and crushed it beneath them.

Sheriff Hayden Duke stood on top of the vehicle, looking out at the swath of destruction around them, holding onto the arm of the Butcher for balance. There were hundreds of dead trife out here. Thousands. More confusing, they didn't all look the same. Some were smaller and more humanoid, like the ones he had encountered at Jake's farm. The others were larger and stronger in appearance, more like the creature that had saved him from Pig, in payment for protecting its nest.

The evolution of the creatures meant something. The fact that some were the same in the closed microcosm of the Pilgrim and out here in the world - that meant something, too. He didn't know what. He didn't know if it even mattered. His fight was with King.

The trife could wait.

The demons weren't the only dead things out here. He

could make out the soldiers intermingled with them, especially as they passed through a small dip where the landscape rose on either side of them. It was clear the Scrappers had encountered the trife here. There were abandoned vehicles nearby, their drivers often slumped over the wheel or back against the seat, their throats neatly cut by razor-sharp claws. More Scrappers were on the ground, some covered in blood, some sliced in multiple places. The sight was horrible. The smell was worse.

Hayden's body shook the entire time, as they picked their way slowly across the battlefield. His eyes scanned back and forth, searching for any sign of Natalia.

The Butcher moved suddenly, pulling its arm away from him and wordlessly jumping off the tank. Hayden immediately leaned over the hatch, calling down to Jake. "Tell Chains to stop!"

The tank paused a moment later. Hayden jumped off, following the Butcher. He tried to keep himself calm, reminding himself the instruction he had given it, to search for a female with dark hair, was vague and would likely lead to a few false positives. Just because it had spotted someone matching the description didn't mean it was her.

The roid stepped heavily through the debris, not minding its feet as they came down on trife limbs, crushing them without hesitation. It came to a stop in front of a corpse with a large gash along the side, pointing down at it.

Hayden leaned over the woman. It wasn't Natalia. A Scrapper. She was seventeen at best. Maybe younger. What was she doing out here? Why had King sent her into this kind of danger?

Not that he was shocked. King didn't care who lived or died, as long as he got what he wanted.

The Butcher started back toward the tank. Hayden remained close to it, feeling safe under its protection.

He came to a stop again when he saw the coat.

It was beneath a trife, dirty and bloody, and hardly any of the white cloth was still white. The trife resting above it had a knife sticking out of its throat. Hayden leaned over it, a sudden panic washing through him, chilling him to the core. Ghost had been out here, in the middle of the trife. That confirmed Natalia had been part of the convoy that was attacked. The Courier was supposed to be protecting her.

Did that mean?

He stopped himself. It didn't mean she was dead. Ghost's coat was here, but his corpse wasn't. He had probably gotten away.

Hayden pulled the knife from the trife's neck, slipping it beneath the belt on his hip. He looked back at the tank, finding the Butcher had continued without him and was already climbing back on board.

He ran to catch up to it, noticing as he scaled the side of the vehicle that a small light had gone on at the base of the Butcher's skull.

He took the control transmitter from his pocket. A matching light had activated on it, too. He wasn't sure what it meant, but he had spent enough time around Natalia to guess.

Low battery.

The timing wasn't the best. Hayden climbed into the tank. Jake was up front with Chains, talking to her about something. They both looked back at him as he approached.

"I found Ghost's coat outside," he said. "And this." He showed them the knife.

"That's his, all right," Jake said. "He has them custom forged. No body?"

"No."

Jake looked relieved. "She's still out there, Sheriff."

"Pozz. I know. She has to be." He paused, looking at the

display. The cameras could see better in the fading light than he could. He noticed a structure up ahead. "Is that the bunker?"

"It must be," Chains said. "There's nothing else out here."

"Our Butcher's batteries are low. Do you think we could charge them in there?"

"Sheriff, we don't know how many Scrappers are inside," Jake said.

"Nope," Hayden replied. "And? What if Natalia's still in there? What if we can refuel this thing?"

Jake's face flushed. "Sorry. You're right. I'm with you."

"Chains?"

"You want to crash the Scrappers' party? I'm totally in."

"Good." Hayden took a few steps back, picking up the uniform they had removed from Commander Ales before they had thrown his corpse out into the wilderness. "I knew there was a reason we held onto this. It should fit you perfect, Jake."

"Are you thinking what I think you're thinking, Sheriff?" Jake said.

"I thought my holding up the uniform made that obvious. Do you have a better idea?"

"No. I can do it."

"Of course you can," Chains said. "We've got your back."

Jake reached for the clasps to his body armor. "Then let's go knock on that massive door."

40

As it turned out, they didn't have to knock.

The large door to the bunker started sliding open the moment the tank got close to it, offering them security within. Chains kept the vehicle in motion, rolling slowly toward the opening door, keeping her eyes on the displays and watching for signs of trouble.

Hayden didn't expect any. The Scrappers thought they were Scrappers. And why wouldn't they? Who else came driving up to the bunker in a tank?

"How do I look?" Jake asked, adjusting the sleeves on Ales' uniform. "I feel naked without the armor."

"You look fine," Hayden said. "Here's the transmitter." He handed the device to the Borger. "You know what to do."

Jake nodded. They had gone over the plan on the way.

The tank entered the garage. Hayden scanned it on the displays, searching for the car that had taken Natalia away. There were only three other vehicles in the bunker with them. A large truck and two of the big-wheeled Enforcer cars. His heart sank a little at the sight. Based on the configuration, it was unlikely Natalia was still here. Not that he had really expected she would be. They were at least three days behind the convoy.

A pair of Scrappers moved out in front of the cameras, waving their arms to direct the vehicle. The garage wasn't large, especially for a tank, and the fit was relatively tight. They guided Chains forward and then to the left, parking her between the truck and one of the cars, facing the wall.

"I don't know how to put this thing in reverse," Chains said when they came to a stop.

"I'm sure you'll figure it out when the time comes," Hayden replied. "Jake, you're up."

"Wish me luck," Jake said, putting his hands on the ladder leading out.

"Good luck," Chains said, smiling and giving him a thumbs up.

"Good luck," Hayden said. "I know you can do it."

Jake started climbing, opening the hatch and then vanishing through it.

"I'm Commander Jackson," Jake said, his voice quaking slightly. "Who's in charge here?"

"I am," one of the Scrappers said. "Sergeant Nil." He paused. "We weren't expecting anyone tonight, Commander. What happened to the rest of your convoy?"

"What do you think happened to my face, Sergeant?" Jake said. "We were assaulted on the way up from Haven. King ordered us north to Ports to reinforce the base, on account of the increased trife activity."

"Your face got bruised inside a tank?" the Sergeant said. "You must be the clumsiest Commander in the grepping army." He started to laugh. Hayden could hear other Scrappers laughing with him.

Hayden winced. This was the part where Jake should draw a gun on the Sergeant, and chew him out keep him in line.

"Are you questioning me, Sergeant?" Jake shouted. It didn't come off as very commanding.

"I don't like the way this is going," Chains said. "Your Deputy is too nice for this."

"Come on, Jake," Hayden said.

"No, sir," the Sergeant replied. "I understand completely if you don't want to admit you hit your face on a seat. Or maybe your girl beats you."

The Scrappers laughed harder.

"You will respect me," Jake said. "Or you'll be dinner tonight."

"Is that a threat?" Sergeant Nil said. "Because from where I'm standing, there are six of us and one of you."

"I'm a Commander in the Scrapper Militia. You'll respect me because I outrank you."

"Respect is earned, Commander. Maybe where you're posted, your kiddies know you. But we don't know you for shit. Hell, you aren't even supposed to be here. You could be King's royal ass-wiper for all we know."

There was a long silence. Jake had no idea what to do.

"You heard him, Sheriff," Chains said. "There are only six of them."

Hayden reached to his left, picking up one of the USMC rifles they had claimed. "I'll take care of it."

"King sent me north to Ports," Jake said. "I stopped here to refuel the tank and recharge my Butcher. Will you accommodate me, or do I have to kill you?"

The Scrappers stopped laughing. Hayden reached the ladder and started to climb. He could sense the sudden tension in the air.

"Why don't you come down here, and kill me?" the Sergeant said.

Jake glanced down, into the hatch. He saw Hayden coming up. He shook his head. He didn't want help with this.

"Fine," he said, hopping down from the tank. "You ever duel before, Sergeant?"

The Scrappers laughed.

"Hell yeah," Nil said. "That what you want, Commander? Because if you want to die, that's fine by me."

"Shut up and make some space," Jake said.

"Sheriff," Chains said, coming up behind Hayden. "You can't let him do this. The Scrappers duel each other all the grepping time, and if you're still here, it means you've never lost."

"He saw me coming," Hayden said. "It was his choice. He's a good shot."

"That won't mean anything if he isn't a quick draw."

Hayden knew it, but what was he supposed to do? Jake knew he was there. He had declined the help.

"He feels like he has something to prove," Chains said. "After Wiz attacked us. After he got knocked out. He's a nice guy, Sheriff. This place doesn't have enough nice guys."

"I can't interfere," Hayden said. "It's dishonest. He made the challenge; he has to live with the consequences."

He didn't like it, but he knew how it worked from the movies stored on the PASS.

That didn't stop him from climbing further up the ladder and peeking out over the top, to where Jake was positioning himself ahead of the garage door.

Nil was at the other end. He was a younger man, dressed in Scrapper robes and thick, brown fatigues. His head was bald, his hair replaced by a large eagle tattoo that covered his entire crown. He stared down at Jake with malice, his hand hovering over the revolver at his hip.

One of the Scrappers moved out to the side, closer to the tank. The others were arranged nearby, away from the line of fire. Every one of them looked amused, certain that Nil was going to come away victorious.

The two men faced one another. Jake's hand shifted, closer to his gun. He had stuck with a revolver even after they had taken the Marine weapons from the Pilgrim, more comfortable and more experienced with the vagaries of the less precisely crafted firearms.

Each second hung in the air, tense and thick. The Scrapper near the tank turned and started to climb, heading for the hatch. Hayden saw him coming, quickly lowering the rifle and squeezing his mechanical hand into a fist. The claws sprung out, and he waited just below the line of sight.

Whatever the Scrapper was doing, he had taken away Hayden's ability to see the outcome of the fight.

Each heartbeat felt like an eternity. Each tick a lifetime. Everything slowed down. The Scrapper's arm came over the hatch, pointing down, gun in hand. His head appeared after, looking in for a target. He saw Hayden looking back at him, and his eyes grew in surprise. He turned his head, as though to warn the others, or to say something to someone. Hayden lunged up toward him, leading with his mechanical hand.

Outside the tank, a shot was fired.

Hayden held the ladder with his free hand, plunging the claws into the Scrapper's chest, pushing upward and knocking the man back. The momentum carried his body off the claws and sent him rolling down the side of the vehicle.

Somebody shouted.

Hayden kept climbing, desperate to see the outcome of the duel. Desperate to find Jake still standing. He turned his head as he cleared the hatch and then covered his face with his metal hand as the bullets started to come, forcing him to duck back down.

Time regained itself.

"Should I find reverse?" Chains shouted.

"Did you see what happened?" Hayden asked.

"No. The cameras back there aren't working, remember?"

"Damn it." He grabbed the rifle again. "Wait here."

"Sheriff, you can't go-"

He didn't hear her. He scrambled out of the tank, rolling to the opposite side as bullets pinged off the metal around him, more than one putting a hole in his coat and striking the armor beneath it.

He set the weapon on the metal, sweeping the display across the scene. He didn't wait to find a specific target. As soon as a body was visible that wasn't Jake, he squeezed the trigger, sending multiple rounds into it.

Three Scrappers fell before the others tried to run, heading for a doorway he imagined led deeper into the base. He didn't want to cut them down with their backs to him. He had a sense of what was right that was hard to deny. But if they got inside, could they call for help? Could they better arm and armor themselves? Did they have a Butcher of their own?

He couldn't risk it.

He adjusted his aim, shooting at their backs, knocking them down one by one.

The last one made it to the door. He slammed his shoulder into it, shoving it open, desperate to escape.

He looked back as he leaned against the frame, adjusting his path to take him down the steps.

Hayden painted the target.

His whole body froze.

The face beneath the reticle was Sergeant Nil's.

The cold sting of the truth slammed him in the gut.

It didn't stop him from pulling the trigger.

41

THE RIFLE CLICKED, BUT DIDN'T FIRE. SERGEANT NIL GLARED up at where he was perched, a smirk appearing on his scarred face before he slammed the stairwell door closed behind him and locked it into place.

Hayden stared at the spot for a few seconds, trying the rifle a few more times. It was empty. Damn it.

He got to his feet, jumping off the tank and rushing where Jake was lying on the ground. He didn't see any blood. Not right away.

He fell to his knees when he reached the Borger. His face was tight. His stomach clenched.

Jake had a single, perfectly aimed hole in his forehead and only a trickle of blood coming out of it. His eyes were open, and they shifted back and forth, trying to focus but unable to do so. His chest rose and fell ever so gently, proving he was still alive.

If you could call it that.

"Jake, can you hear me?" Hayden said. "Jake."

He heard footsteps rushing his way, and he turned his head as Chains met him there.

"Oh. Geez. Oh. Sheriff. Grepping hell."

She knelt beside him, putting a soft hand on Jake's face. His head turned slightly, pressing harder into it. She looked over at Hayden.

"What are we going to do?"

Jake's eyes turned back toward him, showing he understood their words.

"Medical in Metro can't fix anything like this," Hayden said sadly. "Is there any medicine out here that can?"

"Not that I've ever heard of," Chains said, tears in her eyes. "This sucks."

Hayden looked down at Jake. He knew what had to be done. There wasn't another option. "Jake." He paused. "Can you blink?"

The eyes stared up at him. They didn't blink.

"I'll make it quick, okay? You won't feel anything. I just. I just want to say thank you. For saving my life. For giving me a chance to find Natalia. For giving me this." He held up his arm. "You were a good man, Jake. You and your father. I'll make things right for you. The way they should have been. You and your Dad."

Jake's eyes didn't move. The only reason Hayden knew he was still alive was the light pulsing in his neck.

Chains dropped down, putting her face over Jake's. She lowered it until her lips were pressing against his.

Hayden used the distraction, putting the replacement hand on the side of Jake's head. He breathed in, and then contracted the hand, the motion sending the blades shooting out through the bone and into the brain.

Chains sat up, looking at him. A tear trickled down his cheek.

"Grepping bastards," she said.

Hayden nodded in agreement, withdrawing the blades from Jake's head. "He should have let me handle it," he said softly. He dug into Jake's pockets, withdrawing the Butcher's transmitter. He held it out to Chains. "Get the Butcher charged, and see about refueling the tank."

She took the transmitter, and he stood up.

"What are you going to do?" she asked.

"Finish cleaning house," he replied.

He slid the empty magazine out of his rifle, taking a fresh one from the body armor and locking it in.

"I should come with you," Chains said.

"No. I've got it. Stay here."

"Sheriff-" she started to say.

"Stay here," Hayden repeated. "Get the Butcher charging and the tank refueled. Please."

Chains nodded somberly. She put her hand over Jake's eyes, pushing them closed. Then she jumped to her feet, looking around the garage for the things she needed.

Hayden walked over to the metal door. He pushed against it, finding it locked.

"Chains," he shouted.

She stopped and looked at him.

"Get the transmitter. I need some help with the door."

She returned to Jake's body, taking the Butcher's control device from his pocket. A moment later, the roid started to move, climbing off the tank and approaching Hayden.

He stepped aside, letting the machine do its work. It put its hands on the door, flexed its arms, and pushed.

The door bent inward, held in place by a metal bar across the back. It didn't survive the pressure long, the bolts in its anchors giving way, breaking free of the frame and allowing the door to be torn off the hinges and thrown back and into the wall. It made a loud crack as it hit that echoed down the stairwell.

Hayden ducked around the Butcher, putting the rifle to his eyes and sweeping the stairs. He started to descend.

There was only one level down. Hayden paused there, finding this door was barred as well, the Scrappers doing their best to keep him out of the base. Were they so afraid of him? Then why had they been so belligerent with Jake? He didn't understand these people or the decisions they made. There was no reason for it.

He backed away from the door, moving to the first platform on the steps and shifting his finger to the secondary trigger. The explosion would either collapse the stairwell or remove the door. He was fine with either outcome. They probably didn't have another way out.

He squeezed the trigger. The metal ball thunked out of the barrel, hitting the door and sticking to it. He retreated around the corner, pressing back against the wall. The explosive detonated, shaking the entire structure and sending dust and mortar down on his head. He heard a scream from inside the door. A guard?

He counted to five and then turned the corner again. There was so much dust it was hard to see, but it was clear the stairwell hadn't collapsed. The door was twisted and bent, hanging almost sideways, the metal behind it blown away. A soldier was on the ground, a piece of shrapnel through his chest.

Hayden peered through the opening with the rifle. The corridor was clear. He slipped past the door and into the base. The wall beside him had the USSF logo on it, nearly two meters in diameter.

He kept walking along the corridor, pausing at each doorway, tapping the door with his rifle, then pushing it open, then sweeping it for signs of the enemy. As he cleared the second door, he heard footsteps coming toward him from an adjacent hallway. He moved the rifle to the back of the body armor, drawing a USMC pistol from his hip.

The Scrappers stopped at the corner, out of sight. He

heard a tick, and then a firebomb came from the side, bouncing off the wall and rolling toward him.

He ran forward, hopping over the device and making it to the corner, letting his body slam into the wall to stop his momentum, turned to face the enemy.

They were surprised by the maneuver, left having to adjust their aim. He fired into them, one round after another.

The firebomb went off, a soft detonation that spread flame across the hallway. Hayden threw himself from the wall, into the Scrappers, closing his replacement fist and extending the claws. He slashed one of them in the face, taking a round in the gut from another. It didn't pierce the armor, and he turned the pistol and fired, hitting the soldier in the throat.

It was over as quickly as it started. Four dead Scrappers sat at Hayden's feet. He breathed heavily, his adrenaline pumping, his anger and frustration coming out in his assault.

Sergeant Nil wasn't among them. Where the hell had he gone?

He stepped over the dead, continuing down the corridor. He reached a larger door to his right. It was open and led into a dining area. Old metal tables and chairs were arranged inside, and the smell of meat wafted out from the back. What kind of meat?

He noticed a dark spot behind a counter. Black, with a pale star near the front.

He stepped into the mess.

"Sergeant Nil," he growled. "You didn't duck low enough."

The Sergeant didn't move.

"Are you the only one left here, Sergeant?" Hayden asked. "Not much of a defense."

Nil rose slowly. His hands were down, hidden by the counter.

"Who are you?" the Sergeant asked.

"Sheriff Duke," Hayden replied. "I'm looking for my wife. She was here with Ghost. Two, three days ago."

"You're the Insider?" he said. "You're supposed to be grepping dead."

"I'm not," Hayden said.

"Your wife is gone, Sheriff," Nil said. "Ghost took her to Ports. Just the two of them." He raised his head, clearing the counter. He was smiling. "Just the two of them," he repeated. "Ghost has a way with the women. Shit, Ghost has a way with everybody. And anyone he doesn't have a way with always seems to wind up dead." He was talking, but Hayden could tell his hands were moving slightly, edging closer to his gun. "You should thank him when you see him. Oversergeant Grimly was going to do your wife hard. Ghost killed him for it. She's his property now."

Hayden's eyes stayed fixed on the soldier. He was trying to get under his skin. Distract him. Break his concentration. He knew why.

"Three days," Nil said. "Plenty long enough for him to seduce her and get into her pants. One way or another. Sorry, Insider. Must be rough to get introduced to the real Earth like this."

"I'm learning to adjust," Hayden said, lowering his gun. "Why don't you come out into the open? You want to take a shot at me? You can do it there."

Nil nodded. "Sure. Have it your way, Sheriff."

He started to move.

It all happened in a split second. It wasn't Nil's feet that were moving. It was his arm. His gun arm. Hayden raised his pistol again, not slowing the vertical momentum as he pulled the trigger. Nil's weapon came level at the same time the bullet hit him, right between the eyes. The force of it knocked his aim off when what was left of his nervous system managed to send a signal to his finger to take the shot. His round went high, hitting the ceiling half a dozen meters in front of Hayden.

Then he collapsed behind the counter.

Hayden held his pistol in front of his face for a moment, making sure the Scrapper didn't get back up. When he didn't, he lowered it back beneath his coat, snapping it to the armor there. He turned around, walking out of the mess.

He moved down the hall, less cautious but still on alert. He made his way through the compound, checking the rooms as he passed them. He came to a small room with four bunks in it. The bottom bunk was unmade. He stared at it a moment and then stepped in, leaning down over it and lifting a single long strand of dark hair. Natalia's hair. He would know it anywhere. He held it tight before tucking it into the pocket of his coat.

He left the room and continued down the hall. He came to the last door, opening it and entering. This room was large and well appointed. A king-sized bed, nightstands. A bottle of wine was on the dresser along with a pair of glasses. He smelled blood. He walked through it, to the bathroom in the back. He looked into the shower there, finding more of Natalia's hair stuck to the drain.

He exited the bathroom, crossing to a closet and swinging it open. Inside were the best quality clothes he had seen, in the form of a trio of softly spun suits. Dark suits, not white like Ghost preferred to wear. Did these belong to King? A wide-brimmed hat sat on a shelf above the suits. He reached up and grabbed it, taking it down and placing it on his head. The fit was a little snug, but he liked the idea of taking it from the Despot.

He spent a few more minutes searching the room, looking for anything he could use. He found an old copy of a Bible in the nightstand drawer, but little else.

He abandoned the room, finishing his sweep of the

compound. There were no more Scrappers inside. There were no other signs of Natalia, either. He discovered the large generator running the place, and later a small communications station. He could hear the Scrappers chattering to one another over what he guessed was a series of longer-range transceivers, but after thirty minutes none of them mentioned Ports or Ghost or Natalia or King, and he lost interest.

He headed out of the facility, climbing the stairs back to the garage. Jake's body was still where he had left it. Chains was off to the side, sitting on the tank. The Butcher was connected to the wall by a thick wire, a flashing light indicating it was receiving power.

"We'll be ready to go in two hours, Sheriff," she said.

"Did you find fuel for the tank?"

"I found fuel. It smelled the same, so I hope it was for the tank. I guess we'll find out."

"You don't have to come with me," Hayden said. "You see what happens to the people who do. I told Jake the same thing. He wouldn't listen."

"I'm not going to listen, either, Sheriff," Chains said. "You'd be alone without me, now. I've been on my own out there. I know what it's like. But I was alone because I couldn't trust anyone. I trust you. I think you're a little crazy in the head, but I trust you."

"I'm going to get you killed."

"If you plan to do what's right, you're going to get a lot of people killed. But they're going to die willingly because they're doing what's right. That's how Jake died. That's how I'll die, too." She paused and then allowed herself a small smile. "Besides, do you have any idea how to drive a tank?"

"No." He smiled back at her. "Neither do you. You can't even put it in reverse."

She wiggled her fingers at him.

"What does that mean?" he asked.

"Nothing pleasant," she replied. "But in this case, it's supposed to be endearing."

"Then I'll take it that way." He turned his head back to Jake, another pang of guilt causing him to shiver. "We have two hours. We should take care of his body. On the Pilgrim, the corpses are sent to Medical for processing. They get broken down and reused."

"Reused?"

"It sounds awful. It isn't as bad as it sounds. From the videos I saw, you used to bury the dead."

"We still do, when we can."

"Then we'll find something to dig with and bring him outside."

"You want to go outside? What about the trife?"

"We won't be far, and we can call that if we need to." He pointed to the Butcher. "I wish I could bring him back to his farm. This will have to do."

"It's probably a better burial than he would have gotten otherwise," Chains said. She paused a moment. "Sheriff?"

"What is it, Chains?" he asked.

"Casey," she said. "My name is Casey."

"Casey? That's a pretty name."

She blushed slightly beneath the grime. "Thank you. I can't stand hearing it from other people. They've always used it to hurt me. That's why I go by Chains. I know you won't hurt me. You can call me that if you want."

He stared at her a moment. She was putting her faith in him. Was she going to die like all of the rest?

"Okay, Casey," he said. "I'll do my best not to let you down."

"I know. Nice hat, by the way."

42

NATALIA LEANED BACK IN HER CHAIR. THE GLOW OF THE mainframe terminal flared out ahead of her, revealing the logo of a blue eagle with a white star in its grip, against a red background. A small box sat beneath the logo, with simple instructions:

ENTER PASSWORD.

Three days had passed since Ghost had broken her spirit. Three days that were both the best and worst since Hayden's death. Three days spent working on the problem Ghost had presented to her: a room full of computers that would not start.

She used all of her waking hours on the problem. Eighteen each day. It was better than being in her room, naked and alone, left to remember Hayden, left to mourn with no way to end her own life. They took everything from her. They even drained the water from the toilet, so she wouldn't be able to drown herself.

She had examined all of the conduits. She had tested the connections. She went over wiring diagrams and tried to isolate everything. She traced the problem back to a single large box at the front-end of the room. All of the power flowed through it, and at first, it seemed operational. Then she realized there was a thermostat sending a signal out to another device located below the servers, and that equipment wasn't responding. It had taken time to lift up the grated floor of the room, to find the small access hatch and descend into its bowels. She discovered the main control board had burned out. She removed it and brought it back to Ghost with simple instructions:

"Find something that looks like this and bring it back here."

He had looked at her, a small smirk appearing on his face. Was he impressed with her work? Amused by how agreeable she had become? Uncertain of her motives or if she was telling the truth?

Regardless, he thanked her, took the board, and disappeared.

He returned early the next morning while she was asleep. He was dirty and sweaty, and he had stitched a cut above his left eye. He also had a matching board in hand.

"We found two of them," he said. "In case this one is also damaged."

He didn't tell her she had to rise to fix it immediately. She decided she would, getting up and making a quick trip to the bathroom before rejoining him in the hallway, where he returned her clothes.

He didn't usually stay with her when she worked. He usually had Bones come down to keep an eye on her. The woman hovered near her any time she was outside of her room. Bones didn't speak to Natalia, even when Natalia tried to speak to Bones. The soldier kept her distance but was always alert, making sure she was earning Ghost's trust, instead of betraying it.

This time, he escorted her from her room personally.

There was nobody else in the server room when they arrived. She turned the lights on; a series of overhead diodes that provided more than ample illumination to the space. She pointed to a rolling cart with dozens of tools organized on it.

"I'll need that," she said.

Ghost looked tired, but he did as she said, retrieving the tools and wheeling them to the open part of the floor. She climbed down into it before holding up her hand.

"The board," she said.

He passed it down to her.

"I also need a screwdriver."

He handed it down, too.

She screwed the board back into place.

"Soldering gun," she said, holding her hand up.

He didn't react right away.

"Ghost, soldering gun," she repeated, looking up at him.

He was staring into space, distracted by a thought. He looked bothered. Concerned.

About what?

"Chuck," she said loudly, using his name to break him out of his trance.

His eyes drifted toward her. They bore into her in a way that made her shake.

"Soldering gun," she said again, steeling herself against the gaze.

He passed the tool down to her, moving slowly.

"Is there something you want to tell me?" she said.

"No," he replied. "Keep working."

She took the gun, using it to reconnect the thermostat wires to the new control board. She made a few other adjustments and then climbed back up.

He was still there, looking at her intently. She could tell he was worried about something. Worried enough that he was struggling to hide it.

"Let's see what we've got," she said, leaving him there while she made her way back to the main power switch.

She opened the face and flipped the switch. A series of lights began to flip to green on the box itself, and the ground started to rumble beneath her feet. Ghost looked at the floor, surprised by the sudden vibration, which calmed a moment later. Then a blast of cool air began to rise from one side of the vented ground, while a second fan at the other end pulled the warmer air in.

The servers, all two hundred of them, showed sudden signs of life.

That was last night. Today, it seemed ironic to her that she had repaired the HVAC unit beneath the floor and gotten the servers up and running again, only to be stymied by something as simple as a series of letters, numbers, and symbols. Of course, she had seen an interface like this plenty of times before. This software was more up to date than the operating system that helped manage the critical systems on the Pilgrim, but at its heart it was essentially the same thing.

Then again, she had never needed to guess the password to the MEDS; the Metro Engineering Diagnostics Service. She had the administrator codes etched into her brain, and they were the first thing she tried here, unsurprised when they didn't take.

Ghost had asked her how they could bypass the screen. They had come across the security before, and been equally stumped about working around it. He was impatient when he asked, whatever was bothering him lingering in everything he said and did.

She had explained some of the potential methods to him. She had described brute force methods, dictionary-based algorithms, and rainbow table vectors as simply as she could. He had stared back at her like she was speaking another language, and in a sense she was. Then she told him the password was probably written down somewhere or hiding in plain sight. If they had found anything in the rooms of the scientists, that was a good place to start.

He had disappeared immediately after.

He returned now. She noticed he had forsaken his usual white suit for light body armor similar to hers. Even when they had been on the road here, he hadn't been concerned enough about his safety to use extra protection. Why was he wearing it now?

He ignored her questioning glance at the sight of the armor, dropping a thick notebook on the flat surface in front of her.

"This belonged to the head of the facility," he said.

"Where did you get it?" she asked.

"It was locked in King's safe. I would have been back sooner, but I had to get the password from him."

"I thought you don't have long-range communications?"

"We don't from the road," he replied. "But the old military installations all have emergency radio transmission systems, including this one. I've been in contact with King since we arrived. He's pleased with the work you've been doing for us. We're both pleased you decided to cooperate in the end."

"You taught me a lesson, and I've always been a quick learner. My husband is dead. There's no reason for me to keep pretending like I can do anything about it. I can be a prisoner, or I can be a trusted asset, but you're going to use me either way. I'd rather have some freedom, given a choice."

She kept her eyes locked on Ghost the entire time. She noticed him flinch slightly when she mentioned Hayden.

What did that mean?

"I'm glad you're starting to see things my way. As I said, trust is earned, and you have a long way to go beyond simply saying the words I want to hear."

"I know," Natalia replied. "I'll prove myself to you. I will."

She put her hand on the notebook. "There's no guarantee what you're looking for is in here."

"I know if it is, you'll find it. I'm not willing to accept the scientists who worked here wouldn't leave some means for future generations to access what they knew, even if as you say, they hid those clues in plain sight. They had to know the information stored here could be valuable to someone, someday. That notebook was down here when we arrived. It wasn't taken. It wasn't destroyed. There has to be a reason for that."

"It will take some time," she said.

"You have three hours," Ghost replied. "No more."

The statement caught her off-guard. "What? Why the sudden rush?"

He stared at her for a moment before speaking, deciding how much to say.

"We went to the north side of the city looking for your control boards. We saw trife gathering on the other side of the river, in numbers greater than anything I've ever seen. They were coming out of the wilderness in what seemed like an endless tide. I think they may be preparing an attack."

Natalia felt a sudden chill at the news. That must be what had been bothering him earlier, and the reason he was wearing the armor now.

"On Ports?"

"And possibly the other cities to the south."

"Aren't we safe down here?"

"We have been, but it could be they're tired of us having this foothold. Or maybe the energy from the generators will draw them in, and I don't know if the defenses will hold against such large numbers. If we lose power, we lose the servers. We may never be able to recover them. Even if they leave the facility alone, even if they continue south to

Sanisco, we could wind up trapped here, too far behind their lines to get back out. I just don't know."

"Have the trife ever acted like this before?" she asked.

"Not that I've seen, but they're in a constant state of evolution. These trife are larger, like the ones we saw near the bunker. Stronger. More powerful. And there are thousands of them. We need the information on those data stores, now more than ever. The trife were delivered here to wipe us out. Only the appearance of the goliaths saved us from extinction. But what if the goliaths can't stop this threat? If there are weapons caches out there, as we suspect, we need to know where they are. We need to prepare."

She looked at the computer screen, and then at the notebook. She picked it up, opening the first page and quickly scanning it. It was a journal. A handwritten journal.

"There's nothing you can do for me here," she said. "Leave me in peace and let me work. I'll send word through Bones when I have something."

"Natalia," Ghost said. "I want to be able to trust you. Now more than ever. This is more than our lives at stake. I know you care about the people you call innocents. If the trife overwhelm us, they'll die, too."

"You can trust me," Natalia said. "I've made my decision. I've made my peace. I'm yours."

She stared up into his eyes. They locked on one another. Then he nodded. "Hurry."

He left the room. She returned her attention to the journal. If the password were hiding in there, she would find it. She meant it when she told Ghost she was his.

It was a hell of a lot better than any of the alternatives.

43

"That's it," Casey said, pointing at the broken skyline of a city visible through the tank's displays. "Ports."

Hayden swallowed the mix of fear and excitement that caused his heart to pulse. That was where Ghost had brought Natalia, and he had no reason to believe she wasn't still there.

They had taken a direct line from the bunker toward the city, after finalizing the refuel and recharge, burying Jake, and getting back on the road. It was early morning now, the sun just starting to rise to their right, peeking out over the hills. They had made good time, keeping an even speed across the landscape and rolling over anything that would have slowed a lesser vehicle down. They hadn't passed anything of note on the way. No cars. No horses. No trife. The rust-hued landscape had been barren of life, silent and dead.

"How do we find the Scrapper's base?" Hayden asked, his eyes scanning the skyline.

So much destruction. So much death. And yet instead of banding together, humankind had continued to fracture. It was so senseless.

"We'll know we're close when they start shooting at us," she replied.

"If they know we're coming."

"Ales should have delivered us to Sanisco hours ago, Sheriff. You can bet King's gotten the word out that he's missing. And tanks aren't exactly common out here."

"Good point. When we get there, I go in with the Butcher, and you stay in here."

"Sheriff," Casey started to argue.

"No. I need you to distract them while I look for Natalia." He pulled a transceiver from his pocket. "How much range do these have?"

"A couple of miles in ideal circumstances. But they're useless once you go underground."

"We'll stay in touch as long as we can." He put his hand on her shoulder. She glanced up at him. "Promise me you'll stay in the tank. I don't want to lose another Deputy."

She nodded. "Okay, but if you need me, I'll come running. You're the closest thing to a friend I've ever had out here."

"You are a friend, Casey. That's why I don't want you to get hurt."

She put her hand on his for a moment before returning it to the tank's controls.

Another hour passed before they entered the city in earnest. The tank rolled through deserted streets, crushing rubble beneath its treads as it navigated around building after building that had been torn apart either during the war or after it. They didn't see any signs of the Scrappers. They didn't encounter any trife, either. After covering what felt like half of the city, Hayden started to wonder if they had really made it to Ports, or if the Scrappers didn't have a base here after all.

"I don't know what to say, Sheriff," Casey said, her eyes focused on the camera displays, searching for signs of activity. "I would have at least expected some trife to be watching us. There's nothing."

Hayden didn't like it, and he damn well didn't trust it. He needed to be prepared.

He retreated to the back of the tank, grabbing the magazines and rifle he had laid aside and loading up his armor. He checked his pistol and extended and retracted the metal hand's claws to ensure it was all functioning properly. As he did, his eyes fell on Jake's bag, still sitting off to the side in the vehicle. The only way he could make up for the loss of the Borger was to find Natalia, save her, and then move on to helping the rest of the people under King's thumb. He knew his wife would understand. She wouldn't have it any other way.

Once he was done, he picked up the transceiver and pressed the button on the side. "Chains, can you hear me?" he said, using her nickname. The radios weren't private. If anyone else were on the same frequency, they would be overheard.

"I hear you," she replied. "It's working."

"I'm going to head up top and take a quick look around. Maybe get a better perspective on things."

"Pozz that. Be careful."

Hayden moved to the ladder, grabbing the hat he had taken from King before scaling it and opening the hatch. He climbed out beside the Butcher, putting the hat on his head. He looked ahead, toward a building that was mostly intact, save for the windows. They had all been broken out, the interior gutted of anything of value, leaving the other side of the city visible through it. He couldn't see much through the thin slivers of empty panes. It looked as though there was a body of water separating one part of the city from the other, with a rusted old bridge connecting the two banks. The far end was strangely darker, cast in an odd, deep shadow.

"I see a river," he said through the transceiver. "Do you think the base is on the other side?"

"I have no idea, Sheriff. We're looking for a needle in a haystack, I guess. I thought it would be easier."

"Me, too. Turn left up ahead, and then head west for a few blocks before turning north again. I want to get down toward the bridge."

"Pozz."

Hayden pocketed the transceiver and headed back to the inside of the tank, closing it and rejoining Casey on the inside. She steered the tank over a few blocks and then turned it back north. The supports for the bridge were visible ahead, rusted and ugly.

"I don't know if it will support this thing," Casey said.

"We're not going to risk it. I may need to go on foot."

"That's not a good idea."

"We may not have a choice."

"I'm not letting you go out there alone."

"I told you, I have the Butcher."

She glared at him but didn't argue. He had a feeling if it came to it, she would follow him anyway.

The tank crested a hill, giving them a good view of the bridge below and the other side of the city. Hayden's eyes tracked the shadows as they shifted in the streets, moving in a way that betrayed their true nature.

His heart started thumping at the same time a chill worked its way across his spine. Those weren't shadows thrown by the rising sun. They were trife. Thousands of them. They milled around one another in silence, as though they were waiting for something.

"Chains, we need to back off," he said.

"What do you see?" she asked.

"Hell."

The tank groaned as she shifted the gears, reversing the

treads. They started rolling backward. Hayden watched the trife. Why were they waiting there? What were they waiting for?

A sudden hum started rising within their ranks. A solid, steady, throaty hiss. The mass began to vanish beneath the rise, the pitch of their calls intensifying.

All at once, they started to move, rushing forward toward the bridge, hundreds of the creatures thundering ahead. They poured onto it, dashed over it, at least for a few seconds.

The bridge was almost out of Hayden's sight when it exploded.

He didn't know what caused the detonation. One second it was there. The next, it was gone, a ball of fire engulfing it, trife thrown all around it.

When the smoke cleared a few seconds later, the bridge was gone.

"Chains, stop," Hayden said, still watching.

The tank ground to a halt. He moved forward on the turret to get a better view. The trife were still humming, but now hundreds of them from the back were lifting into the sky on large wings, sweeping forward and picking up the others ahead of them to carry them across the chasm.

He had never seen two groups of different trife work together before. On the Pilgrim, they had killed one another.

Was this a new development?

Either way, the trife were coming. If Natalia was here, he didn't have long to find her before this whole place was overcome.

44

"Time is almost up," Ghost said, sweeping into the room.

Natalia looked over at him, the first time she had looked anywhere but at the journal or the terminal display in three hours.

"I've almost got it," she said.

She had tried so many combinations already. The next one had to be the right one. She looked away, typing something else into the password box. Once again, it failed.

"The trife are on the move. We have twenty minutes before they block our escape."

"I'll get it," she insisted. "Just give me a few more minutes."

"Bones, go," Ghost said. "Help the others. I'll take care of her."

Bones didn't argue. She hurried from the room, heading for the lift.

Natalia tried another password. It didn't work. She flipped the page in the journal. Damn it. She almost had it.

A click behind her head distracted her for a moment.

"You have two minutes," Ghost said, putting the muzzle of the revolver against her skull. "And then you die."

"Damn it, Ghost," she replied. "The journal is a key. A cryptographic key. The first letter of each entry is a part of the cipher. I think it's a polyalphabetic, but that's not enough. There may be extra characters."

He reached around her, slamming the journal closed, sticking his face in hers.

"Bullshit," he said. "You're stalling. You've been stalling. I trusted you."

Natalia shook her head. "I'm not. You can trust me, I swear. It should be right. I don't-"

Her eyes fell on the back of the notebook. She could have kicked herself for missing it. An inscription. The first word was "Thank." The first letter was "T."

She reached past Ghost, entering the last letter, transformed to N by the cipher.

The display changed. She was in.

"There," she said, turning to him. "I told you-"

She didn't get to finish the sentence. She felt a heavy smack against the side of her head. She saw the world falling away in front of her.

Everything went dark.

45

Hayden jumped back into the tank, pulling the hatch closed behind him. He turned the manual lock, sealing it in place, before digging the Butcher's transceiver out of his pocket.

"Stay on the tank," he ordered it. "Protect the tank."

The transceiver beeped twice. That was the only acknowledgment he would receive.

"Geez," Casey said, up at the front of the tank. "I've never seen them work together like that. And I've never seen so many."

Hayden hurried to the front of the vehicle, watching the display. The trife were on the move, the wingless demons being carried over the river by the winged creatures. Scrappers had appeared on the buildings nearby, firing down at the aliens, round after round pouring into the front lines. He hadn't seen where they had come from. He hadn't realized they were hiding around them the entire time, watching the trife and waiting for the assault. They were too concerned with that enemy to worry about him.

Hundreds of the creatures were already across, charging

up the street toward the tank. They hissed to one another, assembling in patterns and leaving a wide berth around the vehicle, clearly aware of its destructive power.

What would have been its destructive power anyway, if they had any shells for the massive cannon mounted on top.

"What the hell should we do?" Casey asked, her hands on the tank's controls, ready to move.

"Nothing," Hayden decided. "Let them go past. We don't know where the Scrapper base is. Maybe they do."

"Are you sure?"

"No, but do you have a better idea?"

The first line of trife made it to the tank. Some of them tried to climb onto it, and they heard the thunking of the Butcher's feet on top of them, moving to intercept. Those creatures appeared on the display a moment later, broken and bent, thrown down and into the others.

The demons streamed by, going around them, breaking for the Scrapper positions. They heard a soft rumble further back, and then a car came into view behind them, a gun mounted in its rear. The Scrapper guiding it aimed it their direction, spinning it up and sending round after round zipping through the air, tearing a line of trife to pieces, the slugs pinging off the back of their armored vehicle. It only remained for a few seconds before lurching away, the mass of creatures closing in.

"Grepping gatling gun," Casey said. "Damn."

"Turn us around," Hayden said. "We can't let them get too far ahead. We don't want them to overwhelm the base. They'll kill Nat."

"Pozz that," Casey said, adjusting the tank's controls, getting it to rotate on one tread.

It started to spin back around, drawing the attention of the trife. More of them started climbing onto the turret, challenging the Butcher. Creature after creature was thrown loose, but there were so many it didn't matter. For every one the machine killed, three more took its place.

"Sheriff, I don't like this," Casey said, looking worried.

Hayden didn't blame her. The density of trife was increasing as more and more of them reached the other side of the river.

"We have to find Natalia," he replied. "Nothing else matters."

The tank rumbled down the street, dozens of trife climbing it, the Butcher standing in the center and defeating all comers. They hung from its heavy frame, clawing at its metal form, trying to find a weak spot or tug it away from the vehicle. They reached the corner, the armor pinging as rounds from Scrapper guns went past charging trife and into the sides.

"Turn that way," Hayden said, pointing Casey toward the Scrappers.

The tank started to turn, the adjustment sending them careering past the road and slamming into the corner of an old building. It caused the tank to shudder, giving it just the jolt the demons needed to finally dislodge the Butcher. The entire vehicle shook as the roid fell off it, crashing to the ground with the creatures piling on top of it.

"Shit!" Casey shouted, getting the tank back under control. "Sorry."

"Forget it," Hayden said. "Keep moving."

The trife were ahead of them, rushing toward the Scrappers. They turned and ran into an alley. A moment later, their car burst out from between the wreckage of two buildings, barely avoiding the trife as it spun and headed down the street.

It passed a cross street, turning left ahead. A second car pulled out in front of it, the one with the gatling gun. Two gatling guns. They both swiveled toward the tide of trife and the tank riding within the wave, the gunners opening fire. Bullets hit the armored exterior once more, along with pieces of trife as they were torn to shreds by the rounds. A hundred creatures died within seconds.

It was nowhere near enough.

The gunners fell into the seat as the car peeled away, taking a sharp left and accelerating away.

"Follow them," Hayden said.

"I am," Casey replied.

Hayden looked into the one functional rear camera. The Butcher was there, back on its feet, the trife swarming around it and giving it space.

Up ahead, the gunners in the car had returned to their positions, firing backward at the trife giving chase. They were taking a straight line up the street, heading toward a growing mass of something stretched across the street.

"It looks like they knew the bastards were coming," Casey said.

Hayden's eyes settled on the pile of cars that rested across the road between two buildings, nearly ten meters high. An armored transport sat in the center of it, backing up as the cars approached, making way for the Scrappers to enter.

"That has to be where their base is," Hayden said. "Don't slow down."

"What?"

"Keep going. There." He pointed to the side of the pile.

"We're going to let the trife in."

"I know. They shouldn't have taken Natalia if they didn't want the trife to get through. Do it."

"Pozz that, Sheriff. Hold onto your ass."

The tank shifted vectors slightly, at the same time the car passed through the center of the blockade and the transport moved back into place. Scrappers with rifles appeared on top of the stack, firing down at the demons, killing one after another after another.

There was a point where they noticed the tank coming their way. They raised their arms and cheered, thinking the armored vehicle was on their side and had maybe brought reinforcements from the south.

The cheers were short lived when they realized the tank was headed for their makeshift wall, and it wasn't slowing.

"Brace yourself," Casey said.

Hayden grabbed the back of her seat, holding steady as the tank slammed into the pile of cars. It nearly came to a stop, stymied by the weight of the wall, the force pushing him forward. Casey added more power to the throttle, the engine roaring behind them, the grip of the treads keeping them in motion.

The cars moved, shifting above them. They began to lose balance, flipping off one another and toppling down, some of them bouncing off the armored skull of the tank, the others crashing around it. The impact knocked more than a few Scrappers from their perches, throwing them to the ground where they were pounced on by the trife.

The tank pushed through the barrier. The creatures followed through behind it. They overtook the vehicle, running through the streets, heading toward a building a block away.

Bullets hit the top of the tank, the Scrappers trying to stop their mad dash. On the opposite side of the central building was another blockade, and cars were emerging from a garage beneath it, turning and heading toward it, pausing as they reached the so-far unaffected exit.

Hayden watched as an armored car pulled out of the garage, climbing the ramp and pausing in the street. Someone was standing in the hatch leading into the transport, and for as dirty as the camera lenses on the tank had become, it was easy for him to recognize the large white hat on the man's head, along with the familiar face beneath it.

Ghost. He was here. He was leaving. Was Natalia with him?

"We need to stop that car," Hayden said.

"How?" Casey replied.

"I don't know. We have to catch up with it."

Even now, the trife were closing on the convoy, the Scrappers laying down heavy fire to keep them back. Ghost produced a rifle from the transport, a massive thing that he aimed at the tank. Hayden saw a muzzle flash, and then the front left camera went out. Another flash and the front right disappeared. A third, and they lost forward sight completely.

"Grepping hell," Casey cried. "I can't drive it like this."

"No!" Hayden shouted, slamming the side of the vehicle with his hand. "He's getting away!"

"I'm sorry, Sheriff. We can't catch him like this. Maybe she's still inside?"

Was it possible? Would Ghost leave her behind? He had brought her here for something. What if he had gotten it? Did he still need her?

"I'm going in," Hayden said.

"I'm coming with you," Casey said.

"No, you aren't."

"Try to stop me."

Hayden didn't have time to try. He ran to the back of the tank, climbing the ladder and opening the hatch, pistol in hand. He emerged onto the top, turning as a trife hissed in front of him, pulling the trigger and hitting it right in the face. He ducked as it toppled past him and off the vehicle.

He quickly scanned the immediate area. The trife were surrounding them, some of them rushing into the open garage, others attacking the soldiers on the blockades.

Ghost was already through the barrier, facing back toward him.

Hayden threw himself from the tank, flailing in the air, the round from the N80 whistling past his ear. He hit the ground hard, his body cracking from the impact. He rolled over, picking himself up.

A trife scurried toward him, claws raised to slash his head.

A shot above him, and its head exploded.

"See, I already saved your life," Casey said, jumping down. "Aren't you glad I'm here?"

Hayden smiled. "Pozz that."

They ran toward the garage together.

46

NATALIA'S EYES OPENED SLOWLY. THE BACK OF HER HEAD WAS throbbing, her vision blurry.

What the hell had happened?

She remembered trying the different passwords to access the mainframe. She remembered none of them working. Then Ghost had shown up and said they were running out of time.

After that?

Nothing.

She pushed herself up, reaching out and grabbing the chair, using it to bring herself to her feet. A wave of dizziness passed over her, and she struggled to stay upright, to pull herself around to the seat before dropping.

She closed her eyes again, trying to shake off the vertigo. She listened. There was no sound save for the hum of the HVAC keeping the servers cool. Her eyes snapped open, and she looked around, surprised to find she was alone.

Running out of time. Alone. Had Ghost abandoned her here?

She could hardly believe it. After everything that had

happened? After she had decided to give up the ideals of her past in exchange for a future as more than a slave? And he had left?

She lowered her head into her hand. It didn't make sense. She was an Engineer from a Generation ship. She was valuable. Important. Why would he leave her behind?

Because he didn't trust her. Because he believed it would only be a matter of time before she turned on him, and on King. He had agreed to give her a chance to kill his father, but that agreement had meant nothing. He never had any intention of letting her get near him. He never had any intention of letting her get near either of them, except on his very specific terms. He had been using her from the moment he had picked her up at the Pilgrim's hangar. Manipulating her, even when she thought she was manipulating him.

King was a monster.

Ghost was a snake.

Which one was the true threat?

He could have killed her. He could have put a bullet in her head. He hadn't. He left her there, unconscious. He left her there to be killed by the trife.

That son of a bitch.

She remembered what he had said about Hayden, back in Sanisco. That he had given her husband a chance to live. That if he were a god, like King and himself, maybe he would survive. Was Ghost giving her that chance, too?

She fought to stand, the dizziness settling as she regained her senses. She made her way across the room toward the lift, reaching the door. She froze when she heard small pops echoing down from above. Someone was still in here, and they were shooting at something. It had to be the trife.

She needed a weapon. Something to defend herself with. She looked around. There was nothing, save for the cart with her tools. The biggest thing she had was a hammer. It would have to do. She pressed the button to summon the lift, and then went back to grab it.

She picked it up, turning to the lift again. Her eyes crossed the terminal as she did. She realized then that it was unlocked. When had she figured out the password?

The blow to the head had taken the memory. She glanced at the lift, and then returned to the mainframe. The display was dark, with white text printed on it. She could only see the last twenty lines or so. Each row was a coordinate. Latitude and longitude. Locations for something. The weapons caches? More ships like the Pilgrim? She didn't know.

The final line was different. It wasn't a coordinate. It was a series of letters and numbers, sixteen characters long. What did it mean?

She stared at it for a moment, her body growing colder as the realization set in.

The lift thumped as it reached the bottom of the shaft, making a noise that didn't sound anywhere close to correct. The circuitry sparked a moment later, and the doors opened, a cloud of dust and debris flowing out, following the escape route into the room. She turned away from it, covering her eyes from the dust. She would have to take the stairs.

She waited a moment for the cloud to dissipate and the soot to settle. Then she hurried forward. She had to get out of here. She had to… what? What the hell was she going to do? Ghost had gotten what he came for.

More than he came for.

Damn it.

There was no one to help her.

No one to save her.

No one to save them.

She was alone. All alone.

The stairwell door opened ahead of her. A trife pushed past it, into the room. There were more of them behind it.

Natalia scampered back, ducking behind one of the large black servers, putting her back to it and turning her head to peer out into the room.

The trife were coming. One, then six, then twelve. They were being drawn in by the heat of the servers. Led directly to her.

She lifted the hammer. It shook in her hand. She wished it were a gun. At least then she could use it on herself.

She could hear the trife approaching, their hisses getting louder. There was no way out of this. No escape. There was no reason to pretend otherwise.

She dropped the hammer as she got back to her feet.

She stepped out from behind the server, directly in front of the lead trife. She held up her hands, turned her head to the side to expose her neck, and closed her eyes.

47

HAYDEN LAUNCHED HIS REPLACEMENT HAND AT THE TRIFE, THE extended claws stabbing deep through its neck. He yanked it out, pulling sideways to throw the creature's body to the side as he did.

Casey stood behind him, her back pressed against his. She fired at their rear, single rounds that popped and clinked, the range between them and the targets too close to miss.

They moved down the stairwell, one step at a time. One floor at a time.

Reaching it had been hard enough. The trife had entered the building ahead of them, swarming through it and down. At first, following the creatures had been a benefit, since it gave them the direction of where they needed to go. But now they were surrounded on both sides, with demons in the front and back of them, doing their best to finish off the only two humans left in the city.

Hayden clenched his teeth, firing his pistol point-blank into the next trife's head. He hoped that wasn't true. There had to be three humans left in the city. Three, or all of this was for nothing. All of everything was for nothing, and he was going to bring yet another innocent person down with him.

Casey had saved his life outside, and she had saved his life again in here. There was no way they would be making it down the stairwell without her. She had his back, figuratively and literally, her skill with guns more impressive than he would have guessed. She called herself a Driver. She said she wasn't a killer like the Couriers. Based on how she was dispatching the trife now, he had to wonder if she had lied.

He dropped another step, nearly slipping on a patch of trife blood. He caught himself by slashing into another demon, at the same time he fired the pistol into its chest. He ducked to the left, a heavy claw scraping against his armor, catching the thicker plates that lined it and getting stuck. He yanked the creature to him, ramming his claws into its eye and then kicking it back and into another demon.

Behind him, Casey's rifle clicked empty.

He didn't miss a beat, reaching into one of the armor's pockets and removing a fresh magazine, handing it back her way. She released the old one, grabbed it, and placed in into the rifle, immediately firing again. The warm splash of gore on the back of his head told him that one had gotten way too close.

"Geez. How many floors are there?" Casey said.

"I don't know," Hayden replied.

"Your wife could be on any of them."

"If she's here at all, I know."

"This is crazy. I'm crazy for following you in here."

"I know that, too. We keep going until we get to the bottom. At least then we can fight them from one direction."

"You hope."

"Hope's the only thing I have left."

"Me, too."

They kept going. One step at a time. One floor at a time.

Trife died on both sides of them, the numbers that could attack them at once limited by the tight confines. As they progressed, the density of the creatures ahead of them started to dwindle, though he imagined the density above was only increasing. He didn't have much to compare it with, but he couldn't believe how many trife had been coming into the city. He still couldn't believe two different kinds had been working together, and he definitely wasn't ready to accept what that meant for humankind.

There was a very real possibility that they would reach the bottom, and never be able to get back to the top.

There was a very real possibility that if they did get back to the top, there would be absolutely nothing left to go back to.

Except maybe the Pilgrim.

As if Malcolm would let him back in.

A macabre smile passed his lips at the idea of himself standing in front of the secured hatch, bloody and beaten, pounding on the door and crying out to the Governor while a million trife gathered behind him.

Would it be better to let the colonists live out their days until the food and water finally ran out, or would it be better to let the trife in, and end their species once and for all?

A fresh trife moved toward him. He raised his pistol as he had so many times before, pulling the trigger.

The gun clicked empty.

The demon hissed loudly, sensing the failure, claws slashing toward his face.

He tried to duck away. Too slow. He felt the sharp fingers cutting his flesh, slipping in and through without much resistance. He could nearly feel them skidding across the bone of his cheek.

He cried out in pain, turning his face as the claws passed dangerously close to his eye. He swung his left hand back toward the creature in a heavy metal punch that bashed in its skull and knocked it hard into the wall.

"Sheriff?" Casey said behind him.

It hurt like hell, but it was mostly flesh. He reached into his armor, searching for a fresh magazine for the pistol. There weren't any more.

"I'm okay, keep moving."

They did, covering a dozen more steps until there were no more trife blocking their path.

Until there were no more steps to descend.

They had reached the bottom.

"We're here," Hayden said.

There was a closed metal door ahead of them. He kicked it open, holding the replacement hand ready.

He scanned the room quickly. A glowing display sat on a simple table a dozen meters ahead on the left, a chair positioned in front of it. Further back, dozens of flashing lights were attached to hundreds of tall, black boxes, a configuration he recognized right away. A mainframe, like the PASS.

Dozens of trife were gathered near the servers, absorbing the heat and radiation the computers provided. They raised their heads when Hayden entered, hissing to one another.

Casey passed through the door behind him, throwing her back against the door to slam it closed.

"Shit," she said, seeing the trife.

"Don't shoot me," Hayden said, reaching up, removing his hat and placing it on her head.

"Pozz," she replied, smiling beneath it, raising the rifle and taking aim.

"And don't let any more of them in."

"You do know how much I weigh, right?"

They were banging on the door behind her, trying to enter. So far she was able to keep them from overpowering her, but there was no telling how long that would last.

Hayden returned his attention to the demons. They were moving cautiously, spreading out from the center, using the servers as cover for their approach.

Casey fired, single rounds that hit individual trife, one after another. Three of them fell dead before they could get behind the servers.

It forced the rest of them to move faster, parting from the open space and vanishing into the shadows, hissing to one another in preparation for their attack.

Hayden watched them part, spreading like a curtain in front of him, their exodus quickly revealing something at their center.

A body.

A human body.

A woman.

Hayden's heart stopped. His breath caught in his throat. His hands and teeth clenched.

He could see her face.

He would know it anywhere.

Natalia.

She wasn't moving.

He cried out, a sudden rage overtaking him, freeing his body and soul from the otherwise paralyzing panic that threatened to bring him to his knees. He roared in anger, turning his attention to the trife as they launched their assault.

A bullet hit the first one in the head, knocking it away from him. He grabbed the arm of the second with his human hand, pushing the claws aside and punching it in the chest with the claws of the replacement, lifting and throwing it into another, which fell to a bullet a split second later.

He turned to a fourth, ducking low beneath its strike, coming up hard with the claws and ripping it from sternum to throat.

A hard swipe hit him on the side, the claws digging through his armor and reaching the flesh. He ignored the burn, slamming the metal hand down on the arm and breaking it before backhanding the trife in the face, the force breaking its neck.

A heavy round of gunfire followed, a burst of twenty slugs that cut down four more of the creatures trying to attack him from his flank. He turned the other direction, catching a set of claws on his replacement hand, deflecting them before kicking the creature in the leg. The movement brought it off balance, and he grabbed Ghost's knife from his belt with his human hand, using it to stab the demon in the eye.

His adrenaline was pumping full speed, his heart racing, his eyes threatening to cloud over with tears he couldn't allow to come. His fury and his agony were one and the same, and he charged deeper into the trife, ignoring Casey's cries that he was blocking her line of fire.

He didn't hear her, and he wouldn't have cared if he did. He wanted to be the one to kill them. All of them. He owed them for his wife.

He cut through them, a raging berserker, the knife in his human hand matching the claws on his replacement, tearing through trife flesh and muscle, dropping them around him and casting them away. He felt their claws striking him, skipping off the hard plates and reaching through the softer fibers, slicing his flesh beneath. Every burn increased his anger more. Every fire in his body fueled the fire in his soul.

And then, suddenly and impossibly, it was over.

The last trife fell three meters away, gunned down by Casey. Hayden charged forward, falling beside Natalia, his body shaking so hard he could hardly see straight.

"Nat. Nat, I'm here," he said, the tears finally coming, streaming from his eyes and burning the cuts beneath them.

He leaned over her, putting his hand on her face. "I'm here. I found you. It's okay. You don't have to die alone. I'm here."

He looked up when he heard a crash behind him. Casey had her foot planted against the door and was using the rifle and her chains to lash it closed.

When he looked back at Natalia, she was looking back at him.

She was smiling.

She was alive.

48

"Hayden," she said, looking up at him. "Oh, Hayden. I can't believe it. I can't believe you're here. You look like hell. Your poor face."

She stared up at him. She had to be hallucinating. She had to be dead. There was no way he could have found her down here. No way he could have come. It was impossible. Completely impossible.

But how could it not be real? He was beaten to hell, his face bruised and bloody, a long, deep cut below his eye. He was bleeding from both sides of his body, where claws had pierced a long coat and the armor he was wearing beneath it. Why would anyone dream of someone in such lousy shape?

He leaned down as she pushed herself up. He wrapped his arms around her, holding her close. She could hear his heart pounding. She could feel the warmth of his body and the moisture of his blood and sweat and tears against her cheek. It all felt real enough.

"I knew I would find you," he said. "I knew it. I was never going to give up. Not ever. I love you."

"I love you, too."

She clung to him, afraid to let him go. Afraid the dream would end, and the truth of her nightmare would start.

He pushed back, getting his face in line with hers, leaning forward again and pressing his lips to hers. She met them eagerly, melting into his kiss.

"No offense, Sheriff," a voice said nearby. "I'm happy you found your wife, and that she's still alive. But we aren't out of the shit yet."

Hayden's lips moved away. Natalia watched his head turn. She shifted her gaze, finding a small woman standing nearby. She was the strangest looking girl Natalia had ever seen, with a large, wide-brimmed black hat on her head and chains draping her arms. She smiled when she saw she was being stared at.

"Hi," Casey said. "I'm Chains. Well, my friends call me Casey."

"Am I dead?" Natalia said.

"I hope not," Hayden replied, looking back at her. "If you're dead, that means I'm dead, too. And if this is what dead is like, I'm not happy about it, at all."

He reached out to her, helping her to her feet, holding her arm tight, as though he were afraid he would lose her again if he didn't.

"I still can't believe you're here," Hayden said. "I didn't give up. I didn't lose hope. But I still didn't think you would be here. I didn't think I would find you."

"I thought you were dead," Natalia said. "I saw those monsters, the goliaths. I saw them attacking the compound, where you were. How did you survive?"

"A good horse, and a lot of luck," Hayden said. "What about you?"

Natalia's mind flashed to the gas station, to her night with Ghost. A sudden chill overtook her. That didn't matter now. It was over. Hayden was here. She would tell him later, and when she did, she knew he would understand.

"I don't know," she said. "I thought I was going to die. The trife came in. They surrounded me. I gave myself up to them. I was afraid, and I think I passed out. I shouldn't be alive."

"If they didn't kill you, it means you're either preggers, or you're barren," the girl, Casey, said.

"What?" Hayden and Natalia replied together.

"Weird, right? They don't bother killing women who can't have babies because they can't add to the human population anyway. And they don't kill women who are carrying babies; I guess because they have some weird sense of morality. I mean, they don't like when we kill their offspring, either."

Natalia and Hayden looked at one another. Which one was it, and what did it mean? There was no time to worry about that right now.

'Hayden," Natalia said. "The mainframe. Ghost. The one who brought me here. I gave him access. He did things to me." She stopped, not able to deal with that at the moment. "I let him in. I'm sorry. Oh, Hayden, I'm sorry."

"What do you mean?" Hayden said, looking at her. His face was troubled, reflecting her pain.

"The mainframe. He got data from it. Coordinates to Space Force weapons caches, I think. He also got the code. The Space Force master code."

"Master code?"

"Yes. The password that unlocks everything, everywhere. The scientists who worked here, they must have left it for whoever managed to get in. I got in, and I gave it to him."

"Everything?" Hayden said, his pained expression turning to worry. "Including the Pilgrim?"

"Yes," Natalia said, her voice trembling from the extent of her failure. "He has the master code. He can get Inside."

Hayden stared at her. She wasn't sure how to read the

fresh look that covered his face. He was angry, afraid, determined, strong.

"It's okay," he said. "It isn't your fault. Do you hear me, Nat? It's not your fault. We'll figure it out."

She nodded, even if she wasn't ready to believe that.

"We might need the codes, and the coordinates," Hayden said, looking at her. "I know your memory is second to none. Can you capture them? As many as you can?"

"Yes," she said.

He took her hand in his, squeezing it, and then letting it go. "Do it."

She walked over to the terminal. She could hear Hayden speaking as she did.

"Casey, we need to figure out how to get back out of here. Maybe the shaft?"

She sat in the chair, trying to calm herself as she looked at the display. She read the master code multiple times, looking away and speaking it back to herself out loud. She repeated the process six times until she was sure she had it.

"Shaft's no good, Sheriff," the girl said. "The bastards cut the lines."

"Then we'll have to find a way through them," Hayden said. "Good thing I've still got this."

Natalia didn't know what he was referring to. She kept her eyes focused on the terminal, memorizing the coordinates from the bottom up. They didn't mean anything to her in terms of geographic location, but they could worry about that later.

If they managed to get back out of here.

She closed her eyes, repeating the master code and the bottom five coordinates on the screen out loud.

When she opened them, the display was clear.

"What the?" she said, thinking the power had gone out. Where the hell had the text gone?

Then Hayden was behind her, looking at the screen.

"Nat? What happened?"

"I don't know," she said. "The list was there two seconds ago."

"Did you get the code?"

"I got it, but-"

She stopped speaking, watching in fascination as a new line of text appeared on the screen:

DATALINK BUNKER PORTLAND, ARE YOU OPERATIONAL?

A few more seconds passed, all three of them staring at the screen in shock while another line of text appeared.

THIS IS WESTERN COMMAND LEWIS-MCCHORD.

IS ANYONE THERE?

THANK YOU FOR READING FORSAKEN!

I've said it before, and it bears repeating - if you enjoyed this book and want to support this series, please, please, please consider leaving a review and letting me and others know how much you enjoyed it. A star rating and a sentence is all it takes.

Do you want to know when I have a new release? www.mr-forbes.com/notify

Thank you for your support.

Cheers,
Michael.

OTHER BOOKS BY M.R FORBES

Browse my backlist:
mrforbes.com/books

Starship Eternal (War Eternal)
mrforbes.com/starshipeternal

A lost starship...

A dire warning from futures past...

A desperate search for salvation…

Captain Mitchell "Ares" Williams is a Space Marine and the hero of the Battle for Liberty, whose Shot Heard 'Round the Universe saved the planet from a nearly unstoppable war machine. He's handsome, charismatic, and the perfect poster boy to help the military drive enlistment. Pulled from the war and thrown into the spotlight, he's as efficient at charming the media and bedding beautiful celebrities as he was at shooting down enemy starfighters.

After an assassination attempt leaves Mitchell critically wounded, he begins to suffer from strange hallucinations that carry a chilling and oddly familiar warning:

They are coming. Find the Goliath or humankind will be destroyed.

Convinced that the visions are a side-effect of his injuries, he tries to ignore them, only to learn that he may not be as crazy as he thinks. The enemy is real and closer than he imagined, and they'll do whatever it takes to prevent him from rediscovering the centuries lost starship.

Narrowly escaping capture, out of time and out of air, Mitchell lands at the mercy of the Riggers - a ragtag crew of former commandos who patrol the lawless outer reaches of the galaxy. Guided by a captain with a reputation for cold-blooded murder, they're dangerous, immoral, and possibly insane.

They may also be humanity's last hope for survival in a war that has raged beyond eternity.

(War Eternal is also available in a box set of the first three books here: mrforbes.com/wareternalbox)

Hell's Rejects (Chaos of the Covenant)

mrforbes.com/hellsrejects

The most powerful starships ever constructed are gone. Thousands are dead. A fleet is in ruins. The attackers are unknown. The orders are clear: *Recover the ships. Bury the bastards who stole them.*

Lieutenant Abigail Cage never expected to find herself in Hell. As a Highly Specialized Operational Combatant, she was one of the most respected soldiers in the military. Now she's doing hard labor on the most miserable planet in the universe.

Not for long.

The Earth Republic is looking for the most dangerous individuals it can control. The best of the worst, and Abbey happens to be one of them. The deal is simple: *Bring back the starships, earn your freedom. Try to run, you die.* It's a suicide mission, but she has nothing to lose.

The only problem? There's a new threat in the galaxy. One with a power unlike anything anyone has ever seen. One that's been waiting for this moment for a very, very, long time. And they want Abbey, too.

Be careful what you wish for.

They say Hell hath no fury like a woman scorned. They have no idea.

Man of War (Rebellion)

mrforbes.com/manofwar

In the year 2280, an alien fleet attacked the Earth.

Their weapons were unstoppable, their defenses unbreakable.

Our technology was inferior, our militaries overwhelmed.

Only one starship escaped before civilization fell.

Earth was lost.

It was never forgotten.

Fifty-two years have passed.

A message from home has been received.

The time to fight for what is ours has come.

Welcome to the rebellion.

Or maybe something completely different?

Dead of Night (Ghosts & Magic)

mrforbes.com/deadofnight

For Conor Night, the world's only surviving necromancer, staying alive is an expensive proposition. So when the promise of a big payout for a small bit of thievery presents itself, Conor is all in. But nothing comes easy in the world of ghosts and magic, and it isn't long before Conor is caught up in the machinations of the most powerful wizards on Earth and left with only two ways out:

Finish the job, or be finished himself.

Balance (The Divine)

mrforbes.com/balance

My name is Landon Hamilton. Once upon a time I was a twenty-three year old security guard, trying to regain my life after spending a year in prison for stealing people's credit card numbers.

Now, I'm dead.

Okay, I was supposed to be dead. I got killed after all; but a funny thing happened after I had turned the mortal coil...

I met Dante Alighieri - yeah, that Dante. He told me I was special, a diuscrucis. That's what they call a perfect balance of human, demon, and angel. Apparently, I'm the only one of my kind.

I also learned that there was a war raging on Earth between Heaven and Hell, and that I was the only one who could save the human race from annihilation. He asked me to help, and I was naive enough to agree.

Sounds crazy, I know, but he wished me luck and sent me back to the mortal world. Oh yeah, he also gave me instructions on how to use my Divine "magic" to bend the universe to my will. The problem is, a sexy vampire crushed them while I was crushing on her.

Now I have to somehow find my own way to stay alive in a world of angels, vampires, werewolves, and an assortment of other enemies that all want to kill me before I can mess up their plans for humanity's future. If that isn't enough, I also have to find the queen of all demons and recover the Holy Grail.

It's not like it's the end of the world if I fail.

Wait. It is.

Tears of Blood (Books 1-3)
mrforbes.com/tearsofblood

One thousand years ago, the world was broken and reborn beneath the boot of a nameless, ageless tyrant. He erased all history of the time before, enslaving the people and hunting those with the power to unseat him.

The power of magic.

Eryn is such a girl. Born with the Curse, she fights to control and conceal it to protect those she loves. But when the truth is revealed, and his soldiers come, she is forced away from her home and into the company of Silas, a deadly fugitive tormented by a fractured past.

Silas knows only that he is a murderer who once hunted the Cursed, and that he and his brothers butchered armies and innocents alike to keep the deep, dark secrets of the time before from ever coming to light.

Secrets which could save the world.

Or destroy it completely.

ABOUT THE AUTHOR

M.R. Forbes is the creator of a growing catalog of science fiction and fantasy titles. He lives in the pacific northwest with his family, including a cat who thinks she's a dog, and a dog who thinks she's a cat. He eats too many donuts, and he's always happy to hear from readers.

To learn more about M.R. Forbes or just say hello:

Visit my website:
mrforbes.com

Send me an e-mail:
michael@mrforbes.com

Check out my Facebook page:
facebook.com/mrforbes.author

Chat with me on Facebook Messenger:
https://m.me/mrforbes.author

Made in the USA
Middletown, DE
02 February 2018